A Daughter's Gift

Also by Mollie Walton

The Raven Hall Saga

A Mother's War

The Ironbridge Saga

The Daughters of Ironbridge
The Secrets of Ironbridge
The Orphan of Ironbridge

Mollie
Walton

A Daughter's Gift

Book Two of the Raven Hall Saga

WELBECK

First published in 2023 by Welbeck Fiction Limited,
an imprint of Welbeck Publishing Group
Offices in: London – 20 Mortimer Street, London W1T 3JW &
Sydney – 205 Commonwealth Street, Surry Hills 2010
www.welbeckpublishing.com

A CIP catalogue record for this book is available from the British Library

Hardback ISBN: 978-1-78739-952-5
Ebook ISBN: 978-1-78739-951-8

Printed and bound by CPI Group (UK) Ltd., Croydon, CR0 4YY

MIX
Paper | Supporting
responsible forestry
FSC® C171272

10 9 8 7 6 5 4 3 2 1

This book is dedicated to the memory of the firefighters of the Blitz, who risked their lives and in many cases made the ultimate sacrifice. Ordinary women and men they may have been, but their bravery and duty were extraordinary.

Prologue

Date: 5 August 1940

From: Sgt H. Woodvine

To: R. Calvert-Lazenby of Raven Hall, Ravenscar, North Yorkshire

My dear Rosina,

I'm at a port and about to sail in a few hours. Where I am heading I cannot divulge. All I can reveal is that I will continue to work with radio, but that is all I can say about that. The only thing I can disclose about my present circumstance is that I am bunked with three other RAF chaps, one of whom is sleeping as I write this and snores like a foghorn, whilst another stinks worse than fox excrement and the third is clean and quiet like me, thank the stars.

Some of the lads I'm with have been telling me that the post from our destination can be notoriously slow in getting back to old Blighty, so I thought I'd write to you now, knowing that it will be posted on British soil and therefore will reach you soonest. I've also been told that the best way for me to keep in touch with you regularly is to send you telegrams when I can. I have to pay for these myself, and as the cost is per word, they will of necessity be brief, but at least they will let you know I'm still in one piece. However, I'm a stubborn Shropshire lad and therefore will continue to write letters to you regularly; even if they take months to reach you, you will know that I was thinking of you.

Thank you for your latest letter with news of your five wonderful girls and how their war is going. I'm glad to hear Grace is continuing to do her war work as a Wren admirably and has a nice chap. Not so glad to hear that Evvy is still in London, as we all know it could well be a target soon, as you said. But try not to worry too much. Evvy strikes me as more capable of looking after herself than almost any man I've ever met. And I think the London Fire Brigade are very lucky to have her. I believe they do keep women off the front lines of firefighting (yet from what you've told me of her, I'd half expect her to crop her hair, paint on a moustache and join the front ranks.) Glad to hear too that Connie can now bowl overarm (remind her to keep her eye fixed on the wicket); that Daisy can now play that tricky Bach piece all the way through without error and that Dora has taken to studying the constituents of snail slime; let's hope she can help Jessop and Throp keep the little rotters off their salad crops. It's also good to hear that Ronnie the evacuee is still playing chess (remind him to try opening up the diagonals in his first moves).

Please, PLEASE never feel that your news from home is dull, as you worried about in your last letter. It could never, ever be that to me. You have no idea how comforting it is to hear the ordinary details of your day, your life, your girls and of Raven Hall. (I dreamt last night that I was standing in the grounds of the hall, listening to the seagulls mocking us, looking out to sea, your arm entwined with mine. We were standing on that little triangular platform of grass with the two seats in the corners, the ones you call the king and queen's seat – I'll never forget our first embrace there . . .) Everything there is beloved to me, as are you, my darling.

I know we've discussed this in letters before and on the telephone, but I want to reassure you that I have no qualms at all about the fact that there is a gap in years between our ages. My only fear at first was that as a seemingly green young man in his twenties and you being a wise clever woman in her forties you would not believe the love that I feel for you is real. In the dead of night, I still worry *about this from time to time. It strikes me as miraculous that I am lucky enough to have been not only noticed but liked and even loved by a woman of your beauty, kindness and intelligence. I want to remind you that I am not so green as I might be, that I have lived and faced death in the International Brigades in Spain and now again for the RAF in my own country; also, that I have had romances and such in my somewhat shorter life. And that I can honestly tell you, hand on heart, that I had no idea that love like this existed, that the feelings I have for you were possible. As you know, I've read stacks of novels and poems, as well as watching dozens of plays and films in which the subject of love is paramount and only now do I understand what they are getting at. I never understood why someone could die for love; it seemed ridiculous to me. Until I met you. Don't fret: I don't intend on dying for the love of you, my love. But now I fully comprehend the sentiment. This is my unnecessarily wordy and roundabout way of saying, simply, I love you more than myself.*

Right, my hand is aching after this epistle and I ought to get a nap before we sail as I have an ominous feeling that I might still be a terrible sailor, as I was when I went to Spain, and again will find myself throwing up my guts every five minutes, so I think I should get some sleep now before we go. I'll write to you again upon my arrival. Yet please try not to worry if you don't hear from me for a while. This war breeds fear and uncertainty about everything, I know that. But rest assured that the one thing I have not one iota of uncertainty about is you. In my darkest moments, the vision that keeps me going is the thought of a future with you, where we can be together, free of the constraints of war and duty, devoted to each other. Whenever I can, I shall be in touch.

All my love to you, my darling.

Yours always,
Harry

P.S. As we agreed the last time I saw you at the railway station that we should never say goodbye, but something else instead, then I have decreed that is the way I'll finish all my letters to you, because if it wasn't for this damned war, it's my deepest desire. Thus, I shall end, as we did in Scarborough, your glorious auburn hair etched against the wispy white cloud of steam:

See you Sunday.

Chapter 1

August 1940

The late-afternoon sun, low in the London sky, streamed in through the staircase window, temporarily blinding Evvy as she shifted her heavy bag from one shoulder to the other. It was digging into her bra strap and she was fed up with it already. But her destination was only a few minutes' walk from Judd Street, where she shared a flat with Beryl, her actress friend who had just joined the Women's Auxiliary Air Force, signing up to be a WAAF. Both had decided to give up the Judd Street flat and put their stuff into storage, Evvy's in a London friend's garage. Beryl had already gone off for training the week before and it was strange and lonely for Evvy to be left in their tiny place alone, even though she'd quite looked forward to a bit of peace. She realised she liked constant company. Well, she imagined she'd certainly get plenty of that when she arrived at the fire station. For Evvy had joined the AFS, the Auxiliary Fire Service, supporting the London Fire Brigade.

Up till this point in the war, it had been largely voluntary and when she'd signed up a few weeks before, she had done a bit of training in the evenings at Station 73, Euston Road, after working as an artist, painting public information posters and helping out at a local theatre designing sets. The training had included showing her the basic equipment and procedures of a fire station, from bells to hoses, ladders to couplings, hydrants to pumps. She'd also learnt basic first aid and how to use stirrup pumps to put out smaller fires. Despite women not being permitted to actually fight fires, they all had training with the hoses just in case. Holding on to the hose as it pumped out gallons of water was exhilarating; it seemed a thing alive with its own inclinations. The power of the water shocked her and she tried to picture how it would feel to douse flames with it. She loved the physical challenge of it, as Evvy was not one for desks and chairs. She needed to be doing something, with muscles and sinews involved, preferably. That was one way in which being an artist suited her and this work fighting fire with water seemed elemental, which fully appealed to her poetic sense. And now, the AFS had called her up officially and she was to work for them full-time, with a weekly wage of two pounds. That morning, she had received a letter instructing her to report for duty at 6 p.m. that evening, with full kit, prepared to work and to move in to the AFS accommodation located at Substation 73V, Argyle Street School, WC1.

A school? she'd thought when she read it. *Will we have to sit on those tiny chairs?*

It was a five-minute walk, if that, but her kitbag was digging into her other bra strap now and making her cross. Yet she'd carried more and far further, travelling around France as an artist what seemed like a lifetime ago but was only a year back. She'd been fearless then and was fearless still, yet what she'd had to fear in this first year of the war was boredom with the whole Phoney War business. The doom merchants had predicted instant raids on London, which had never transpired. She'd liked her job as a painter for exhibitions and her work at the theatre till now, savouring the lively London nightlife. But her disappointment was intense at how drab and ordinary wartime felt after nearly twelve months of it.

'Nothing's happening,' she would moan to Beryl, as they read the daily papers.

But Beryl would give her a disapproving look and say, 'Nothing's happening to *you*, Evelyn Calvert-Lazenby. But plenty is happening to the poor Polish people, and the French and the Belgians and all sorts. Don't be so selfish!'

And Evvy would feel cross with her but knew that Beryl was quite right and she was being a spoilt brat. Evvy had always had enough self-knowledge to understand perfectly well that she was probably behaving badly but wanted to carry on doing it anyway, as long as nobody was hurt, of course. She had her limits. Her own freedom was paramount to her, but she was never knowingly unkind and wanted everyone to feel as jolly as she did, most of the time, though she kept a sharp tongue for anyone who disrespected her or those she loved. Life was a lark to her and she wished everyone could feel the same way.

She was halfway along Judd Street now and turning into Cromer Street. She focused on the task ahead and began to feel excited about the prospect. She still had not received her AFS uniform – a very smart dark blue with red piping. There was a shortage apparently and she had to wait, which she didn't mind too much as she did love her own clothes, mostly living in slacks with blouses or pullovers. She disliked skirts and dresses, except in the hottest days of summer, when they were a relief. But she did get funny looks from people sometimes. Although she had a very feminine frame and face, with longish, wavy, golden hair (she knew she'd never be mistaken for a chap), she often wished she'd been born a man. They had so much more freedom in the world, and freedom was Evvy's sole aim in life.

As she turned into Argyle Street, she peered along it, squinting to see where this school might be. And before long, there it was, a shabby little brick building with doors labelled for boys and girls, now somewhat ghostly since all the children had been evacuated and the school had been requisitioned by the fire service. The railings had all gone for the war effort and Evvy imagined for a moment the children streaming over the low wall from the playground and running into the streets like a very short mob. She chuckled to herself as she walked through the brick archway into the entrance to the school. She did have a vivid and weird imagination.

'Who are you, girl?' came a male voice and she stopped. She turned and saw a middle-aged man in the buttoned-up, dark-blue tunic of the fire service, standing in the corridor, staring at her.

'Evelyn Calvert-Lazenby, reporting for duty at Substation 73V, Argyle Street, WC1.'

He raised his eyebrows at her, seemingly impressed she'd got its full title correct. Evvy was good with detail; perhaps it was the artist in her – observant with an extremely good memory. She always beat her four sisters hands down at card games, because she could remember which cards had been put down and which hadn't. This particularly infuriated Connie (who invariably threw her cards in Evvy's face when she lost, again and again).

He squinted at her. 'How old are you?'

'Twenty. How old are you?'

He gave her a look and did not deign to give a reply.

Evvy inwardly told herself, and not for the first time, *Steady on, lass.* She knew her cheeky ways did not go down well with her superiors – oh, the years of battling with teachers at school! – and now in wartime she knew she'd have to bite her tongue far more often. But wasn't it so much more fun not to?

'You're early. S.O. ain't here and might not be back tonight, I dunno. You'll have to see him tomorrow morning. There's meals for AFS staff for a shilling in the café opposite and bedding in that classroom there and you'll have to bunk down in the bus round the back. The beds haven't turned up yet.'

'Can't I just go home for the night?' The flat was bare, but she'd rather sleep on the floor there than on a school bus, for heaven's sake!

'No, you cannot! You're on duty now.'

'But what am I supposed to be doing?'

'Whatever you're called upon to do. But S.O. deals with new recruits and, like I told you, he ain't here. So get yourself fed and rested and – if you're not called for before – be back here 6 a.m. sharp.'

With that, he walked off down the corridor and turned into a room, from where Evvy could hear a hubbub of talk and a bit of laughter, seemingly all male and a bit rough. She considered going down there and presenting herself again, but what was the point? The man would be annoyed she'd ignored him and she might have to face a bunch of rowdies, and she really wasn't in the mood. And who was this S.O. he kept mentioning? Their boss, she supposed. Must stand for station officer or something like that. And if he wasn't here right now, there wasn't much she could do about that. So, she did as she was told, for once, and went to the classroom to collect some bedding.

There were, indeed, twenty or so tiny chairs in there. On two of the tables, piles of sheets, a range of blankets and a few narrow pillows were piled up. It was summer and warm at night, so she only took a thin blanket and a pillow and stuffed them into her bag. She was disappointed that she wasn't being shown the ropes straight away. Now she'd arrived, she just wanted to get on with the job. She didn't know what the job involved yet, but more than anything, she wanted to climb ladders and fight fires. The trainer chap at her evening sessions on Euston Road had made it very clear that women didn't do any such thing in the fire service, mostly answering phones or driving people and stuff about. Being a driver would be preferable to the tedium of answering phone calls, Evvy had felt, but she'd still rather be a proper firewoman. As usual, the world didn't want women to do what they wanted to do, she mused.

She decided to dump her stuff in the bus and then go for something to eat. She walked down the corridor, thoroughly sick of her heavy bag by now, and found a back door that led out to another playground, its surface chalked up with the spectral remains of hopscotch squares and other games. Behind the low wall at the end, she saw the bus parked up in a three-sided open garage. It was quite a small vehicle, but as she peered in through the mucky windows, she could see that a person of her limited stature (she was five foot four – a full four inches shorter than her elder sister Grace) could stretch out along the back seat all right. She tried the door and, of course, it was locked. The man hadn't given her a key.

She tutted and shook her head, then dropped her bag on the ground, steeled herself and marched off back inside. She noticed a sign on the wall that read WATCHROOM 73V with an arrow that pointed down the corridor. So, the mysterious room beyond, from which had emanated all the male noise earlier, was called the watchroom.

Evvy appeared at the door and, in comic fashion, everyone in the room stopped talking and stared at her.

'Who's got the key to the bus, then?'

The room was quite sizeable and there were about eight or so men in there, all in their fire service tunics, sitting on a variety of chairs and tables in a room with desks, a couple of telephones and maps on the wall. It must have been the staffroom once, complete with a sink and tea urn, and many of them were holding cups in mid-air as she stood there, waiting for an answer.

'Now then, darlin'!' shouted one man from the back. 'Want a willing bloke for a tumble on the back seat of the bus then?', to which Evvy shook her head and folded her arms.

'That's enough of that,' said a stern voice, to which someone replied, 'Sorry, S.O.!' and forward came another man, younger than the one she'd spoken to before, perhaps in his mid-thirties. He was tall, very slim, long-legged, with prominent cheekbones, dark eyes and black sideburns poking out from beneath his cap.

The man she'd spoken to earlier stepped forward and said to him, 'You weren't here when she arrived, sir, and I didn't know you'd be back so soon. So I told her to sort herself.'

Evvy looked at this new chap and said, 'Do *you* have the keys then?'

He stood and stared at her, glanced at the floor, gave a deep sigh, then folded his arms. 'I'm your new boss. So perhaps you'd better start again, with calling me "sir".'

An eruption of sniggers went around the room and she could feel all eyes on her.

'Do you have the keys, *sir?*' she said, with clear emphasis on the final word.

He took a bemused look around at the others in the room and they all made a noise together, a kind of high-pitched 'Ooh!' that suggested Evvy was in trouble, but she didn't care. She'd had to deal with nasty classmates at school who hated her and creepy men in France who wanted her and she had dealt with both the same, with contempt or humour.

'You lot sound like a bunch of gossipy schoolgirls,' she said.

This drew uproarious laughter from the room and caused her boss to shake his head and raise his eyebrows.

'Follow me,' he said to Evvy and walked swiftly past her out of the room, which drew more uproar from the men.

Evvy's response was to lift her chin, close her eyes, turn in a stately fashion and walk steadily out of the room, which was much appreciated by her audience. She heard a few whistles and more laughter as she followed her boss down the corridor until he opened another door and went inside, closing the door behind her as she came in. It was most likely once the headteacher's office, complete with desks and bookshelves and the shield-shaped marks left by removed prizes that had once been mounted on the walls. He sat down at the desk and she stood before him, her hands behind her back. She knew she'd pushed it just now and should have been far more respectful, but it had become clear to her instantly that this was going to be an exclusively male environment and she'd have to put her foot down firmly and early on, so that these blokes didn't think they could take any liberties whatsoever with her and that she definitely meant business.

'What's your age?' he asked first, just like the other man. Her mother had always said she looked younger than she was, an innocent face (always a great joke at home, as everyone knew she was far from innocent underneath).

'I'm twenty, sir.'

'Really? And what's your name?' he said, now sitting with his hands laced together on the desktop.

'Evelyn Calvert-Lazenby.' She decided not to use the same cheek as before and ask him his name. After all, this was her new boss and she needed to start playing the game. But she couldn't help adding, 'People call me Evvy.'

'I'll be calling you Calvert.'

She wasn't sure what to say to this, so simply said, 'Yes, sir.'

'My name is Lewis Bailey. I'm the station officer of this substation and district officer for this area. The men call me S.O. or sir. We run this station properly, with discipline and with gumption.'

'Yes, sir,' she said again.

'You don't need to speak up, unless you're told to, Calvert.'

She went to say *Yes sir* but stopped herself at the last second, left with her mouth open to speak. She closed it and shook an imaginary lock of hair out of her eye, an old habit from when she'd had long tresses in France. Her hair was fashionably shorter these days and pinned back for work that evening.

'Why did you apply to join the AFS?'

'Gold Flake cigarettes, sir.'

'Come again?'

'I saw a rather fine piece of painting of a pretty girl on a Gold Flake advertisement and while I was appreciating the artwork, I noticed it said about men and women "with wills to win" and the girl on it was in AFS uniform. And it said in a little box that I might get to drive light lorries about and that appealed to me, as I'd much rather be out and about than cooped up on the phone or whatever godawful female thing the war would like me to waste my time on.'

Bailey frowned at her and she stared blankly back.

'You're going to have to learn to curb yourself a bit, Calvert.'

'How so?' she said, blithely and wilfully pretending not to know.

18

'All this . . .' he waved his hand vaguely, 'talk and this . . . cheek. You're a very quick-witted and clever young person. And that's all well and good. I can use skills like that. But this isn't peacetime now. This is wartime. And you're in the AFS now. You're expected to work hard and follow orders to the letter. Are you prepared to do that? Because, if not, I'll tell you straight, Calvert, you'll be neither use nor ornament if you can't follow orders. Lives are at stake, my men and women's lives and those of the public. Understand? This might feel like a jolly to you, a bit of excitement. Ooh, look at the pretty sparks and the orange flames! But it's not. It's an emergency service. It's about damage and death and preventing those things. So I need you to be the very best version of yourself that you can be. Are you up to that, Calvert?'

Evvy admired that. Some straight talking. Not rude, just factual. And, to be honest, he'd given her a verbal dressing-down that she most likely deserved a bit. She did feel she definitely needed to stand up for herself where that gang of men in the watchroom were concerned. But she knew too that her cheeky mouth had got her into trouble in the past. This chap needed her to toe the line and do her job, for very good and persuasive reasons. He had made all that clear without making her feel small. And she liked him for it. 'Yes, sir. Absolutely, sir.'

She stood up straighter and lifted her chin.

'Good. All right then. Now we're on the same page, you want to be a driver for us, then?'

'Yes, please, sir.'

'Can you drive?'

'Yes, sir. I learnt to drive in France. I've driven cars, vans and I once had a go on a motorbike, though I was a bit wobbly.'

'That's useful, Calvert. We need both drivers and motorcycle despatch riders, or DRs. Some girls do both, they're drivers of staff cars or trucks and they're also DRs.'

'Yes, sir. Thank you, sir.'

'So . . .' he began, then paused, as if deciding whether or not to continue this train of thought. 'What were you doing in France, then?'

'Painting, mostly. Studying here and there, painting here and there. Travelling about.'

'You were an artist before the war?'

'I still am. It never leaves you.'

'Yes,' he said thoughtfully. 'I suppose it doesn't.'

'Yes, sir,' she said, though he had a faraway look in his eye and she wasn't sure what she was saying yes to. She only said it to fill the silence that had momentarily descended upon them. Then he came back to himself.

'Right then. Tomorrow I'll send you off to start your driver training. You'll be practising on heavy goods vehicles too and then you'll take a test. We'll think about the motorcycle side of things a bit further on. Need to get you driving first as we have stuff to shift about all over town and I need a driver sometimes to drop me places in the district, so we need girls like you to do it.'

She wanted to ask, would she be the only woman at that station? Would she be sleeping in a bus every night? But she knew better now not to interrupt.

Yet, it was as if he read her mind, because the very next thing he said was, 'And just so you know, two more girls should be arriving tomorrow, to man the telephones and assist in the watchroom. So you won't be the only female here for long. I have sixteen men under me, so there will be seventeen men and three girls. Quite a ratio to get to grips with. Can you cope with it, Calvert?'

'Yes, sir,' she said with certainty.

'Yes, I believe you can. And I want you to know that I'll be having words with my men too, that none of that nonsense we just saw in the watchroom will be repeated in future. Every bloke and every girl in my station will show decorum and respect whilst on duty. I expect that of everyone.'

'Yes, sir.'

'All right, Calvert. You can go.'

With that, he gave her the keys to the bus and enquired if she'd eaten, and as she hadn't and everyone else had, he sent her to the café across the road, which turned out to do a very good fry-up of eggs with bubble and squeak.

When she came back to the station, it was quiet and she decided to get an early night, to prepare for the early start. She wasn't entirely sure how she'd wake herself up at 6 a.m. without an alarm clock, but she hoped someone would come to find her if she slept in. She was a light sleeper anyway, habitually dreaming all night and waking up after each one. So she was pretty sure she'd be awake at dawn and get herself into the girls' toilets to freshen herself up a bit before she was on duty.

She bedded down on the back seat of the bus and, despite being in central London, the area behind the school was pretty quiet. Though the seat was a bit springy, she was tired enough to drop straight off. She'd wake up at first light, she was sure of it . . .

Famous last words. She woke up because she fell off the back seat. She fell off the back seat because the bus was moving. The bus was moving because someone was driving it around the streets of London.

'Oi!' she cried, scrambling up from the floor and stumbling forward, as the bus tilted around a tight corner and she fell into the seat opposite.

'Blimey!' said the driver, peering in the rear-view mirror. 'What is this vision I see behind me?'

Evvy felt ridiculous as she made her way up the bus aisle, swaying and jolting against the seats. 'I'm in the AFS and this is where I'm sleeping! I'm supposed to report for duty at 6 a.m. Where are you taking me?'

'Didn't know you were there, did I? I'm off to Shaftesbury Avenue to pick up some equipment. It's only half five now. We'll get back in time. Take a seat! Enjoy the ride!'

Evvy came forward, taking a seat nearest the driver on the opposite side, so they could talk more on equal terms. She could see now that he was a youngish chap, somewhere in his twenties. His hair was thick and parted at the side, a mid-brown, toffee sort of a colour. And as he turned to glance at her, she saw his eyes were the most extraordinary light blue.

'I know you,' he said. 'You're the new girl.'

'I may be new but I'm no girl. My name is Evelyn Calvert-Lazenby and I'm twenty years old. Who are you, anyway?'

'Pleasure to meet you. I'm Sam. I drive Heavy Unit One and risk my life fighting fires so people with double-barrelled names like you can sleep safely in their beds.' He said all this with a cheeky smile that simultaneously annoyed and appealed to her.

'Well, I don't think that little dig about my name was necessary. Double-barrelled or not, I'm here, aren't I? I'm not sleeping safely in my bed. I slept unsafely in a bus last night and S.O. said I'm to start driver training today.'

'You're right. My apologies. And we do need more drivers. Good to see girls getting in on the act. No reason you can't do nearly as good a job as a bloke at driving.'

'A better job, I dare say,' muttered Evvy, as the bus lurched to a halt.

Now the bus had stopped, Sam turned to her and she got her first proper look at him, head on. The colour of those eyes struck her again, like the sky on a cloudless winter's day, bright and clear. There was a mischievous glint in them and a curve in his smile that he seemed to know made his lips look awfully tempting. Overall, Evvy saw that he was devilishly handsome and – oh boy! – did he know it. Her least favourite kind of chap usually.

'It's a pleasure to meet you, Evelyn Calvert-Lazenby. Did I get that right?'

'You did,' she said, begrudgingly. 'And what's your full name?'

'Sam Bailey, at your service.' He held out his hand.

As she extended her hand to shake his, she said, 'Bailey? Any relation to the S.O.?'

'Indeed I am. I'm his baby brother.'

They shook hands and looked at each other silently for a moment. So, another Bailey. He didn't look much like his elder brother, though both men had the same chiselled cheekbones and dimples in their chins. Sam was prettier than his brother, yet Lewis Bailey was handsome in a rugged, older man kind of a way, Evvy thought. She wondered how it felt for the elder brother to have an Adonis for a younger brother. She had noticed that neither of them wore a wedding ring.

'Let's get on with it, eh?' said Sam. 'Or my brother will be having a go at me for wasting time fraternising.' There was that cheeky smile again.

'I fully intend to get on with it,' replied Evvy, haughtily. 'I'm here to do my job, nothing more.'

'Right you are,' said Sam cheerily, as he opened the driver's door.

Evvy could see he knew he'd had an effect on her. He was the sort that knew he always had that effect on most women he spoke to. But she was determined to do her job well and not be distracted by any silly flirting nonsense with the men here, however handsome they were. She realised at that moment that she wanted, more than anything, to be taken seriously.

Before long, they'd collected a few steel helmets and rubber boots and stashed them on the bus, before returning to the Argyle Street station. Evvy enjoyed bringing them in, to the delight of the AFS firemen there who complained that it was 'about bloody time' that they got some proper safety gear. Evvy noted that Bailey must have spoken to them since last night, because everyone was properly respectful and polite to her, which made a nice change. She just had time to slip to the ladies' room to have a quick wash and brush her teeth before reporting to Bailey at 6 a.m. He immediately sent her for breakfast with a few other chaps and they were all friendly and asked her about herself. She noticed a couple of them were shy with her, surreptitiously glancing at her when they thought she wasn't looking. It was nice to talk to them and interesting to hear more about Bailey and the others at the station. There was a mixture of social types: the career firemen were mostly the born-and-bred working-class Londoners, while the AFS ones were a mixture, some working-class and a couple who appeared more well-heeled and one who spoke with a much posher accent. Evvy could see that the dominant males of the group were the London Fire Brigade blokes, and the posher ones of the AFS were definitely seen as a few rungs below on the ladder, treated like new boys in the school playground. They called the one upper-class AFS chap 'the rookie' and ribbed him a lot. He took it well, considering. An interesting turn of events in wartime, with the social hierarchy being turned on its head. Experience had become the new currency.

One chap told her a bit more about the Bailey brothers, that Lewis Bailey was eight years Sam's senior but treated his brother more like a son, since their parents had died when they were quite young. The Bailey brothers were 'thick as thieves', it was said, yet equally 'wind each other up something terrible'. *A love-hate relationship then*, thought Evvy. *Sounds like me and Connie.*

After breakfast, they went back to the station and Evvy was introduced to the two new women who had just arrived, dressed in civvies like her.

'Camp beds just turned up for you three girls. Down in the library. And your uniforms got here all right,' said a fireman and pointed down the hallway to the classroom where the bedding was.

The other women were called Lynn and Pauline, chatty and nice. Lynn was young and eager, early twenties, while Pauline was older, perhaps in her late thirties, and had clearly taken Lynn under her wing. They both said how glad they were there was another woman at the place, 'as we're a bit outnumbered, aren't we!' said Pauline.

They went into the classroom to find a table with a heaped pile of AFS uniforms, all mixed up and wrinkled and, quite frankly, a mess. Pauline got the three women organised straight away, dictating a list of each item they would need: smart tunics, skirts and very nice jockey caps with a bow above the peak, all of the uniform in blue with red piping. It was an attractive uniform and Evvy liked it better than Grace's Wren uniform and much more than the other services. She wanted to do her duty, but she'd much rather not look like a frump while doing it. But after sifting through the piles, they realised that there was not one complete set of everything and only two skirts and two pairs of trousers, both of which were huge at the waist, as if they'd been made for barrels to wear.

'Oh dear, only two skirts,' said Lynn. 'What shall we do?'

'I'll be wearing trousers,' said Evvy. 'I hate skirts. And anyway, I'll be driving, so trousers will suit me much better.'

'But you can't wear those, love,' said Pauline.

'It's all right,' Evvy replied. 'I'm pretty good with a sewing machine.' Hers had been left at her friend's house, along with her sewing bag of scissors, needles and pins and so forth. She'd pop round there later when she was off-duty and get those trousers cut up and sorted in no time. She held them up against her and they all laughed at how wide they were.

'You could fit three of you in one leg!' said a male voice and they all looked up. It was Sam Bailey, tall and slim, leaning casually on the door jamb, smiling gently, with his arms folded. He held his cap in his hand, tapping it against his arm, watching Evvy.

'Don't you have a fire to put out?' she remarked and turned away from him, sifting through the pile of uniforms, pretending to look for something when she already had what she needed.

'Only in my heart,' he replied. '*My foolish heart*,' he sang, sweetly.

Lynn and Pauline stood silently and watched them both, waiting for what Evvy would say next.

'Steady on, Bing Crosby,' she said and glanced up at him. He still had that delicious little smile playing around his lips and she had to look away, he was so beautiful. Damn these good-looking men! Not for the first time, she wished she didn't like men. She'd had plenty of experience with them, never had any trouble attracting them. She knew how pretty she was but tried never to be arrogant about it. She despised arrogance, her most hated characteristic in a person. Evvy had been surrounded by arrogant girls at boarding school – full of money and privilege and snobbery – and couldn't wait to escape the prison camp, as she called it, and run off to France. She had met such different types of men there – artistic men, poor men, writers and musicians. Some were still arrogant, but she learnt that the men who had real talent were often those who were least sure of themselves. The conceited ones were invariably talentless.

'Sam Bailey, actually,' he said, addressing Pauline and Lynn. 'Pleased to meet you two ladies.'

Pauline and Lynn both said 'pleased to meet you' back, but Evvy still poked about in the clothes, refusing to reward him with a glance, let alone a word.

When she finally looked back up, he had gone.

'What a *dish*!' whispered Lynn, eyes agog.

'And doesn't he know it,' said Pauline, with a knowing look.

'My thoughts exactly,' agreed Evvy. 'Doesn't he just,' she added and pensively bit her lip.

Chapter 2

Just over a week later, Evvy walked swiftly towards Lyons'
Corner House on Tottenham Court Road, where she'd
arranged to meet her elder sister Grace for a quick cuppa
while on a break. Grace had just recently been moved from
being stationed near the family home at Scarborough all
the way down to Hertfordshire, but she came into London
when she could. They hadn't seen each other for months
and Evvy was looking forward to seeing her sister, but she
was running late, as usual.

'Darling!' called Grace as Evvy hurried in through the
door.

Her sister looked so different from the last time she'd seen
her that Evvy almost didn't recognise her. Grace had always
had long, dead-straight hair which she wore as a curtain in
front of her face. To hide from the world, Evvy had always

thought. But now, her hair was shoulder-length and curled beautifully off her face, with a lovely bounce to it. She was nicely dressed, with a smart frock and good shoes, in sharp contrast to the baggy old day dresses she used to wear when she was at Oxford studying all that ancient stuff she buried her head in, all that Greek and Latin. Since she'd joined the Wrens, Grace had transformed into a confident woman. Evvy assumed it was the Navy work she did that had given her this self-assurance, but, just like the rest of the family, she had no idea what kind of work it was, as it was all top secret. All Grace could say was that it was an indoor job. Plus any passer-by could see that the station she'd worked at in Scarborough had been surrounded by aerials. But's that all they knew. Well, whatever it was, it suited her down to the ground.

'Gracie! You look glorious!'

'Oh, shut up,' said Grace good-naturedly, though clearly pleased.

They had a quick but heartfelt hug, then sat down for tea and scones with currants in, which were as hard as rocks.

'You look marvellous too, Evvy. I love your uniform. The red piping is smashing, especially on your lovely cap. It really suits you. And those trousers fit you like a glove!'

'And so they should, because I adjusted them myself. The original pair were made for King Kong.'

Grace laughed and said, 'Tell me everything. How's London life? I hear Mummy wanted you to come home, but I knew you wouldn't.'

'Oh, God, no. I love Raven Hall, of course, but I don't want to live out in the sticks, for heaven's sake.' Evvy thought for a moment about her beloved home at Ravenscar, perched on a cliff overlooking the sea and its serene views across to Robin Hood's Bay. Evvy had been trying to escape it all her life, as she was prone to adventures, yet the hall would always be her bolt-hole, her port in the storm. But for now, she was eager to face the storm and all its challenges. 'No, I knew the painting work was starting to dry up, so I decided to join something before I got told by the government where to go. I couldn't bear to join one of the services – the ATS girls, the Wrennies and the WAAFies and all that nonsense. No offence. You know how ill-suited I am to discipline.'

'Oh, I do,' said Grace. 'A perfect terror at school. I think they were pleasantly surprised when Connie and the twins were well-behaved, after the stunts you used to pull.'

'So, I thought if I'm going to have to do war work, I want to be in London where it's fun and if I must wear a damn uniform, then at least let it have a bit of style, and to be part of something that's not too dull. So the AFS seemed like a good bet.' Evvy spread some margarine on the scone to try to improve it, but it could still crack your teeth. 'Why are the scones so awful? Lyons is usually good. I'm guessing it's shortages. Maybe it's half made with sawdust.'

'Here, just daub it with jam and stop moaning,' Grace chided her, always the slightly bossy older sister. 'So, tell me, how is the AFS? You certainly look bright-eyed and bushy-tailed. Does it suit you, the work?'

'Yes, I believe it does, so far. Before I got called up full-time, they gave us lectures on hoses and nozzles and water pressure and such things, as well as how fires work, how they start, how they spread. And about the different bombs the enemy might use, especially the fire-starting ones, the incendiaries. They taught us comical names, like male and female couplings and goose necks. It was all rather exotic! They showed us how to hold the hoses correctly, because even though they won't let women near any equipment in a real fire scenario – heaven forbid! – they have at least realised that women will be manning the stations when the chaps are out fighting fires, so if the station gets hit, the gals will need to be trained to put fires out, instead of sitting there screaming or filing their nails!'

'Oh, don't get me started on women in the forces. And I mean it – don't. Because I can't tell you anything anyway. But, suffice to say, I know exactly what you mean and I've had my own battles in recent months, just to be taken seriously.'

'Yes, it's infuriating, isn't it? But, to be fair, they are starting to take me seriously now I've had a bit of driver training.'

'Ooh, is that what you'll be doing, then?'

'Yes, they've had me training as a driver all week. I started on the school bus at our station, which was easy enough, and yesterday I had a go at a pretty big truck, but I did have a bit of trouble when I went down quite a narrow street and there was a van coming the other way, so I had to manoeuvre up on to the pavement and somehow the top corner of the truck got attached to the awning over a hardware shop and as I blithely carried on down the road, I stripped the whole thing off with a great ripping sound! The owner came running out, screaming at me! "Sorry, guv'nor!" I shouted and carried on.'

Grace laughed and said, 'Only you, Evvy. Only you!'

'Yes, I know. Another one of my famous scrapes. The AFS will pay him back, they said, but weren't best pleased with me. Well, I'm not used to how big these vehicles are yet, great lumbering things, like prehistoric creatures. Yesterday, they sent me to New Cross speedway to do some motorbike training and that suited me far better. I got really quite fast on the thing and really enjoyed the speed. Such fun! So, I'll be doing a mixture of jobs for the chaps. Driving messages and equipment and things and men around London, sometimes on two wheels, sometimes on four.'

'Oh, Evvy, that sounds jolly good for you. Just perfect. I can't imagine you sitting for hours inside answering phones.'

'Well, *exactly*, darling. As you know well, that would drive me absolutely cuckoo. I have to get out and about. Now look, enough about me. I know you can't tell me about your work, but can you tell me about your man, Jim? Mummy wrote and said he was awfully nice. She really likes him, you know.'

Grace gave her a faraway kind of smile and her eyes veritably sparkled, which showed Evvy that her sister was head over heels in love.

'Oh, I say,' said Evvy and grinned at Grace. 'You've got it bad!'

'I have rather. I know we've only been together around four months or so, but I've spent a lot of that time with him, not only at work but out of it, every moment we can get. And I feel I know him better than I've ever known anyone. Jim is the nicest, funniest, sweetest person I think I've ever met. I didn't know you could feel this way about a man.'

Evvy was genuinely thrilled to see Grace glowing like this. Evvy had always found boys and men flocked around her, which could be annoying, but she knew how shy Grace had been and how difficult she'd found making any sort of connections with the opposite sex.

'He better be the nicest man in the world,' said Evvy, taking Grace's hand and squeezing it. 'Or he'll have me to answer to. Truth is, *you're* the nicest person I've ever met, Gracie. And you really deserve a nice bloke.'

'Thank you, darling,' said Grace and blew her sister a little kiss. 'Now, what about you? Any nice fellers on the horizon?'

'Oh, you know me, sweetie. Men are easy come, easy go in my book. So tiresome, most of them.'

'Working with firemen sounds rather dashing. Are there any dashing ones?'

The Bailey brothers immediately sprang to mind, especially the younger one.

'There is a very pretty boy at my station. I mean, he's prettier than most girls I know. Ridiculously handsome. He's been trying to talk to me all week, but whenever he does, he has nothing to say. Absolutely nothing! A bit of banter, but when that runs out, he just dries up. Most disappointing.'

'How dull. Is he a bit thick, do you think?'

'I don't know! Maybe!' laughed Evvy. 'He might just be trying to look like he isn't really bothered, in front of the others. Perhaps if we were alone, he might open up a bit. But, honestly, I wonder if he might just be a dud. All the lights are blazing, but nobody's home. Know what I mean?'

'I've met a few girls like that too in my time,' said Grace. 'But some men don't seem to mind that!'

'Well, I damn well mind. I can't be spending my precious time with an idiot.'

'Why not give him a chance? I can see you've taken a bit of a shine to him, darling,' said Grace, giving her sister a knowing look.

'No, I haven't!' insisted Evvy. 'You asked about fellers so I told you who was about. I've not really had time to bother with flirting, to be honest. The driver training has been pretty full on. And our boss – who everyone calls S.O. – is very strict and keeps us busy. If I'm not driving, I'm helping organise supplies and cleaning equipment and so forth. He's a bit of a taskmaster. But he runs a tight ship and I appreciate that. Nothing worse than an incompetent boss. If I have to answer to someone, at least let him be good at his job. And he is, our S.O., Lewis Bailey, he really is. He's the pretty one's brother actually. But they couldn't be more different. I have a feeling Bailey's got hidden depths.'

'You like him too, don't you?' smirked Grace.

'Oh, do shut up, Gracie! You'll have me married off before the tea goes cold. Speaking of which, it has a bit and I must get back in a minute. Sorry it's such a short visit.'

They finished off with a quick discussion of home.

Just before Evvy was about to leave, she made a throwaway comment about their mother. 'And I wonder if before long Mummy won't be married off again.'

'Who on earth to?' said Grace, clearly perplexed.

'Harry, of course, that dishy young officer.'

'The RAF chappie who stayed at the hall a while?'

'Yes, of course. They were like two peas in a pod, Connie said.'

'Connie never told me that!' cried Grace.

'Connie never tells you anything. She thinks you'll look down your nose at her. She calls me up and tells me all her secrets. And her secret is she's got a crush on Harry, but she was annoyed because he was always hanging about with Mummy in the evenings when she wanted to talk to him. She's too naïve to realise they were up to something, but I read between the lines.'

'Well, that's a big assumption to make!' said Grace. 'And anyway, it's ridiculous. He's twenty years younger than her.'

'Not quite. And so what? Love doesn't give a damn about age. They've got something juicy going on, I'm sure of it. And good for her! What a catch! He's lovely, isn't he? Gorgeous to look at and, by all accounts, marvellous with children and fascinating to talk to.'

'Oh Evvy, you do talk such rot sometimes. Mummy would never do something so reckless, so . . . unusual. She's highly conventional, you know. You've cooked this whole thing up in your head. And I don't think you should say such slanderous things so lightly.'

'Don't get your knickers in a twist!' Evvy said, rather loudly, causing a couple of other diners to look round disapprovingly.

'Evvy!' Grace whispered sharply.

'All right, all right. Don't go all matronly on me. Think what you like about Mummy. But I say, good for her. She deserves a bit of fun after being married to that cad of a husband and useless father we had all those years and then becoming a widow so young. Why shouldn't she? It's not against the law for her and Harry to have something going, for heaven's sake.'

But Grace was perturbed by the whole thing, Evvy could tell. So there was no point in pushing it. Grace was actually the highly conventional one. And she'd always got on better with their father before he died. He approved of Grace, as he liked women to be subdued, and pliable to his whims, whereas Evvy was too wild, the same as him, and so they always knocked heads on the rare occasions he was home from gallivanting. And when Evvy had heard he was dead, in a skiing accident, flattened by an avalanche a few years back, she didn't cry like all the others did. She had loved her father, but she had not liked him very much. Sometimes the thought of him made her feel angrily sad and that annoyed her. She hated to show any sign of weakness. And so, she and Grace always disagreed about their father and thus the subject was best avoided between them. Evvy immediately regretted bringing him up.

'Look, I'm sorry. That was bad form. Can we forget all that and part as good sisters? I hardly see you and don't want to fall out when we do.'

'Of course, darling,' said Grace and reached across to squeeze Evvy's hand. 'It was lovely to see you. I must get back too. Got a train to catch. On duty tonight.'

They stood up, paid and left. In the street, they had another quick hug, but Grace held on a little longer than Evvy and Evvy let her, feeling her arms squeeze tighter around her.

'Everything all right, Gracie?'

Grace stood back and tossed her hair, just the same way Evvy always did. 'Everything's fine, darling. I just, you know . . . I just think a lot about wartime and danger and so forth. Mummy and the girls are all safe where they are. But I worry about you, here in London. What if the bombers come? I just hope you know what you're doing, joining the fire service. It scares me, darling. It does.'

'Ah, don't worry, sis. You know me. I'm always in some scrape or another and I always fight my way out. Besides, if Hitler was going to bomb London, wouldn't he have done it by now? I'll be grand, you'll see. You take care of yourself too, though I suspect you'll be quite safe in rural Hertfordshire.'

'There's a possibility I might be sent abroad, perhaps in the new year. We're not sure yet. But I'll let you know, as soon as I do.'

'Gosh, well, I'm quite envious, Gracie. That sounds jolly exciting!'

'Yes,' said Grace, in a small voice, not sounding at all convinced. Evvy wondered if she was thinking of Jim and leaving him behind.

'That man of yours will wait for you, if he's worthy,' said Evvy and kissed her sister on the cheek. She saw Grace had a tear in her eye. Always got emotional at partings, that one. 'C'mon, cheer up, sweetheart.'

'Oh, I'm all right,' replied Grace, putting on a brave face and tossing her hair again. 'Let's meet up again when we can and try not to leave it so long next time, hmm?'

'Oh, you know me, darling. Always larking about. But we'll find a spare half-hour here or there. Goodbye, sis. See you soon.'

'Yes, darling,' said Grace with resolve. 'See you soon.'

Evvy walked back to the station thoughtfully. She really did love her sister so much, but always felt awkward showing her just how much. Evvy hated to show her feelings to anyone, really. Again, like her father that way. She had quite envied Grace's look when she'd talked about Jim. All those men buzzing about Evvy for years and she had never felt a damn thing for any of them. Grace meets one nice man and he turns out to be the love of her life, by the sounds of it.

Well, Gracie deserves that, more than anyone, Evvy thought and told herself to stop wallowing. *Love is not for me,* she reminded herself. She believed she was too selfish for love or marriage or babies and any of that girly nonsense. She had the world to see and art to create and no time for female things. With pride, she thought about how she was walking back to her job as a driver for the AFS, and in doing so, blazing a trail for women everywhere. *Perhaps after this bloody stupid war,* she thought, *the world will realise women can do everything a man can do. And then we'll get on in the world without being perpetually held back.* She was determined to start this revolution herself, in her own way.

* * *

'Waste of money,' someone said loudly, beside her, just as she was about to go into the fire station entrance. She turned and glanced back, thinking it was just an overheard snippet from a passer-by's conversation. But she saw a middle-aged couple, arm in arm, who had stopped in the street and were staring at her indignantly.

'Are you addressing me?' she asked, in her best imperious voice.

'Yes, I am,' replied the woman. 'You're a waste of money. Two pounds a week, I read in the paper. Two pounds a week to swan around in that get-up and no fires except the usuals and the fire brigade can take care of those. Terrible waste of public money, you AFS lot. And you, walking along the street, bold as brass in your uniform without a care in the world. I'm not surprised with two pounds a week in your pocket. It's a disgrace!'

'Oh, do put a sock in it,' said Evvy scathingly.

'How dare you!' snapped the woman's husband.

'No, actually, how dare *you*. What are you doing for the war effort, eh?'

'Our son's in the Navy!' cried the man.

'Good for him, but that's not you, is it? And you won't be whining about the AFS if Hitler starts bombing London, will you? You'll be crying out for them, in your slippers, when your house is set on fire from a hail of incendiary bombs. We'll see who's a waste of money then, won't we?'

Evvy turned away from the couple, who walked off muttering about how rude she was, what a disgrace it was et cetera, et cetera. She looked up and saw Lewis Bailey watching her from the main door.

'You give as good as you get, don't you, Calvert?'

'Better, I'd say,' she quipped, then remembered her place and added a hasty, 'sir.' He gave her a stern look and she added, 'Sorry, sir. Mouth engaged before brain, as usual.'

'It's all right, Calvert. Lots of my men get an earful when they walk down the street in their AFS uniform. Worse than the girls get, mostly, as they call them army-dodgers and suchlike. Most of them change into their civvies after a shift so they don't have to walk home in their uniform and get yelled at.'

'It's not right, sir. It's not. We're all training like mad and getting ready for when it happens. If it happens . . .'

'Oh, it'll happen, all right. It'll come. The Luftwaffe have kept themselves busy with the RAF stations, but that won't last forever. They'll come for us soon. You can count on it.'

Evvy hadn't really believed herself when she'd said to Grace that Hitler would've done it already if he was going to start bombing London, but she had wanted to reassure her sister. She was ashamed to admit to herself that in the past few days, during all this training for the eventual battle for London, she had hoped that it came to something tangible, that she could use her skills in a real-life emergency rather than all these drills and ifs and buts and maybes. And then she realised how foolish it was, to wish for destruction. Hearing it from Lewis Bailey made it feel real. Somehow, whenever he spoke, whatever he said, she felt it was accurate and fair, trustworthy and absolute. He had that kind of a voice, not bossy, but steady and true.

'Then it's a good job we're prepared for it, isn't it, sir?' she said. 'Everyone here is smashing. They all know what they're doing and they're all keen as mustard.'

'Thank you. I reckon that's true. I've done my best to get this new station up and running and keep all you AFS lot in check.'

'Have you always worked for the fire brigade, sir?'

'Yes, man and boy. My brother too. Our dad was a fireman before us. When we learnt about the AFS joining the service, I volunteered to set up substations and train and supervise the new blokes. It felt a worthy thing to do. We'll need you all, I'm sure of that. And soon. Feel it in my bones. Hitler hasn't even got started on us yet. Fire will rain down upon us.'

Evvy felt a little chill run down her spine. But she was determined not to show a glimmer of fear. 'I'm ready, sir.'

'Yes, I reckon you are. But I'm not convinced all of the other substations are. And, actually, that's something you could help me with. Later on, I'll be giving you a shout. I need you for a little trip. Sleep with your uniform on tonight, Calvert, all right?'

'Yes, of course, sir,' she replied, intrigued for a moment as to what this trip could be, then focusing back on her work, as she had arrived at the station just in time for duty.

She was sent off to collect more equipment from another station. She took the school bus and the wrinkled map of London she kept in her pocket at all times. She'd been told to begin memorising the streets in the local area, because if London was bombed wholesale and fires were everywhere, there would be blocked roads all over the place – either buildings collapsed and debris in the street or criss-crossed by hoses and ankle-deep in water. So, she needed to learn the directions all around the area so that she could get her despatches quickly to her destination, taking alternative routes if necessary.

After she'd dropped the stuff off, she asked permission to do a recon of the local area and spent a couple of hours driving around Bloomsbury, Fitzrovia and St Pancras, noting down shortcuts on the back of the map with a stubby pencil. She felt ideally suited to this aspect of the job, due to her excellent, almost photographic memory. She could have been a London taxi driver in another life, she mused. She felt a great pride in the fact that she had already committed to her visual memory quite a few of the streets between her own substation and four other main stations nearby, in Soho, Camden Town, Clerkenwell and Islington. Her next task would be to memorise the locations of the several substations attached to these main fire stations, dotted around in the streets surrounding each of them. After that, she intended learning all of the other main fire stations in the next circle of boroughs surrounding Bloomsbury. She had been instructed that if the war from the air came to London, all of the stations might be called upon to direct equipment to anywhere in the city that needed it, so she'd need to be absolutely sure where she was going, as she'd have to get there in a hurry at a moment's notice. Lives would be at stake and she'd never had a better reason to learn something quickly. *If only they'd said it's a matter of life and death at school*, she thought, *I might have bothered to concentrate.*

When she'd finished her recce, she went back in to the station and had a chance to chat to Lynn and Pauline for a while, telling them in great detail everything the rude couple in the street had said to her and everything she'd answered back. They seemed to love hearing her stories of how mouthy and brazen she was with people; they always laughed and clapped when she told them such things, which encouraged her even more. Sometimes she hoped that someone would give her cause to be sarcastic and daringly witty, just so she could tell it to Lynn and Pauline when she got back.

Soon after, it was dinnertime, then time for sleep. Evvy bedded down beside the other two women in their camp beds in the school library, surrounded by children's books. Each bedtime that week, she'd taken something down from the shelf and read an old favourite to herself. It was comforting to return to the characters of her childhood. Of all the girls, she and Daisy were the ones most obsessed with storybooks. They would snuggle up together and read and reread *Cinderella*, *Pinocchio*, *The Elves and the Shoemaker*, *The Musicians of Bremen*, *The Ugly Duckling*, *The Twelve Dancing Princesses*, and so on. She loved fairy tales and stories of toys coming to life or elves and brownies and other sprites sneaking into houses and causing mischief. Lying on the stiff, unyielding camp beds in the school library, still getting accustomed to the odd sensations of this new life she'd begun, it was nice to read a few pages of *Alice in Wonderland* or *Peter Pan* before she slept. It made everything seem a little unreal and in this time of war, where the world and its troubles were all too real, a little imaginative escape could help a lot.

Knowing something was going to happen that night, this 'little trip' Bailey had told her about, meant she could not sleep at first. She lay awake listening to Lynn and Pauline's breathing, but before long, the rigours of the day caught up with her and she was fast asleep.

The next thing she knew, there was a little shove on her shoulder, which she ignored, dreaming of being lost in the woods and leaning against trees that came to life. Then came another shove. She woke up with a start to see Lewis Bailey looking down at her.

'Fancy a little drive, Calvert?' he whispered.

'Yes, sir,' she said, too loudly, forcing herself to wake and sit up.

'Go and get the bus up and running and bring it round the front. I'll join you in a minute.'

Evvy did as instructed and jumped up, hearing Pauline and Lynn grumbling from their beds but – lucky them – turning over and getting straight back to sleep. Yet, though she loved her sleep, Evvy was rather excited about whatever this was going to turn out to be. She liked the idea of a midnight drive to who knew where.

She fetched the bus keys from the hook she used behind the library desk and went out to the back. The moon was high and bright, throwing sharply diagonal shadows of unlit street lamps across the playground. She started up the bus and drove it round to the front. She was getting used to this vehicle now and really quite fond of it. She'd christened it Suki in her head – Suki the school bus. She liked to give her vehicles names. The big lumbering truck she'd driven the other day was Nellie (the Elephant). Suki was much easier to drive, small and neat with a nice little chug-chug sound when she was idling, as she was now in the street.

Bailey came out of the station and hopped into the bus, all dressed up in his full uniform with smart cap and rank displayed and everything polished and neat and tickety-boo. He did look impressive like that, she admitted to herself.

'Head for Camden Town, Calvert. We're going to pay one of our substations a surprise visit. See how ready they are.'

Off they went, driving through the blacked-out, deserted streets of London. It was eerie and thrilling all at once, with Lewis Bailey beside her, not speaking a word. Evvy concentrated hard on her memory of the streets running north towards Camden Town, waiting to hear from S.O. where their final destination would be. There was an atmosphere in the bus she couldn't quite put her finger on, a kind of electric charge in the air, an expectation of something, but she could not decide what. She tried to focus only on the road ahead, as all she had to see by was a thin strip of light emitting from her shielded headlights and the moon that shone down on them. Yet, there was a bit of breeze that night, and at times, clouds were blown across the moon and the night fell into black darkness, and she had to focus fiercely on the way ahead to avoid the shadowy shapes looming up on each side and in front; a memory jumped into her mind of reading a detailed description of Snow White fleeing through the midnight woods to escape the evil queen, the jagged shapes of trees threatening her as she ran.

'Concentrate,' she muttered to herself. She had a marvellous capacity of mind when the conscious part of it was in charge, but too often she'd drift off into the reveries of the subconscious when she really needed to be wide awake in the real world. She scolded herself inwardly for her daydreamy ways.

As if he knew, Bailey said, 'You're doing just fine. Turn left down here, then first right . . . Now pull up there.'

She saw another school to the right, similar to theirs, and saw a space just before it, where she pulled in. It was shrouded in darkness due to the blackout and looked as if it were empty.

'Is this place operational, sir?' she asked.

'Indeed it is, Calvert. There should be seven men and three girls in there, all ready for action, with their equipment organised, their appliances parked up behind and everything prepared for immediate movement in case of emergency. The last time I came, the whole venture was in a right mess and I gave them a stern dressing-down and told them I'd have their guts for garters if they hadn't got themselves shipshape the next time I came. Shall we see if they are ready? Or if they're still in a right mess, as I suspect?'

He had a wicked smile on his face and Evvy couldn't help but smile back.

'Oh, yes, sir. Let's see!'

'Come on, then. Softly, softly, Calvert.'

They crept up to the front door and stopped. Then Bailey raised his fist and pounded on the door, pushing it open and storming in, shouting, 'Inspection! Inspection from your district officer! Look lively!'

Evvy followed behind, hearing the skid of chairs scraping back and spotting alarmed-looking blokes appearing in doorways. Bailey marched around the facilities as Evvy waited in the corridor, standing to attention. Some of the men had clearly been asleep on the job, but Bailey said he was pleased to see that all the equipment was in order, the maps were now correct on the watchroom wall, the women were wide awake and waiting at the phones and everyone was in the correct uniform, except one fellow whose tunic had not yet arrived and he wore a donkey jacket instead with what looked like Ovaltine stains down the front, for which he got a good telling-off from Bailey.

Then he swept out as swiftly as he had descended upon them, Evvy behind him, stifling laughter as she heard the mutterings behind her of disgruntled AFS staff, who'd given her dirty looks the whole time she'd stood there. Back out to the bus, Bailey waited by the door and she unlocked it and opened it for him, watching him climbing in with a secret smile on his face at their successful night-time raid.

Driving back, Bailey did not speak and Evvy ventured to say, 'They didn't do too badly, did they, sir?'

'Well, I've seen worse. And I've seen better. But, yes, they weren't too bad. Sometimes it's good to put the wind up people. Especially in this waiting-room period of wartime, folk can get lazy. Get complacent. So I keep everyone on their toes, because the enemy never sleeps, Calvert. Those bastards never sleep.'

It was shocking to hear a man swear in conversation with her. She'd heard plenty of colourful language in France, but in England she found that men were often loath to use profanity in front of a woman. She felt a little privileged that Bailey had chosen her for this mission and had been relaxed enough with her to speak as he felt. It heightened the strange atmosphere between them even more and again she told herself to focus on the streets. The last thing she needed right now was to lack concentration and clip the wing mirror of a parked vehicle on the way back. She did her best and got them back safe and sound.

They walked in silence across the darkened playground and when they reached the door, Bailey opened it for her and stood aside, motioning for her to walk through, following her after. She turned to receive her next instruction and he pulled the door shut, the corridor in shadow so deep, she could barely see him, just a glimmer of light from the next corridor thrown across the far wall giving shape to his form. She noticed the curve of his back, his long legs.

His profile was etched in the dim light and he looked like a statue of a man standing there, stalwart and strong, decidedly handsome.

'You did well, Calvert.'

'Thank you, sir.'

'You're . . . you are . . .' He ran out of words and she held her breath. What was he trying to say? 'You're a brick.'

'Thank you, sir.' It was not the word she'd expected, although, to be honest, she had no idea what she expected from this mystery of a man, her superior officer. 'I do try.'

'I'm . . . glad you're here.'

'Me too, sir.'

'Good . . .' he said, quieter. 'Good.' And with that, he turned away and strode up the corridor, calling back without turning his head, 'You're off duty now. Get some shut-eye.'

But back in her camp bed, thinking about the events of the night and Lewis Bailey's phrase 'shut-eye' that made her think of the Hans Christian Andersen story about the Sandman who came to sleepy children with his dreams painted on umbrellas, she wished Old Shut-eye would come to her, because, for a range of reasons too complex to figure out that night, she could not sleep for all the tea in China.

Chapter 3

August 1940

It was early morning at Raven Hall. Rosina sat at her desk, gazing at the view from her window. Despite living in this house all of her life, she never tired of that vista. The neat, tended grounds, part laid to clipped lawns and bordered by pretty shrubs, sloping down to the walls that held back the encroachment of the wildness beyond, the bracken fringing every barricade, as if reaching over to peer into her gardens. Her eye was always drawn to the curve of Robin Hood's Bay, opposite her own headland at Ravenscar, surrounded by moorland and higgledy-piggledy farms marked out by hedges and patches of every shade of green. At this hour, Rosina's study was bathed in yellow light. She sat amidst this display of nature's gold, staring down at a telegram she held in her hands, reading the few, simple words, over and over. It had arrived two weeks before, saying only that Harry had arrived in port. He couldn't say where, but he'd cheekily constructed what sounded like a cryptic crossword clue. She had smiled at his cleverness when she'd received the telegram and delighted in settling down to try to work it out. The clue in the telegram read: 'On the contrary STOP captivity village lowlands queen of jungle STOP'.

Harry knew she did a crossword every day and had done for years. 'On the contrary' probably meant she had to look for opposites. So, the opposite of captivity was . . . liberty? Freedom? Village became town or city? Lowlands were highlands, hills, mountains? Queen of jungle was king of jungle, perhaps – the lion? That gave her liberty city mountains lion, which she puzzled over for a few minutes, then got out her atlas. Where might Harry be going that was not occupied, that could be reached by sea and took about a week or so to get there and that was a British territory? Various scribblings and searchings later, she got it: Freetown, Sierra Leone. She looked back at the atlas and placed her fingertip on the city, obliterating it. That was where her love resided. But for how long? It seemed awfully foreign and far away. It gave her a shiver of fear, but at least she knew where he was and that was a blessing. The clever thing, using a cryptic clue! Cheeky too, but Rosina guessed the likelihood of German spies being familiar with the workings of English cryptic crossword clues seemed suitably small.

She folded the telegram carefully and opened the bottom left-hand drawer of her desk, the one with the lock on it, where she now kept all of Harry's correspondence. She had kept his early letters in her handbag, as nobody would ever look in there and she wanted to keep them private. Now, there were too many to cart about in her handbag all the time, so she locked them away in this drawer and kept the key in her handbag instead. Sometimes, she'd retrieve them when she couldn't sleep and would read over them in bed. At those times, in the quiet of night, she'd thought often of the deep, delicious kisses they'd had beside the king and queen's seats, the stone chairs on the outcrop that overlooked the gardens. She pictured what might have happened if there had been nobody at home, no war, no responsibility and instead just the two of them, him leading her inside to her bed and . . . all of the rest of it . . . They had only kissed in reality, but in her mind, they had gone so much further in thoughts that were divine yet frustrating. After these night-time imaginings, when she had looked at his dear script and touched the page where his hand had guided the pen, she made sure she locked the letters away again in the morning.

Her relationship with Harry was still a secret from everyone except dear Bairstow, her housekeeper and cook, who had guessed at their love recently. It had turned out that Bairstow, who had never married, had had a secret love of her own as a young woman, thus they had bonded over this. Since then, Rosina felt their relationship had shifted from employer–employee to something more akin to friendship, though, of course, she had lived with servants all her life and was not naïve enough to believe that true friendship was possible with someone who was paid to be there. As kind as Bairstow was, and as much as Rosina relied on her, she would always be her employee.

Now, sitting in her study in the early morning, thinking with an ache of how much she missed Harry, Rosina realised again how isolated she felt in Raven Hall – a widow, a mother of five, sole land agent of her family estate and responsible for it all. She was wise enough to know how lucky she was, to have a home at all, to have five daughters who loved her, to have at least a few staff left to help her run the place and – as yet – little disruption from the war, aside from the depleted staff and the senseless shooting of some cows by a German aircraft. She knew she was more than lucky not to be working in a factory or a coal mine or any other hard-labouring job she could picture, but she did find herself feeling exhausted much of the time, the burden of responsibility for everything weighing more heavily than ever on her shoulders. Whenever she felt sorry for herself, however, she chided herself, thinking of the other theatres of war, in Czechoslovakia, Poland, France, Belgium and the rest, labouring under occupation. At least she still had her freedom, her liberty, as the crossword clue reminded her.

It was time to stop musing and to get on. Breakfast should be started soon. Her two eldest daughters away down south, she had three left at home. It was the very last day of the summer holidays and she needed to get the girls up to tackle their packing for going back to boarding school on the train the next day. Rosina had had her small breakfast early with Bairstow and now must get the girls to eat. Rosina found sleeping tricky these days: too many thoughts. She went upstairs to look in on each of her daughters in turn. Constance – called Connie by everyone – was still fast asleep, on her side with her arm flung back over her straw-coloured head, as if throwing a ball, which she probably was in her dreams, being obsessed with all things sporting. Though such an active girl, she loved her bed. But it was because all that activity wore her out and she always fell asleep in seconds and slept like a log. Rosina nudged her shoulder and Connie grunted awake, looking hazily at her mother, then turning over abruptly and hiding her face.

'Come on, sleepyhead,' said her mother, gently. 'Packing day today.'

Connie grunted again and said, with eyes screwed tight shut, 'I hate school.'

'No, you don't. You've been moaning all summer about how much you miss your team sports and can't wait to get back. Come on, the sooner you're up, the sooner your next hockey match will be.'

Connie forced herself to sit up, rubbing her eyes. 'But it's stupid. I'm just about to turn eighteen at the beginning of September and I can leave school and go and do something useful for the war. Why on earth do I have to go back?'

Rosina sighed and sat down on Connie's bed, briefly recalling yesterday's meagre birthday celebrations they'd held early for Connie and the twins, all born in September, though a year apart. (Rosina would never forget the shock of finding she was pregnant again when Connie was only three months old, compounded later by the discovery that two babies were coming instead of one!) Bairstow had managed to cobble together a small cake and the girls had swapped mostly handmade gifts and some bits of their mother's jewellery (along with Rosina giving all three girls a cash donation to their trust funds), so at least they'd had a bit of celebration at home before doing it for real back at school.

'As we've discussed a thousand times, everyone turns eighteen at some point in their last year of school. It just so happens you have a very early birthday on September the fifth and so you turn eighteen much earlier than most. So you still need to see out your last year of school. And you have exams to take.'

'But I'm hopeless at exams and school stuff, you know that. I just want to get out there and start earning a living and helping my country. School is a complete and utter waste of my time, Mummy. You know that!'

Connie was staring at her now, wide awake. The girl's mid-blue eyes glared fiercely, her long, angular nose and sharp cheekbones giving her a determined look as she dug her heels into her perpetual arguments against her mother's logic, only slightly lessened by the bed-spoiled mess of blonde hair that stood up in clumps all over her head, giving her a somewhat comical appearance in her attempt at fortitude.

Rosina stood up and folded her arms. 'I'm not discussing it again, Constance. You will go back to school and finish this academic year and then we will look at war work. Please do stop causing arguments when you know my mind is made up and my answer will not alter.'

Rosina left the room and had to stop herself from slamming the door. Of all her daughters, Connie gave her the most provocation these days and was a devil for her stubborn nature. Once she'd made up her mind about anything, Connie was a terrier for not letting go of the bone. It used to be Evvy who was the most troublesome, but now she'd left home, Rosina had given up trying to tame her. Connie was successfully taking over the mantle of rebellious daughter and, with her older sisters Grace and Evelyn absent, had assumed amongst the sisters the leadership role in the war against their mother. It rankled Rosina to know that Connie was largely right about leaving school – she'd never been academic, always far more successful at anything practical, involving either her feet, her hands, or both. It made sense for her to leave early and do something more useful. But Rosina felt strongly that not only was it her duty to keep her daughter safe and sound at school until the last possible moment, but it was also what she strongly desired, as the thought of a third daughter out in the dangerous wartime world was too upsetting to contemplate. Two was bad enough. For now, her other three chicks were cooped up in the countryside and Rosina would keep it that way as long as she could. All Connie had to do was grin and bear it for another year. But Rosina fully expected, one day in the not too distant future, that she would receive a telephone call from school to say that Connie had absconded. She just hoped they, and she, could keep Connie there for a few months at least. Maybe the war might resolve itself in that time – who knew? Highly unlikely, Rosina surmised, from reading the newspapers' accounts of Europe's fortunes darkening by the day. But whatever happened, she hoped Connie would stay put for the time being.

Rosina went on to Daisy's room, expecting to find her quietest twin also fast asleep, as Daisy adored bed and would sleep all day if she could. At sixteen years of age, about to turn seventeen, Daisy was not lazy so much as a dreamer, who loved to find quiet places to lie and read or think or look through orchestral manuscripts, playing the music in her mind. Rosina opened the door to find Daisy's bed vacated and her nightie strewn across the unmade bed. She guessed that Daisy must be out with Ronnie, the evacuee, lately her newest and closest bosom friend.

Ronnie Holt had been around the estate since last winter, as he lodged with a farming family nearby who had recently adopted him after the untimely death of his parents in a bombing in Hull. This summer, Daisy and Ronnie had bonded over games of chess and for the past few weeks had become inseparable. They were opposites in some ways, kindred in others. Both shy and quiet, Daisy had brought out his intellectual side and Ronnie had encouraged her to get out and about, as he loved clifftop walks and roaming the moors further afield, as well as trips down to see the seals at the beach below the hall.

When Rosina had first met Ronnie, wandering about the grounds of Raven Hall, she'd thought him about ten years of age, so small and malnourished he was, when, in fact, she'd been amazed to discover later that his true age had actually been fifteen, around the same age as the twins. But these last few months of country living and devoted care from his adoptive parents had transformed the boy and he'd shot up by inches and really filled out. He was the same height as Daisy now and starting to look like a young man, instead of the skinny, short, silent boy Rosina had first met. She wondered about the wisdom of allowing Daisy and Ronnie to spend so much time together alone . . . but the point was moot now, since Daisy was back to boarding school tomorrow and Ronnie would stay here, continuing to attend the local Ravenscar school.

Rosina went to fold up Daisy's nightie neatly and only then saw a scrap of paper on the counterpane, which read, *Gone off scrumping with Ron.* They'd bring back a basketful of random late-summer fruits, no doubt, and later they'd make a pie or crumble with Bairstow.

Lastly, it was her other twin's turn to be roused. Rosina went into Dora's room, to find her sitting up in bed with a book on her lap, scribbling notes on a pad. As she went closer, Rosina could see it was some sort of chemistry work, with a series of equations looping across the page. Her mind boggled that a daughter of hers could be so scientific, when Rosina, though quite good at mental arithmetic, had never found science easy and Dora's late father had been hopeless at anything so academic.

'You're at work early!' said Rosina and came to sit at the end of Dora's bed. Few could tell Daisy and Dora apart, but, of course, as their mother she knew how utterly distinct they really were – the texture and feel of their hands, the moles and other blemishes on their skin, the very subtle differences between the way they looked at her, the quality of light in their eyes, the way their eyebrows and lips moved when they were annoyed, or thoughtful, or amused. All these tiny details of life were embedded in a mother's consciousness and by now Rosina almost found it surprising that anyone could mix them up.

Dora looked up at her mother and smiled briefly, before turning her attention back to her scribbling, her long, wavy, yellow hair framing her face that was frowning in concentration. Dora had always been a bad sleeper, like her mother, though Rosina's mind was usually riven with worries or else ideas for short stories (or, in recent times, lovely thoughts of Harry). Instead, Dora's brain was always at work on some scientific theorem or other and Dora often claimed that sleep was a waste of brainpower and she wished she never had to sleep at all.

'Just in the middle of . . .' Dora said vaguely, before trailing off.

'All right, darling, but you must get up soon and have breakfast. No more lazy mornings. Packing to do.'

'Good-oh,' said Dora, her pencil never ceasing to scribble numbers and letters across the page.

Rosina left her to it, knowing that she'd most likely end up doing most of Dora's packing for her, as this twin so often shunned mundane activities as beneath her, when her mind could be focusing on much more cerebral pursuits.

While the two girls in bed gathered themselves, Rosina went outside to the chicken coop to collect eggs. The day was going to be glorious, warm and breezy, the sun shining down on the pale stone of the battlement-style walls that encircled the grounds. Swallows and house martins dipped and curved through the air over the lush green lawns, while bees buzzed in the bushy lavender that sent its sweet scent on the zephyr. Beyond the walls of Raven Hall, over the ever-present sea, the seagulls swooped and chattered.

On the way to the coop, Rosina saw her gardener Mr Jessop and his under-gardener Mr Throp, who until recently had been a vagrant living in the old brickworks and was 'rescued' (as Connie claimed) by her daughters and given a job and lodgings by Rosina, since both Bairstow and Jessop vouched for him. It had been a risk but turned out to be an excellent decision, as Throp was a hard worker and got on well with Jessop and everyone else.

As Rosina walked towards the gardeners, she noted again how odd it was to see Throp dressed in the clothes of her dead husband George. She had kept them all for the four years since his death in a skiing accident, but when Throp had turned up with nothing on him except one ragged set of clothes, she had decided it was time to put them to use. She had given him several of George's trousers, jackets, shirts and shoes, as well as a couple of coats, scarves and pairs of gloves. She had kept a few items behind to use as material for mending or adapting for herself and her daughters. She had also given him various pullovers, again keeping some for herself to unravel for the wool to knit other items her girls might need. Another widow might have felt some emotion at seeing her dead husband's clothes on someone else, but Rosina had married George Calvert as a rebellion against her father, soon discovering that the infatuation she felt for him was not reciprocated, at which point it popped like a soap bubble. Thus, to see Throp now wearing George's old clothes, the expensive slacks and jackets incongruous in the garden, actually gave her cause to smile. How horrified the snob George Calvert would have been! How nice to think that he would have disapproved. A petty little revenge for all his infidelities and selfishness, but a pleasing one, nevertheless.

Rosina chatted with her gardeners for some minutes about the jobs for the next week or so, then saw Daisy and Ronnie appear from behind the far wall, carrying a basket laden with plums. Rosina waved at them as they made their way towards the kitchen, both of them biting into plums and struggling to keep the juice from running down their arms as they did so, Ronnie licking his wrist. Rosina passed the beehive they'd recently acquired and smiled, as she did every day at the comforting sound of humming that emanated from the little wooden house and looked forward to the fresh honey that Jessop collected and brought to the kitchen table in neat jars from time to time. She'd considered getting a cow last year, but the thought of caring for it and milking it herself felt too much to deal with on top of everything else. Also, she could not get out of her head the image of those poor cows shot up by a German fighter that she'd recently seen in one of her farmer's fields. Harry had put one out of its misery, but she'd never forget its mouth opening and closing silently before it died. She didn't want to be reminded of that every time she went outside. The chickens, however, had proven to be an excellent decision, providing eggs and the odd chicken meal here and there.

The chickens clucked like mad as Rosina approached and – as she did every time she saw them – she thought of Harry and the day they had collected eggs together when she had first known him and together they had given all the chickens movie-star names.

'Come on, Bette,' Rosina said. 'Leave Ginger alone.'

There was a good crop of eggs that morning and as she carried them back to the kitchen, Rosina smiled all the way, feeling that this was a good morning, in a good place, in a good time and that all was right with the world.

But, as often happens at such halcyon moments, it didn't last, because soon after breakfast, there was the sound of a vehicle approaching. Rosina went to the window to see a car pull up and a man and a woman step out, smartly dressed, with folders in their hands.

'Who on earth?' she muttered and Bairstow peered out of the kitchen window too, adding, 'Looks official. That usually means trouble.'

'Oh, God,' moaned Rosina and primped her hair as she walked down the corridor towards the hall, hearing the sound of someone knocking boldly on the door as she approached. A knock on the door these days could mean anything, from mild annoyance to the most devastating kind of news – was it about one of the girls? Grace or Evvy hurt . . . or worse?? Could it be about Harry, but who would know to send word, since their relationship was secret? Rosina felt anxiety rise in her and fought to swallow it down before reaching the front door.

She opened the door to see the woman and man standing smartly on her doorstep, their folders with sheets of paper attached with large, rusty bulldog clips. The woman had a pencil behind one ear.

'Mrs Lazenby?' said the woman.

'Mrs Calvert-Lazenby, yes,' replied Rosina.

'Ah, good. We're from the Office of Works as part of the Directorate of Lands and Accommodation. We're here to inform you that Raven Hall is to be requisitioned by the government for use by the armed services.'

Rosina felt as if all the blood immediately drained from her head and pooled into her shoes. She must have looked it too, as the man said, 'You look quite ill, madam. Should you be seated?'

The woman was not so kindly, as she merely added, 'We need to come in and look around the place, see what best use it can be put to.'

Rosina stepped back without a word and motioned for them to come in. She was lost for words. Of course, she'd considered that this would happen, as the newspapers and friends' letters from different parts of the country had talked of large houses being requisitioned. But when it hadn't happened at the beginning of the war, somehow she wondered if perhaps they'd got away with it and Raven Hall had been forgotten about. But here they were, the government types, ready to shatter that foolish illusion and take over her house and her land. So many questions leapt into her mind, she felt dizzy with them, and again the man asked if she wanted to sit down. Rosina told herself to buck up and pull herself together, as she disliked the woman already and did not want to look weak in front of her.

'I am fine, really. I'm obviously somewhat taken aback, but—'

'No idea why you should be,' said the insufferable woman. 'The war affects everyone and now it's your turn to serve. As I was saying, we need to start a tour of the premises.'

The woman's officious demeanour and pinched little mouth made Rosina want to swear at her. But she kept her cool and answered simply, 'Of course. But can I offer you some tea before we begin?'

'Yes please,' said the man and smiled, but even as the second word left his lips, the woman – who appeared to be his superior – replied that they didn't have time for that and they should get on with a tour of the house.

'Well, I must say that despite the likelihood of this occurrence happening to my family home, it is nevertheless rather a shock and even if you can't imagine that, madam, then hopefully you can comprehend that I have a list of questions that is burgeoning by the minute. Thus, I'd much prefer if we pretended to be civil and sat down for a moment, with a nice pot of tea, rather than plunge headlong into an intimate examination of how my home is going to be invaded and occupied by His Majesty's armed services. I will return shortly. Please wait here.'

This little speech made the woman squint at her and the man half-smile.

Rosina left them standing in the hallway and headed towards the kitchen. As she turned into the corridor and couldn't be seen from the hallway any longer, she stopped and caught her breath, leaning against the wall and closing her eyes as she fought to breathe deeply. A wave of panic came over her. She had fought for years to make Raven Hall and its grounds, land and tenancies a success. And now, since the war began, she had continued alone, making the land as useful as she could and ensuring that the RAF visitors they'd fed for weeks were wonderfully looked after when they were resident, as well as showing kindness to an evacuee and a local vagrant. She had not done nothing, was her feeling, even though such people as the local ARP man Wigfall made her feel her efforts were meaningless and chided her about her blackout and made her feel that landowners and women like herself were automatically unhelpful to the war effort just by their very nature of being wealthy and female. And now came proof that whatever she had done so far in this war, and whatever her daughters had done or were doing, none of it was nearly enough and she'd have to give up her home and land and everything that came with that, to a horde of marauding soldiers.

Would she have to move out? Where would she go? What would the girls do in the holidays? What would happen to her staff? What would happen to the gardens? Would she be reimbursed? How much would it all cost? The tidal wave of questions threatened to overwhelm her as she fought to quell her anxiety and calm down. She breathed slowly and opened her eyes, determined not to crack up under the pressure.

She walked steadily down to the kitchen and the moment Bairstow saw her, she knew it was bad. Rosina explained and Bairstow said, 'We'll sort it. Whatever's coming, we'll face it,' then set about making up a tea tray. Rosina felt instantly better, despite her fears, and knew that in Bairstow she had a tower of strength who would get her through this, whatever happened.

Rosina walked with more fortitude and haste back to the visitors, who were still standing in the same spot in the hall, looking annoyed they'd been left there so long, but Rosina didn't care. If they came with no notice, what did they expect? She took them into the drawing room and soon Bairstow appeared with the beverages. The man thanked Bairstow and Rosina saw Bairstow give the woman a sharp look when she didn't say thank you too.

The woman had not even taken a sip of her tea, when she started up again. 'So, as I was saying, it can't come as too much of a surprise to you, Mrs Lazenby.'

'Calvert-Lazenby,' Rosina repeated, unsmilingly.

'Mrs *Calvert*-Lazenby. I am Mrs Geraldine Clarkson and this is Mr Richard Swift-Croft.'

Rosina nodded at both. Civil servants from London, she assumed. She wondered, what had either of them been obliged to give up in this war? But that was uncharitable, as who knew what sons or daughters the woman had, being of a similar age to Rosina, whereas the man was quite young and Rosina wondered how he had got away with not joining up.

'As I was saying,' Mrs Clarkson said again, her catchphrase, it seemed.

'May I ask some questions, before we launch into anything else?' said Rosina.

'You'll find that your questions will probably be answered as we go along, if you'll allow me to make my explanation of the process of requisitioning. Thus, I'll continue. Your house and grounds are hereby to be taken without notice and used by the armed services for whatever best usage can be made of them. Mr Swift-Croft and myself will need to see around the entire house and grounds today in order for us to ascertain what kind of operation can be based here. It is likely to be the Army, as this area is part of the Northern Command and it is currently necessary to have large houses that can serve as a base for communications, including office space and officer accommodation inside the house, as well as accommodation for the men in the grounds, largely with tents and so forth to begin with and later in temporary yet robust structures the Army will build themselves as to their own needs.'

Rosina felt sick. The thought of every downstairs room turned over to offices and officers sleeping in every upstairs space was bad enough, but the prospect of the grounds being dug up and built upon, then inhabited by ordinary soldiers really was the last straw. It felt like a nightmare. But it was real and it was happening and she had to focus.

'I see,' was all Rosina could reply.

The young man put his teacup down on to the saucer and caught Rosina's eye, saying, 'It must be an awful shock. But we'll try to make it as painless as possible for you, Mrs Calvert-Lazenby.' He had dark circles under his eyes and looked a bit ghoulish as he smiled at her, but she could see he was trying to be nice, unlike his superior, who soon piped up.

'The fact is, madam, that if you had offered up Raven Hall for war use a year ago at the start of the hostilities, you would have had much more choice about what might have happened to it. You could have had your pick, more or less, or far less intrusive visitors, such as a girls' school.'

'Oh yes,' said Mr Swift-Croft. 'Everyone wants a girls' school. They're far less disruptive than boys' schools. And neither are anything compared to the disruption of the armed services. Navy and RAF are seen as less troublesome than the Army, but I'm afraid it is the Army who'll most likely be coming, I'm very sorry to say.'

'As I was saying,' added Mrs Clarkson. 'If you'd offered up the house earlier, you could have avoided the Army, perhaps. But you didn't. So here we are.'

Rosina felt as if the top of her head would explode and steam come rushing out with a scream. Was this woman blaming her for this catastrophe? 'I had no idea that I would have a choice in the matter either way. And besides, I was merely trying to keep the whole thing going, with staff disappearing off to war work – and before you berate me for complaining about that, of course I know they had to do their duty and that is how it should be. But the fact is I have land and tenants and a house to keep up and all of that costs money and time and organisation and a lot of effort. My hands were full and it didn't occur to me to invite further complications, and I don't feel I should be punished for that.'

'Oh, not punished,' said Mr Croft-Swift, obsequiously. 'I'm sure that's not what we meant to say at all.'

'You plead ignorance of such things, but surely the house was used during the Great War?' said Mrs Clarkson in a scoffing tone. 'Most wealthy houses like this were. Wasn't it a hospital or similar?'

'No, a few officers came to stay from time to time, but I thought they were friends of my father's.'

'Well, if your father had bothered to serve the wartime need by offering up this house for requisitioning in the Great War, then you'd know all about it. The sins of the fathers, I suppose.'

Rosina wanted to slap the damned woman. 'I'll have you know that this house offered the ultimate sacrifice to that war as my two elder brothers were killed in action.'

Mrs Clarkson lowered her jutted-out chin then and looked askance at her companion, who shook his head slowly and offered, 'And the nation is so grateful for their sacrifice, I'm sure.'

Rosina felt her eyes blazing with hatred at these two intruders who had caused her to think on the terrible loss of her brothers. Even all these years later, every thought of them was shot through with sadness and pain. Her beautiful, bright, wise, funny, silly, clever brothers. Killed in their prime, then her father drinking himself to death in the wave of grief that came in the wake of their tragic deaths. How dare these people come into her house and make her speak of such things! Rosina felt a rage bubbling up in her she hadn't felt in years.

Mrs Clarkson glanced over at her and nodded agreement to her colleague's trite words. 'Indeed,' she muttered. Then, 'Shall we start the tour?' She put her teacup down, not having touched the tea, seemingly on principle.

It was probably the best idea, as Rosina feared they'd descend into a fist fight if they carried on talking for much longer. And so the tour began.

Rosina led them through the whole of the downstairs – the two sitting rooms (the family called one the lounge, where the wireless was, and the other they termed the drawing room, still comfortable but used more for guests than the lounge), the games room (where the piano was and where Ronnie and Harry used to play chess), the study (with Rosina's desk), the library, the other leisure areas, such as the ballroom and billiards room now shut up and swathed in sheets. Then on to the dining room and through to the kitchen, the servants' hall, scullery, pantry and outhouses. Bairstow was nowhere to be seen. Then Rosina took the interlopers upstairs to the girls' sitting rooms, Evvy's art studio and their bedrooms, in none of which the girls were anywhere to be seen and Rosina wondered where everyone had gone. They then went on to the many guest bedrooms and servants' quarters, most of which were also covered in dust sheets. At each room, Mr Swift-Croft scribbled down furious notes and Mrs Clarkson merely made a list of cryptic numbers and nodded without saying a word. Rosina then took them outside and pointed out the grounds, the areas below the walls that belonged to the hall, as well as the farmers' fields beyond. Rosina spotted Bairstow sipping from a mug of tea with Jessop and Throp in the greenhouse, while the girls and Ronnie stood nearby, gossiping by the looks of it. They were all staring at the unwelcome visitors with distinctly unfriendly looks on their faces.

At last, the visitors seemed satisfied and headed towards their car.

Rosina asked, 'When am I likely to know your decision, about who's coming and when?'

'Oh, this is your week's notice,' said Mrs Clarkson, smiling insincerely. 'Didn't I say that?'

'A week?' Rosina heard herself utter and felt limp again. 'Somehow I thought it would take longer to get it all organised.'

'Think yourself lucky,' said the tiresome woman. 'Some householders get no notice at all and simply wake to the sound of marching feet. Goodbye then. We'll be in touch, never fear.'

With that, she turned and got into the passenger seat of the car.

Mr Swift-Croft held out his hand, almost as a peace offering. He looked embarrassed. 'Goodbye, Mrs Calvert-Lazenby. Thank you for the tea. You do have very nice teacups, you know.'

'Do I?' said Rosina, completely nonplussed, staring at this strange, thin man with the dark shadows under his eyes. He smiled in an oily kind of a way and climbed into the car, driving it away as Rosina watched them leave, standing alone in the driveway.

Chapter 4

Rosina woke up with a gasp, due to some desperate occurrence in the dream she was having. All memory of it left her mind, as she realised she was in the waking world again. Her first sensation was surprise, that she'd slept at all. Since the visit of the civil servants the day before, she had spent a miserable afternoon and evening discussing the awful possibilities with Bairstow, the other staff and the girls. The latter had been most excited at the thought of hundreds of soldiers all over the place. Rosina had wanted to scold them, but thought it better to let them be excited if that's what suited them, as she did not want to infect them with her own fears. That night, she had attempted to sleep and found herself awake till the early hours, wracked with worry. Thus, she woke up aware that she had no memory of falling asleep.

In the next few moments, yesterday's anxieties began to crowd in, before her conscious mind began to realise that there was an unusual noise emanating from outside. She tuned in her ears to try to isolate what she'd heard. There it was again, the sound of male voices. Was it Jessop and Throp? Ronnie? Some of her farmers, perhaps? With alarm, she realised it wasn't any of those people, as the voices approached the house and grew louder, then were joined by the revving engine of a vehicle, driving so close to the house it sounded as if it were driving on the lawn.

Rosina sat bolt upright in bed. 'Oh God,' she said aloud. 'They're here.'

She leapt out of bed and lifted the edge of the curtain to peer out of her bedroom window. There was an Army truck parked up in the middle of the lawn and a group of men were standing near it on the path talking, one pointing to various places around the grounds and another taking notes. It was only just dawn and too early for even Bairstow to be up, let alone Jessop or Throp, so nobody was there to stop them.

Delayed for a moment by shock that yesterday the Clarkson woman had said it was a week's notice but the Army had decided to arrive less than twenty-four hours later, Rosina galvanised herself and grabbed her dressing gown, flinging it on as she hurried downstairs to find a similarly attired Bairstow in the hallway.

'They're here,' said Bairstow.

Then came a loud knocking on the front door.

'Get thissen back upstairs,' said Bairstow. 'I'll deal with this.'

'No, no, it's all right,' replied Rosina, who was wavering between shock and anger. 'I need to face up to this and get on with it. But thank you, Bairstow.'

Rosina steeled herself and marched up to the front door, throwing it open, her arm outstretched, proudly and defiantly standing there with her floral dressing gown tied at the waist and her plaited auburn hair over one shoulder. She knew she probably looked a fright, but she did not care. If the Army were going to show up unannounced, then the Army would have to expect the resultant chaos.

'Erm . . .' said the man she faced. He was an officer, about her age and very tall indeed, with a thick brown moustache.

Rosina was quite pleased to see him lost for words. 'You are the Army, I presume?'

'Well . . . yes.' He cleared his throat and looked annoyed. This pleased Rosina even more. 'I am Colonel Vaughan. I believe you were informed of our arrival, were you not?'

'I was not. I was visited yesterday out of the blue by two civil servants who told me I had a week's notice. Nobody said anything about the Army arriving at dawn the very next day.'

'My apologies, madam,' said Vaughan, his eyes attempting to focus anywhere but on Rosina's dishevelled night-time attire. 'This sounds like a communications mess-up.'

Behind him, Rosina could see two trucks coming up the driveway, the open backs laden with soldiers, while two more staff cars followed. The feeling of invasion was almost overwhelming, but she was determined to stand her ground.

'We're not in the slightest bit ready for you. Nobody will be coming into the house except by invitation. You'll have to wait until I'm dressed and ready. And then I will invite you in to discuss proceedings.'

'As you wish, but I will need to meet with you urgently, Mrs . . .?' He reached into his breast pocket to pull out a couple of sheets of folded paper, scanning them for the information he had clearly deemed too unimportant to memorise.

'Mrs Calvert-Lazenby,' she said, before slamming the door in his face. She turned round to see a delighted Bairstow rubbing her hands together with glee.

'Start as we mean to go on!' she crowed.

'Indeed, Bairstow. I'm not going to be bullied by military types!'

Bairstow joined her as they went back upstairs.

'Now, while I'm getting ready, could you wake the girls – if they're not imminently awoken by the sound of that lot outside. Please tell them not to wander the halls in their nighties. They need to get up and ready. Their train isn't until midday, so they've time, but I won't have any of this Army lot seeing my girls in disarray.'

Bairstow nodded and went off down the corridor, while Rosina went back to her room. She checked her reflection in the mirror to see that she did look a fright, her plait messy and some of the grey hairs that were scored in silvery tones through her auburn locks were free, giving her a somewhat wild look. Why was it the grey hairs were always the feral ones? Also, her eyes had deep shadows beneath them, her eye bags more pronounced today than ever. She wondered what Harry would make of her appearance at this moment! Would he run a mile? But there was something that told her he would not care a jot. Now, this Colonel Vaughan had seen her like this and she was annoyed about that, but also defiant. She was glad she had faced him like this, faced him with the truth of his presumption, banging on her door at the crack of dawn. How dare he! How dare they, this invading army! Well, if this was her war work, then so be it. She would do her duty. But she wasn't going to be a pushover about it.

As she brushed through her hair, washed and dressed, she could hear the growing sounds of military life amassing outside, with more vehicles arriving all the time.

She feared what she'd see when she went outside to find Vaughan. As she left her room, she heard the girls down the corridor, talking excitedly. She went along to find they had all assembled in Connie's room that faced the lawn and were standing in their nighties with the curtains wide open, staring and gossiping at all the men assembling on the lawns. Rosina rushed to the window and drew the curtains hurriedly.

'Girls! Get dressed this instant!'

'Oh, nobody cares, Mummy!' laughed Connie. 'Don't be a spoilsport.'

'I care,' said Rosina. 'I very much care about strange men seeing my girls in their nightwear. Have some sense of decorum, for heaven's sake. Now, you are not to go outside at all today.'

'What?' cried all three girls in unison.

'But I've arranged to meet Ronnie at seven for our last morning together,' pleaded Daisy. 'I have to go! Please, Mummy!'

'Ooh, Dai-sy and Ron-nie!' Connie taunted her sister in a sing-song way.

'Oh shut up, Connie,' retorted Daisy. 'You're just jealous!'

'I am not!' Connie cried, horrified.

'Girls, girls!' said their mother firmly. 'Listen to me. You're acting like babies. You're young women now, all of you. And outside, lining up on our very lawn, are likely to be hundreds of rough-and-ready soldiers. You are *not* to venture outside today, any of you. Daisy, you may ask Bairstow to get Sheila to take a message to Ronnie to come to the house. You will all get dressed and have your breakfast as usual, then ensure that all your packing is done. You'll be leaving for your walk to the railway station at 11.30. Come and find me before then to say goodbye – I'll arrange for Throp or Jessop to escort you out on to the road. But for the rest of the day, I will be very busy dealing with the sheer and utter chaos that has descended upon us. I need to know that you will support your mother in this difficult time by following my orders to the letter. Do you all understand me?'

'Yes, Mummy,' they all said solemnly, suitably chastised.

Rosina left them, wondering if she'd been too harsh, but realising that the mixture of three young women and what felt like the entire British Army on her front doorstep was a bloody awful one. She wondered about Sheila, the young maid that worked for them, and if she would need protecting from this onslaught too. Mary, the daily, was a married woman with children and Rosina assumed she could take care of herself. She just wished the Army had arrived a few hours later, after the girls were safely off to school. Well, she'd just have to keep her daughters out of the way until then.

Now, to face this Vaughan man. She had not eaten yet, but her stomach was churning with alarm and she felt she could not face breakfast.

Rosina went out of the front door and was met with the most extraordinary assault on the senses. The lawns of Raven Hall were completely covered with masses of men in army green setting up tents, or standing around in clumps smoking cigarettes, or being shouted at by various superiors, or running to and from trucks parked up in the driveway. The smell emanating from all this activity was a pungent mixture of sweat, engine oil and other unidentifiable, yet hardly pleasant, odours that could only be described as a combination of dirt and masculinity. The sounds were a cacophony of orders, chatter, shouting and laughing, cut through with the revving of engines and the clatter of equipment being set up or moved about. The usual sweet sounds of Raven Hall were annihilated. Rosina could not even hear the sea, their perpetual guest. Gone were the baaing of moorland sheep, the cries of the roguish seagulls and the twitter of summer birds in the trees. Gone were the sweet scent of roses and the earthy smell of bracken. Gone was the beloved view to the sweep of Robin Hood's Bay. The invaders had obliterated it all, the only note of normality being the chickens and greenhouses that remained untouched around the side of the house, beside the family garden.

Rosina stood and surveyed the scene with her arms folded, trying to look forthright when all she felt was horror. She knew these were the brave lads of the British Army and that they would no doubt be going to fight a terrible foe at some point in the near future. She had every sympathy with them for that. But to see their hundreds of boots and tent poles already churning up the grounds of the hall, as they flicked cigarette butts into the grass, made her forget all her national pride and want to scream. Even worse was that, as she stood there watching them, some of the men began noticing her and just stared, with no decorum. She stood her ground. She wouldn't be intimidated by any man, not any more. She'd had to deal with a bully of a father and a manipulator of a husband and she would not submit to any of that nonsense any longer.

'Mrs Calvert-Lazenby,' said a voice and she turned to see Colonel Vaughan. 'Please let me apologise for the fact that you had received no notice of our arrival. This must be quite discombobulating for you.'

'Quite,' said Rosina, in a clipped voice, her arms still folded against him, though she was impressed that he'd got her name right.

'There is so much to discuss and I am eager to ensure that our stay at Raven Hall provides the least disruption to you as possible, though I'm sure you understand the immensity of the task I am called upon to oversee. I would like to go through all the particulars with you of our requirements, so that I can answer any questions you may have and provide you with all the information you might need.'

She was somewhat taken aback by this. Vaughan seemed to have found his voice since their first meeting. She did not trust him or his army, nor any man amongst them. But she appreciated his politeness.

'Very well. Please follow me, Colonel.'

She led him into the house and took him along to the formal drawing room. Once seated, he began his spiel. She noticed his moustache hardly moved as he spoke. He really was the epitome of stiff upper lip.

'I am formally notifying you of the requisition of Raven Hall for the usage by the Army for the foreseeable future, yet this may alter at any time and other uses may be made of the premises throughout the duration of the war. According to the Compensation Defence Act of 1939, you, as owner of Raven Hall, will be compensated for the usage of said premises, according to guidelines outlined by the Office of Works following their visit to you last week.'

'Yesterday,' Rosina corrected.

'Yes, of course, my error. Yesterday. Thus, the visit yesterday would be in order to assess the premises for Army usage, yet also to value it, thus you will be informed separately by the Office of Works of a reasonable rent according to the current market rate. Further expenses, such as the rates and power, as well as telephones, and even wages of certain essential employees, will be decided upon between you and myself.'

'Will I have any say in the matter, as to what this rent might be?'

'That you will need to take up with the Office of Works, madam. Now, I'm sure you have many other questions. I am eager to answer any queries you may have. After that, we will need to discuss the organisation of the house.'

Rosina appreciated that he could have steamrollered his way in here with no time for discussion, but instead seemed genuinely keen to make her feel part of the process. 'If I'd had more time, I would have made a list. But, suffice to say, I do have a number of pressing queries I'd like answered first, before we go on.'

'Please continue. I am at your disposal.'

Vaughan had not smiled once. It didn't seem in his nature to do so, but his light brown eyes were focused directly on her and she did get the sense that he wanted to help.

'Will we have to leave?'

'No, you do not have to leave. Some homeowners choose to vacate when requisitioned and take up residence in other properties.'

'I don't have another property to take up residence in. The estate owns various houses hereabouts, but they are all full of tenants. I wouldn't dream of putting them out on the street.'

'Quite right. So you will be remaining resident at the hall.'

'Yes, absolutely, we will.'

'That is acceptable and we will discuss later and in detail precisely how the house will be split, with private areas for your family and servants, and public areas for Army use.'

How this would work boggled Rosina's mind, but she had other questions first.

'My gardeners and I have land to the side of the house where we grow produce for the hall and to sell on to others in the community. We also have chickens and a beehive. Can I be given assurance that these will not be used by the Army or otherwise trampled on and destroyed through carelessness?'

'I cannot promise that the land will not be taken in the future for other uses. So no, madam, I cannot assure you of that. However, I do not intend to take that land at present, as I can ascertain that the lawns will be enough room for the accommodation of the men. As you've seen, they are setting up tents for the moment, yet, in the near future, they will be tasked with building Nissen huts for both the accommodation of soldiers and the defence of the camp.'

'You'll be building on my lawns?' said Rosina aghast. She had thought of this invasion as temporary and that, despite the disruption, they would at some point leave to go and fight somewhere else and Rosina would be able to pick up the pieces.

'Yes, the camp will need some structures, but having said that, this kind of installation will be able to be dismantled without too much trouble in the future when they are no longer required. As well as accommodation for the men, there will need to be cookhouses and latrines constructed.'

Rosina turned her head away from Vaughan and gazed out through the drawing-room window for a moment. She was barely aware she was doing it, but the shock of it all made her lose her concentration and look out to her beloved grounds. She could not see the line of lovingly tended rose and fuchsia bushes that Jessop had cared for through the many years of his tenure, yet she imagined them being ripped out and burnt by these careless men and the thought made her shudder.

Vaughan did not seem to notice that her attention had left him, because he ploughed on with the Army's requirements. 'We will also take over your stables and garages for these purposes. You'll have to find someone to take your horses and move your cars to the side of the house. It is also likely we'll install a new range in your kitchen to deal with demand from the number of officers who shall be accommodated in the upstairs rooms here. The downstairs rooms will mostly be turned into offices. New telephone lines will be installed throughout the house. Now we come to the matter of entrances and exits, as in, which will be used by us and which by the family.'

Rosina focused back on this tiresome man and his monotonous list of demands. His voice was beginning to sound like a typewriter, punching out its words with no nuance or sensitivity as to their devastating effect upon Rosina. 'Entrances and exits?'

'Yes. In my experience of such matters so far, I have found that things run much more smoothly when the family and the services accommodated there have separate areas in which to function. Therefore, I am recommending that a certain number of downstairs rooms be taken by the family towards the latter end of the main corridor and a temporary partition constructed across this corridor to separate the two factions. Also, the same will be constructed upstairs to separate the family and servant bedrooms from those in use by officers. Furthermore, I recommend that the family use all servant entrances, corridors and staircases, while the Army use the main door and all main throughfares and staircases. Are we in agreement?'

'Are you saying . . . are you telling me that I can't use my own front door?'

'Yes, madam. That is exactly what I'm suggesting.'

'Suggesting? Or ordering?'

'In truth, it has been decided.'

'Note the use of the passive tense there. It has been decided? Or *you* have decided?'

Vaughan paused for a moment and regarded her. She regarded him. That top lip and its immobile moustache remained as static as ever, yet there was a minor twitch there, a hint of a possibility of a smile at one corner.

'You are quite right, madam. Let us call a spade a spade. It is my order that the thoroughfares of the house be organised thus, in order to allow a free flow of staff to and from the premises with ease. As there will be many more of us than of you, I hope you'll see the logic behind this decision.'

'Logic, yes,' said Rosina and turned her gaze outside again. She saw a seagull swoop down near a group of soldiers and one of them pretended to shoot it down with a phantom gun.

'Mrs Calvert-Lazenby.' His voice was softer now and it drew her attention. She looked at him. His eyes were clouded with concern, the first human emotion the man had seemed to exhibit. 'I have been in requisitioned accommodation before. I saw the distress it caused the owners. I would like to assure you that I have every intention of minimising the distress to you, madam, and to your family and employees. It would never be my intention to cause you pain.'

This quite amazed her, as she had thought of him as some kind of machine until this point. Now he was beginning to sound more human.

'Thank you.'

'Please also be assured that I am at your disposal, whenever I am able, to answer any queries you have or issues you may face. It is in all our interests that we run this show with as much smoothness as we can muster. So, please do feel free to call on me any time and I will do my best to assist you, if I am not otherwise engaged.'

Rosina regarded him with new eyes. Now the shock was beginning to settle into inevitability, she believed she could hear sincerity in his voice and even see a shred of it in his eyes. More cynically, she supposed part of his job was to get the houseowners on side, as it was easier to deal with pesky people if you made them believe you gave a damn about them, rather than treating them like pests to be eradicated. Perhaps that's all it was, or maybe this man actually had a soul beyond his Army uniform, who knew?

'I do appreciate your words, thank you. This whole business has been a dreadful shock, I will admit. But I am determined to make it work. I have faced many challenges over the years as sole owner and manager of this house and its estate and, rest assured, I will face this one with the same resolve. I hope we can work together to make it a success.'

She had listened to herself make this speech and wondered where on earth it had come from. She still marvelled at how she seemed to have this reserve of strength inside her, even when she was feeling at her weakest. She was glad of it now and knew she'd need it in spades for the next challenge of her life. Despite losing her two daughters to war work and Harry to his posting abroad, as well as staff to the services, she knew that she had got off lightly so far. Now the war had really come home to Raven Hall. And she was going to deal with it, her way.

Chapter 5

September 1940

Evvy loved motorcycles. She'd always adored horse riding and bicycles when she was younger and this was a wonderful amalgam of the two, as motorcycles felt like bikes but also had the energy and speed of a horse – and then some. She took to it pretty easily, though she had yet to master corners completely, as she found it difficult to get just the right angle. Yet she was getting better every day, during her motorcycle training. As well as the general skills needed to start the bike and change gears, knowing how to turn it and stop the thing, she was also being taught how to ride through difficult terrain – in the despatch riders' case, potentially winding their way through bombed streets strewn with debris. They were also told how to take cover behind their machine if needs be. It was all fascinating to

Evvy and also rather thrilling, though she kept scolding herself for finding it so, trying to keep Lewis Bailey's words in mind at all times, that this was no adventure, but first and foremost, it was about preserving lives.

By September, she had not only passed the London Fire Brigade driver's test on their vehicles, she was also feeling quite confident about how to ride her motorcycle. She had been taught basic maintenance skills, about which she borrowed an instruction manual for her Royal Enfield motorcycle, and read up in her spare time on how it worked and how to look after it. So far, she knew how to fix a chain and change a flat tyre, as well as how to check the tyres' pressure and the oil levels. In her usual tradition, she chose to name her Royal Enfield and decided to call it Betty: since it was Royal, she thought she'd name it after Princess Elizabeth. Betty was a lovely bike to ride, handling lightly and easily, and was not too powerful or fast, which was reassuring for a beginner.

On 7 September, Evvy stood in the playground behind her fire station, giving Betty a good clean and carrying out her by now usual maintenance checks. Evvy was wearing her fine-weather gear, the motorcycle rider's kit for the summer: trousers with laces at the shins, shirt and tie, a close-fitting jacket, long leather boots, and beside her on the ground in a canvas bag were long leather gloves and a cap.

She was really pleased with her new despatch rider outfit and thought she looked smashing in it, especially since the trousers actually fitted properly this time. She also had some wellies and a waterproof greatcoat for wet weather. Bailey had found her a helmet, as the cap she'd been issued with was, in his words, about as much use as a chocolate teapot. He reminded her that masonry or shrapnel might fall on her head at any minute or she might meet an obstacle and come off her bike, so she must wear her helmet whenever she was riding. She agreed and also thought it was nice to feel that Bailey was looking out for her.

And Lewis Bailey was not the only Bailey that had taken her under his wing, or tried to. As she was finishing up cleaning Betty, putting away her tools in the afternoon sunshine, she saw Sam Bailey approach her across the playground, puffing thoughtfully on a cigarette as he strolled towards her. They were both on nights this month, meaning they had a couple of hours in the late afternoon free after waking up from an erratic daytime sleep. Evvy chose to spend these hours mostly with Pauline and Lynn, when they were around, or working on Betty, or reading books from the library. In the last week of night shifts, she'd found day sleeping nigh on impossible and was always tired before reporting for duty, too tired for larking around town as she used to. But, actually, she quite enjoyed the night shift, as she'd always been a night owl, loving the hushed and secretive hours after midnight.

She yawned loudly as Sam approached. She really did not care a jot what he thought of her and actively sought to make herself look as ordinary as possible in his company. She didn't want to be one of those girls who were desperate to impress. Or at least she told herself that.

'Now then, Ev,' he said as he reached her, grinning through a cloud of smoke.

'Now then, Samuel,' she replied, wiping her oily hands on a rag.

'Want some help with it? I'm a big fan of Royal Enfields. I know a bit about them if you want a hand.'

'I don't need a hand, thanks. I'm quite capable of doing it on my own.'

'It's a good machine – 350cc and single cylinder,' he said, giving Betty the once-over, adopting the air of an expert.

'Everyone knows that,' said Evvy and yawned ostentatiously again. 'And anyway, she's not an it, she's a she. Meet Betty.'

'Pleased to meet you, Betty Enfield,' said Sam. 'You've got some nice curves, but you're not half as pretty as your rider.' And he winked at Evvy.

'Oh God,' she sighed. 'You really are terrible at this, aren't you?'

'At what?'

'Chatting up girls. I suppose you think you're too handsome to bother with actual conversation. I suppose they just fall at your feet like skittles.'

'You think I'm handsome, then, Ev?' he said, teasingly.

'I said *you* think you are.'

'Am I though?' he said and smiled at her.

She glanced up at him and had to look away. Damn him, he was too handsome by half and she was forced to admit to herself that she did love to look at him. But she'd never admit that to *him*.

'Looks aren't earnt, they're randomly assigned by nature. Telling someone they're good-looking isn't really much of a compliment. It's basically saying, well done on your face.'

Sam laughed and puffed again. 'Want one?' he said, holding out his packet of cigarettes.

'No, thanks,' she replied and wheeled Betty back into the garage, beside the school bus.

Sam followed and watched while she did it.

'Was there anything else, Sam?'

'Yeah, Ev, there was. We've been bantering a while now and I like a bit of banter, you know that. But I like you, Ev. I like you a lot. And I want to take you out. If you'll come out with me, it'd make this London lad the happiest man in England. Don't you like me, Ev? Just a little bit?'

Evvy sighed and looked up at him again. He was not only gorgeous, but he was fun to be around and they did have a laugh together. 'I like you well enough, Sam, I do. But I'm not sure we've much in common, do you?'

'You mean, you're a posh girl and I'm a rough-and-ready type?'

'No, not that. I'm no snob.'

'What then?' he said. 'I suppose you're into books and paintings and sunsets and cocktails and fine dining and expensive jewels and all that sort of stuff. I can get you some stockings and make-up and things like that. I know a bloke or two.'

'I'm not interested in your black-market nonsense. And clearly, you know very little about me! Just because I have a plummy accent, it doesn't mean I don't know about other stuff, like motorbikes.'

'And just because I don't have a plummy accent, that doesn't mean I'm an idiot.'

'I never said you were an idiot. Or thought it either, for that matter.'

'All right then. So, do you think a bloke like me could win your heart then, ducks?'

'Urgh, don't call me ducks! I only like men who don't think they're God's gift. And who do like art and books, yes – what's wrong with that? Don't be a snob the other way.'

'Well, Ev. Something you don't know about me is that I write lovely letters.'

'Oh really?' she said, highly sceptical.

'Yeah, I do, as it happens. I'll write you one. I'm better on the page, me. I feel much more comfy writing than talking. I get all tongue-tied in real life when I have to gab with a girl as pretty as you are.'

She rolled her eyes at another empty compliment and he took a step forward and looked at her quite seriously.

'And I mean it, Ev. I've never seen a girl like you before. It's not just how pretty you are, but you are – oh boy, you are! But it's something about *you*. You've got the way of a bloke about you. You're not like a bloke, but you handle yourself, you know? Handle yourself like a bloke. Like, you know what you're about.'

'You mean, I have confidence?'

'Yeah, that's it. None of this simpering and shy looks and all that feminine stuff, which I can't stand, by the way. You look a person straight in the eye. And you don't take any rubbish off men.'

'So you like bold women, then?'

'Not bold, as much as . . . no messing about. You know what you want. I admire that in a girl. In anyone, really.'

There was a moment where they stopped talking and looked at each other. If an artist had conjured the perfect face to draw, the face that encapsulated the golden ratio, the most satisfying symmetry, that artist would conjure up Sam Bailey's beautiful face. It really was a work of art. As an artist – and as a woman – she could not deny she was drawn to his beauty. The physical pull to this man was almost irresistible. Almost.

She looked away. 'What I want right now is for you to leave me alone to get on with my jobs.'

'All right then, ducks— I mean, Ev. Or Evvy or Evelyn or Miss Calvert-Lazenby or whatever milady would prefer me to call her.'

She was impressed he'd remembered her full name, at least. 'Ev is fine. I'm not stuck up, I told you that.'

'Ev it is, then. I'll be good to my word though, Ev. I'll write you a letter and it'll blow your socks off, you'll see.'

'I won't hold my breath,' she said, but he was already walking away, gently strolling across the playground. He stubbed his cigarette out on the wall before flicking it to one side, then ran his fingers through his luscious hair and disappeared inside the school. Evvy was annoyed at herself for watching him but also immensely enjoyed every moment of it.

She looked at her watch. She had about three-quarters of an hour before her shift began at 5 p.m. She popped over to the café opposite and had her meal of vegetable pie and gravy, then crossed over the road to go into the school's front entrance. The crews were changing shift, the blokes coming out of the front door, civvies on, to avoid the name-calling in the street. Behind them came the three women who worked the other shift, all billeted in a B&B nearby.

Evvy's crew were turning up, chatting with the day watch. Lewis Bailey was there, checking over the fire engine parked up in the street, which was being washed and tinkered with. Everyone in the fire crew called the engines 'appliances', which to Evvy sounded like a kitchen whisk or similar. But that was the official term.

She saw Lewis talking to his brother, asking Sam, 'This heavy unit got everything it ought to have on board?' To which he replied, 'Yeah, Skipper. All present and correct.' Then Lewis muttered something to Sam and they both laughed loudly, Lewis clapping Sam on the back. Sam turned and pointed at the van's engine and they talked animatedly, chuckling and gesticulating as they did. It was clear that the brothers shared a deep bond and enjoyed each other's company. Evvy thought of them marooned in the world after their parents' early deaths and how hard it must have been for the elder brother to make up for that loss. But whatever he'd done had worked, for the two of them looked like best friends, the way they were so at ease together and clearly enjoyed each other's company. Just as she was losing herself in this vision of the two brothers, Lewis Bailey suddenly turned and caught her eye, then nodded at her. She nodded back, immediately looked away and hurried her step into the building.

Once inside, she walked along to the watchroom, where she found Pauline and Lynn settling down at their telephone tables for the duration. The man in charge of standing watch was there – the chap she had met on her very first day who had asked her how old she was. His name was Sid and he was all right, actually. After that somewhat rocky beginning, they got on well now. He was very good at his role, very efficient at running all of the administration of the station and keeping on top of inventory and organising the appliances during fires.

Evvy said, 'All right, ladies?'

'Evening, Evvy,' replied Pauline. 'Any stories to tell us?'

'Any more fellers after you, Evvy?' said Lynn, grinning. She loved to hear of Evvy's exploits, though most of Evvy's tales were of past extravagances, as these days she was too busy and tired for any gallivanting. 'And what about you and Sam Bailey? He's mad for you, they say. We all think you'd make such a lovely couple.'

'Ooh yes,' added Pauline. 'You look so good together! Both stunners. Everybody says so.'

Evvy laughed and said, 'You'll have us down the aisle next!'

The three chatted awhile, bonded by close proximity, time spent in each other's exclusive company and being the only females in their crew. Pauline was a voracious reader and talked a lot about books with Evvy, while Lynn was a very young and naïve twenty-two-year-old who was desperately excited about her new life and the freedoms it offered. Before joining the AFS, she'd lived with her parents and worked in their confectionery shop, which she barely left by her account, so she was often a bit giddy about bunking down with other women and being around all these men. Pauline thought she needed a firm guiding hand and so became her work mother. Not so much for Evvy though, as Pauline could see how independent Evvy was, but even then, she did come across as a bit Mother Hen with Evvy at times, but in a nice, caring way, not in a bossy manner, so Evvy liked her a lot. Evvy liked all of her crew really, though some blokes didn't say much to her or the other women. In general, they were all good-natured and did treat them with respect, largely due to the tremendous influence of Lewis Bailey, who everyone admired and did just as he asked. Evvy felt she'd landed in a great team and felt very lucky to be a part of it.

Pauline was looking a bit pale that evening, so Evvy said, 'You feeling all right?'

'Yes, I'm all right. I just have an odd sensation tonight. Like the hairs on the back of my neck are all standing to attention.'

'Ooh, don't!' said Lynn and visibly shuddered. 'You and your premonitions.'

'Well, I was right, wasn't I?'

'What's this?' asked Evvy, her curiosity piqued.

'Well,' Lynn piped up, 'you know the two bombings we've had in London already? Pauline had a queer feeling right before both of them. She said it to me, she did. She said, "I've got a queer feeling, Lynn."'

'It's true, I did,' said Pauline, shaking her head, looking somewhat troubled by the fact.

'That is queer,' said Evvy. 'Are you our canary down the mine, Paul?'

Pauline chuckled and replied, 'Well, I don't mind that, as long as I don't keel over from gas!'

The two bombings had put the wind up everyone. The first one had created a feeling of panic that it was the beginning of the end for London. But then nothing had happened for ten days, until a couple of days ago. So, Evvy and the others thought that perhaps Hitler's assaults might be few and far between, fingers crossed. Yet the random nature of those two attacks had left everyone feeling unsettled; the worst thing was not knowing when it might come again.

Evvy went to grab a pot of tea for Pauline, Lynn and Sid. She was waiting for orders, so she had a bit of spare time. As she brought over the tray with the teapot, cups and saucers and a milk jug and spoons, she heard them going through the telephone checks they did at the start of every shift.

Pauline was talking to another station on the phone, asking, 'Can I have your return of appliances, please?' Then she spoke the names out as Sid chalked them up on a blackboard behind her. 'One heavy unit, two trailer pumps. Thank you.'

'How many TPs?' queried Sid.

'Two trailer pumps,' said Pauline. She winked at Evvy as she brought a cup of tea over, whispering, 'Cheers, lovey.'

Then Lynn spoke out her details from another station and so it went on, as Evvy sipped her tea, listening to the women's voices call out the list of equipment. It was strangely hypnotic, hearing the repetitive words in Pauline and Lynn's nice, clear voices: 'One ramp lorry, one water unit, one turntable ladder, three TPs.' Evvy sipped her hot tea and allowed her mind to drift a moment, thinking of how she'd like to sketch the two women just the way they were now, sat smartly up straight, their hair pinned back, their pencils scribbling: efficient and modest, yet doing important war work. Evvy thought of the war posters she'd seen, encouraging women to join up, where mostly the models in the pictures were glamorous and red-lipped with perfect, coiffed hair. She'd like to sketch women as they really were, a bit dishevelled, a strand of hair falling here, a broken nail there, but heroic in their way, getting on, night after night, day after day, quietly saving the world from the fascists. But Evvy's little reverie didn't last long, as suddenly Pauline's voice changed and became strident, as she called out to Sid:

'OP control. Air raid, yellow warning!'

The sirens hadn't sounded yet, but it wouldn't be long.

Another call came from an Observation Post to Lynn this time: 'OP control. Air raid, red warning!'

And before she'd even finished the final word, the siren began to ring out over London, swiftly followed by the sound of boots clomping down the corridor to the watchroom. Lewis Bailey was first, wanting the report straight away. But they were still awaiting details. The lads were in the corridor, pulling on their gear: their jackets, with a scarf crossed over their neck beneath, and long waterproof boots with the flaps folded down.

'Gear up!' called Lynn urgently, to which someone replied, 'What'd'ya think we're doing, missus, baking scones?'

Bailey made a couple of phone calls and got some more information about where planes and incendiaries had been spotted, which Sid chalked up, and then put pins in the corresponding spots on the map boards.

The men hung about in the corridor for a while, then went outside for a smoke while they waited. More calls came through with further information, but, as yet, the crew of Substation 73V had not been called upon to attend.

Another call came and Lynn spoke out: 'Incendiary bombs at Angel Lane. Fires in progress. Heavy Unit One required.'

'Right, we're up!' said Bailey and rushed out. Evvy followed to see him call to the men outside, 'Lads!' while, at that moment, Pauline was right behind them and ringing the fire bell clamped to the wall with all her might.

Bailey saw the crew of Heavy Unit One on to the appliance and sent them off. He came back in and said to Evvy, 'I'll need you soon to . . .' But he didn't finish his sentence as they both froze: the bombing had started. They stood and listened to the boom-boom of the bombs hitting their targets. They ran to the door and looked up at the sky. 'Coming from the docks I reckon,' he said. They stood together for a moment, their heads cocked, listening to the approaching destruction. Evvy glanced at him and caught him looking at her. Her insides were swimming with nerves about the incoming raid and seeing him standing there, solid against the sky, grounded her. He seemed to understand this somehow, as he nodded at her and said, 'You'll do fine, Calvert.' She nodded and they looked at each other a little too long, which started her stomach twisting up again.

They headed back inside. In the watchroom, the womens' phones were ringing off the hook. They were shouting out information to Sid and the second they replaced the receiver, it would ring again.

'Fire on Three Colt Street!'

'Fire on Thomas More Street!'

'Heavy Unit Two to Brightlingsea Place!'

'TP to Northey Street!'

Sid was rushing between the blackboard and the maps, doing his best to keep up with the flood of information.

Evvy ran out of the room, rang the bell and a couple of lads came back in.

'HV2 to Brightlingsea Place and TP to Northey Street!' she called and they nodded and off they went.

Bailey came back and they went into the watchroom together, listening to the burgeoning reports of fires and frantic requests for crews.

'All ours are out now,' said Bailey and Evvy could see the pained expressions of Pauline and Lynn as they had to tell those at the other end of the line that they had no more equipment or men to help. 'Calvert,' said Bailey. 'Get on your bike and get down to the docks. See if they need as much equipment as they've asked for. If anyone's spare, tell them to call us from an OP phone or get back here to be reassigned. Let's hope there's just a bit of overenthusiastic calling going on and it's not as bad as it sounds.'

'Yes, S.O. Right away,' said Evvy and rushed off down the corridor towards the back door that led out to the playground.

Before she got there, she heard Bailey calling her. She stopped and turned to see him chasing after her.

'For God's sake, wear your helmet, girl!'

'Yes, Skipper!' she said.

Once at the garage, she wheeled out Betty, strapped on her helmet, pulled on her riding gloves and started up the old gal. She was so intent on the business of readying herself that only then did she recall that the booming sounds that pierced her eardrums every few seconds were actual bombs dropping on London, not that far away, and she was about to ride into the thick of it. She gulped down her nerves as she set off on her trusty bike, giving Betty a little pat. She knew the streets between the substation and the docks very well by then, as she'd continued her map-memorising habits. People had said the Luftwaffe might well go for the docks first, so she'd made sure to learn those routes particularly well.

What she experienced next were, without doubt, the most extraordinary sights and sounds she'd ever seen and heard in her life. She could hear the guns firing hopelessly at the German planes above and the constant crump-crump-boom of the bombardment. These immense sounds grew as she approached the dock area, to an almost deafening bellow, sliced through with the horrible shrieking sounds of high explosives. Ahead, she could see the south side of the River Thames was consumed in fire upon fire, the great stacks of timber providing the perfect kindling for a roaring hellfire on earth. The air was hot, hard to breathe deeply and her eyes and nose began to itch then run. Glowing sparks floated everywhere and the very sky seemed aflame. She dared not ride too close to the fires, but she had to get to the fire crews and see how they were doing.

She went down some back streets and came across hoses stretched across roads leading to a water supply at the river. *Follow the hoses*, she thought and thereby discovered their crews at either end. She pulled up here and there, calling out to men manning the pumps and asking them which station or substation they'd come from, fetching out her little notebook and pencil she kept in her jacket pocket and scribbling down names, numbers and details of vehicles and equipment being used. Finally, she came across her own crew, fighting a fire at a warehouse on a street set back from the river, though it was difficult to differentiate the firemen at first, as they all looked the same in bulky protective clothing and faces blackened by smoke. She saw

Sam Bailey's face for a moment, his profile outlined against the red glow of the fires beyond, ascending a ladder, a rope over his shoulder. When he reached the top, he tied the rope to a railing and shouted, 'Stand clear below!' then he threw it down, whereupon a lad tied it firmly around a hose, shouted 'Haul away!' and Sam pulled it back up. Then he took hold of the hose and moved off across the roof of the building and she lost sight of him. The thought of Sam Bailey – and all the lads of 73V she'd bantered with, played cards with and shared a cuppa with – facing that mighty conflagration with nothing to protect them but a helmet with flaps . . . it was awful.

For the first time, Evvy feared for their lives in a way that had not come home to her before. This was it and this was real.

Chapter 6

Evvy felt she had enough information for Bailey by then and turned tail to make her way home. By the time she arrived at the substation, the all-clear was sounding. She wondered how long she'd been out and was amazed to see as she pulled up and looked at her watch that she'd been gone for two hours. She parked Betty and went inside to find only Sid, Lynn and Pauline all talking about the phones.

'Blimey, Calvert, you look a sight!' said Sid. 'You all right?'

'Yes, I'm fine. I have a report for S.O.'

'He ain't here. He's liaising with the main station at Euston. What did you find out? Too many pumps out there?'

'Absolutely not. All the pumps and hoses and men in Christendom wouldn't be enough. Every man jack of them is working his feet off. I've never imagined such fires. It's hell on earth down there at the docks.'

Sid looked grim for a moment, then Pauline spoke. 'I say, my phone still isn't working.'

Lynn added, 'Mine neither. Dead as a doornail.'

'The phone lines must be down,' said Sid.

Then they heard the sound of boots approaching and Bailey appeared at the door.

'Calvert,' he said. 'You have your report?'

'Yes, sir. Every substation attached to 73 is down there: U, V, W, X, Y and Z, with all heavy units, TPs, ramp lorries, turntable ladders and water units at full capacity and all being used. I have the lists here if you want to see them.'

'That's enough, Calvert. You did well. Sid, have the other watch turned up yet?'

'Yes, S.O. They've all been and gone. Every man is out at the docks and I sent the women to 73, seeing as we've only got two phones here, and by the way, the phones are down now, S.O.'

'What? Right. Calvert, you're up. You'll be our phones tonight. You'll be taking me and carrying messages to and from all of the substations in lieu of the telephones, until they're working again. Fires are still burning out of control and there's rumours that this was just the start. They say the planes will use the burning docks as a beacon and come in again tonight.'

Sid said, 'Since the phones aren't working, permission to gear up and go down and help the lads, S.O.'

'Agreed,' said Bailey. 'Girls, you're to stay here and await further instructions and in the meantime, Pauline, you're in charge of the watchroom in Sid's absence.'

Pauline looked really pleased with this and Evvy was happy for her. She knew Pauline would do the job admirably and was glad to see that women were being given more responsibility like this.

Then Bailey added, 'Calvert, you're with me.'

* * *

The rumours soon proved true. The next raid started around 8 p.m. and again came the roaring of planes that brought the next wave of deadly cargo falling from the sky. Evvy took their new staff car that Bailey had been assigned that week (much easier to manoeuvre down damaged streets than Suki the school bus) and drove Bailey between stations as he assessed the needs of each one, coming out looking more and more grim as the evening went on. He told her to drop him at the main station again and then get back to her own, where she should take the motorcycle and spend the rest of the night going between the substations and taking messages back, to keep Pauline and Lynn informed.

As the light drained from the sky, replaced by an unearthly red glow, the streets became more difficult to negotiate, especially with only a thin seam of light emitting from Betty's headlight, which Evvy had painted black, leaving only a narrow strip to see by in the blackout. Her head ached, her ears rang and her eyes and nose streamed from the sooty air. She did not stop for the whole night, taking constant information on numbers of appliances that were out and where they were, numbers of pumps needed and at what locations, and messages from firemen about more help required or if fires were under control at the various sites at the docks and nearby. Before dawn, the all-clear sounded at last and she headed back to her substation to see what else might be needed. She arrived to find the phones were back on and she could finally take a breather.

She collapsed in a chair in the watchroom and saw Pauline and Lynn inundated with calls now the phones were up and running again. The calls came as cries for help, from air-raid wardens, from the fire alarm phones found in the streets, people desperate for assistance, and yet Pauline and Lynn had to turn them all down, saying there was no help here, as all the men and equipment were out. It was grim work and left them all feeling helpless and miserable. Evvy thought everyone needed a pot of tea and went about sorting that.

At a brief lull in the phone calls, Lynn said, 'We had a despatch rider turn up earlier saying a parachutist had been seen nearby and to guard our stations in case of invasion!'

'Blimey!' said Evvy, looking over her shoulder suddenly, as if the German airman might be looming over her at that very moment.

'But she came back later and said it turned out it was a parachute mine caught in a tree!'

'Thank heavens for that!' cried Evvy.

Lynn continued, 'It was all rather frightening for a moment there. Invasion! Imagine it!'

Pauline had just finished on a call and added, 'Well, yes, but I suppose these sorts of things happen in war, lots of rumours and panic and half-truths bandied about.'

Then the phones rang again and the two women were back on. Evvy took a sip of her tea and thought she probably ought to take the staff car over to Euston and see if Bailey needed her services. But the point was soon moot, as Bailey appeared at the door, grimy-faced, his eyes shining white through the grease and soot that had obscured his face.

Evvy stood to attention and said, 'Are you all right, sir?'

'It's a bit warm down there at the docks.'

Evvy wanted to smile. Talk about the understatement of the year!

'How are our lads?'

'One injured.'

Without thinking, Evvy asked urgently, 'Not Sam?'

There was a momentary pause from Bailey, a look in his eye that showed he was curious that she'd asked about Sam in particular. Evvy wondered if he'd think she was enquiring because Sam was his brother or for her own sake. She didn't have time to consider what the truth of that was for herself.

'No, Jackson from the day watch. He'll be all right. Just a bump on the head.' Then Bailey winced and dabbed his fingertips on his cheeks and winced again.

'Are you all right, sir?' Evvy repeated.

'It's nothing. My face feels like it's on fire though.'

Pauline was scribbling something on the board when she turned and said, 'That sounds nasty, sir. You should have it looked at. It might be fuel oil poisoning – I've heard about it from my brother who works for an oil company. You need to flush your face with lots of water for fifteen minutes, then get yourself to a nurse. There's a doctor's surgery on the next street.'

'Well, I'll give it a wash, but I've no time for a nurse.'

He disappeared to the men's room and came back wincing even more. He agreed to go and find a nurse. Evvy offered to take him, but he refused; he'd walk. Evvy took over the phone for each woman in turn so that they could go and have a toilet break and a stretch. Bailey reappeared after a while, saying that Pauline had been right. The nurse had told him to stay a good distance away from the fires for a day or so and he wasn't allowed to shave for a few weeks.

'I'll be sporting a beard for a while,' Bailey said.

'You'll suit a beard,' remarked Evvy, then remembered her place. 'Sorry, sir.'

'It's all right,' said Bailey gently and screwed his eyes shut, then yawned. 'It's been quite a night. You've done your shift now, Calvert. You can go and get some rest. I'll be needing you in a few hours, so get some kip while you can.'

'I'll rest when my ladies rest,' replied Evvy, 'if that's all right with you, sir?'

'Good work, Calvert,' he said.

But it wasn't to be for long, as the women from the day shift arrived to relieve Pauline and Lynn. All three women of the 73V night shift tramped back to the library and, without a wash or even a word, climbed on to their camp beds and shut their eyes. Evvy heard the familiar sound of Pauline and Lynn's breathing change as they instantly dropped into a deep sleep. But Evvy's eyes had seen too much that night to rest straight away, as shattered as she was. For a while, her thoughts hazy with exhaustion, flickered across her mind's eye a glittering parade of fire, flames, explosions, booms and thunderous roars, ankles deep in water streaming down roads, Betty soldiering on around rubble and hoses,

Evvy's lungs aching as the air filled with spark and soot. She watched it glimmer and flash in her mind as she tried to relax, recalling the moment in sharp relief when she'd seen Sam's face carved out of the crimson sky. She would never forget what she had seen, heard and felt that night. She thought it was enough excitement and danger for a lifetime in a few short hours that seemed to last forever. But then it dawned on her that this might be the first of many, that it was only a prelude of what was to come.

She turned over in her rickety camp bed, hearing it creak, and buried her face in the pillow to shut it all out. She did not remember losing consciousness, but it came swiftly, her body deciding it was high time her active imagination shut up shop for a while and, for heaven's sake, sleep.

*   *   *

The women did not sleep for long, as activity at the fire station had not stopped and they all surfaced after a couple of hours, knowing that they felt their place was back in the watchroom or, in Evvy's case, in whatever vehicle she was required to drive. They all had a quick wash and change of underwear, then went back to work.

Many fires at the docks were still burning and for those fires that now only smouldered, the act of 'damping down' was needed, where drenched firemen, quivering from the cold, doused the ruins in water to ensure every last ember was drowned. Also, for any equipment now not in use, there was a clean-up mission underway, which firemen called 'making up'. Hoses needed collecting, rolling back up and mending – and it was devilishly hard to roll up long, cumbersome, sopping-wet hoses, often with sprinklings of shattered glass stuck to the wet surface, lying in wait to slice through hands – while pumps and vehicles needed cleaning down and checking to see if they needed repairs. Everyone knew that if the fires carried on till the evening, they would provide the perfect beacon for any further wave of bombers.

They prayed that the night before might have been a one-off, but around the same time of early evening, the yellow warning then the red came with the sickening sound of sirens and the madness of the previous night returned, the only difference this time being that everyone was exhausted from the night before – some not having slept at all, including Lewis Bailey – and so everything was more effortful and more difficult, as bodies were heavy with fatigue and minds were fogged by worry and lack of rest.

The eighth of September was as hectic as the seventh, then followed by the ninth and the tenth and still the bombers kept coming. Some days, they managed to grab a bit of sleep, other days they worked for thirty-six hours without a break. It dawned on Evvy – and all of London – that this might never end, that this was their way of life now. Evvy found that once she accepted that this was her new reality, she could somehow cope better with it. Everyone behaved as if the death raining down on them night after night after night was the most routine thing in the world.

Thus, this new phase of their lives began, where the abnormal became normal. And so, Sam Bailey began his renewed attempt to woo Evvy, when a letter appeared on her camp bed in the library one afternoon. In the organised chaos of their new existence, she had had little time to banter with Sam, but she had become increasingly aware of his presence in any room she was in. She would sometimes turn to look at him and the heat that passed between them when they caught each other's gaze was unmistakeable.

She picked up the envelope and opened it, to find a page filled with words.

Dear Evvy,

In these extraordinary times, it seems that everything in my life is thrown into relief. Looking around myself in London during this age of war, it feels like I'm part of a painting, something that might one day appear in a gallery and be titled 'Aerial Bombardment of London, 1940'. I can picture how it might look: the blood-red sky filled with flames, maybe the figure of a lone fireman silhouetted against this crimson backdrop as he ascends a ladder into the unknown. There is great beauty in these terrible nights, where death falls down upon us from the sky. Every day, I go to sleep and thank heaven I'm still alive, and every night, I wake up and steel myself for the challenges ahead.

So, against this backdrop of madness, I look for something to ground me, to guide me. And as I look around my life, the only thing I find I want to look at again and again is you. You are beautiful, as I'm sure you must be aware – not that you are at all vain, for I would say you're one of the least vain women I've ever met – or at least, the least vain beauty. You have an inner beauty that shines out from your eyes, your hair, the tips of your fingers. You shine. You are luminous. And it's as if it hurts my eyes to look upon you sometimes and I must look away.

I know you might not harbour feelings like these for me. But in these dangerous times, I also feel that if I don't write down these feelings, they might very well die with me and that would be a shame. At least this paper and ink will know the regard I have for you. That may have to be enough.

Well, to say you could have knocked her over with a feather would have been a gross underestimation. Evvy actually sat down on her bed with a thump after reading it, stared into space for a while, then read the whole thing a second time. And then a third time. It was quite extraordinary. Who would've thought in a thousand years that the mind of Sam Bailey was hiding these treasures? *It's pure poetry*, she thought. And it seemed to echo some of the things she'd thought herself. To think that such a beautiful frame could house such a beautiful voice was incredible. And certainly something she'd never come across in a man. As she'd often thought, the really gorgeous ones were so often vain and empty, the beautiful souls so often housed in ordinary packages. It seemed the way of the world. But here was the perfect package, all in one man. Well, if she'd been deliberating whether or not to let Sam Bailey take her out, the decision was decidedly made!

She put the letter carefully away inside a copy of *Black Beauty* that she'd liberated from the school library and was rereading after loving it in her childhood. Then she put the book under her thin pillow. She didn't want anyone to see it. The perfectly crafted letter was her treasure. She'd never received anything quite like it.

She was eager to see Sam again, to connect with her visual sense the mental picture she now had of Sam's mind. This incredible person was taking shape and she was eager to get to know him more. When she reached the watchroom, all the lads were around, some in the makeshift 'pub' they'd set up in the canteen, with a piano wheeled in from the school hall, that one of the lads would play songs on and they'd sing along. There was a dartboard fixed up in front of the blackboard the school dinner ladies would have written the day's lunches on. The crews would bring food and beer from the café opposite and the real pub on the corner and get a bit of respite from the gruelling hours they spent on duty.

Evvy saw Sam in there and caught his eye. He looked eagerly at her and she nodded briefly and left the room, waiting in the corridor. He came out quickly and she nodded at him again, then turned and walked away down the corridor, hearing him follow her. Her throat felt tight, her mouth felt dry. Her stomach was churning. Men never usually had this effect on her. In general, they bored her. Was this what falling in love felt like? She'd never experienced it and had come to the conclusion, in the high cynicism of her advanced age of twenty, that there was no such thing and it was all a myth dreamt up by the entertainment business. And yet now, here she was, nervous and skittish, as if she could quite easily duck out a side door and run off. She dreaded stopping and facing him and yet simultaneously was desperate to do so.

They'd walked past the communal areas and down to the back door that went out to the playground. Nobody usually came down here, except Evvy to get to Suki or Betty. She turned and he stopped. She thought he might be smirking, pleased with himself that she was succumbing to his charms at last, which she felt might put her off. But he didn't look like that. He actually looked as nervous as her.

'I read your letter.'

'Did you like it, Ev? What did you think?'

She paused, then said, 'I thought it was beautiful.'

'That's praise indeed!'

'Sam, I . . . I really thought it was tremendous.'

'See?' he said. 'I told you there was more to me than meets the eye.'

'You were right. I'll give you that. You were right.'

'I find it so hard to tell you how I feel about you, Ev. But when I write it down, I can find the words I need.'

'You certainly can. It was poetry.'

'Do I win my date then?'

'You're getting there,' she said and smiled at him, probably the first genuine smile she'd ever given him. He answered in kind, then they both broke out in laughter. It was a bubbling over of joy and excitement, their eyes shining for each other. Evvy covered her mouth and shook her head, a little overcome, and this seemed to touch him, as he frowned at her and reached out to touch her hand.

'Evvy,' he said, gently.

'Yes, Sam?'

'May I kiss you, please?'

'You're very polite, all of a sudden,' she said and smiled nervously.

'May I, though? I know we should wait till our date, but . . . God knows when we'll have the spare time to go out and, Evvy, I'm dying for you. I've wanted to kiss you for so long. Since that first second I saw you. Never seen a girl pretty as you. And fiery, you know? You never stood for any nonsense from me. I want to kiss you so bloody much.'

'Yes, you may kiss me.'

He paused, she paused. They were steeling themselves. Then he leant in and kissed her. His mouth was soft, his hand sliding around her waist. She closed her eyes and let it wash over her. A bloody marvellous first kiss.

* * *

After that, they caught moments like these with each other whenever they could – a quick kiss and cuddle behind the bike sheds or the bus – but, mostly, they had to get on with work – exhausting relentless work, night after night. The lull they all hoped for never came. Just wave after wave of Hitler's Luftwaffe, never tiring, never running dry. The bombers continued to focus on the docks and industrial targets and yet more civilians were caught up in the devastation that destroyed homes and lives. The crew of Substation 73V battled on. There were injuries and near misses, but luckily no fatalities. It was not something any of them wanted to think about. They were just doing their jobs and trying to do them well.

The public certainly seemed to think they were succeeding, as their pre-bombardment ridicule in the streets had transformed, literally overnight, after the first night of this wave of bombing. Now, when people saw the AFS in the street, they would clap them on the back in gratitude, women brought pies and men bought beers. Evvy wished she could see that couple again who'd insulted her, and say, *I told you so!* She was particularly proud of the women of 73V, who had begun their time with the London Fire Brigade as a curiosity and were now completely accepted as essential crew members. Evvy got friendly with the day-shift despatch rider, a plucky woman in her mid-twenties called Vera. They'd briefly trained together at New Cross speedway, but Vera hadn't really needed the training, as she was a keen motorcyclist before the war and was brilliant at it. Evvy had felt a bit outshone by her and tried to keep up, despite her nerves about driving too fast. It was fun to see Vera again, now they were doing the job for real. Sometimes as they changed shift, she and Vera would compare bikes and chat in the playground, exchanging notes on their rides and experiences.

'I heard we're getting new motorbikes soon,' said Vera, bright-eyed with excitement.

'Oh no! But I adore my Betty!'

'These'll be much better though. I hear they're American and twice as powerful!'

'But I know Betty and all her quirks now. We've bonded. We're sisters in arms. I don't like the idea of scrapping her for a shiny new American model.' And then she whispered, to spare Betty's feelings: 'It feels like infidelity.'

'Imagine the speed though!' Vera exclaimed. 'I tell you what, when I get mine, I'll meet you back at New Cross and we'll have a race. I bet you a quid I win by a mile. And then you'll be converted.'

But Evvy wasn't sure about that. After all, who needed power when it was manoeuvrability that counted, worming her way around debris and hoses in the bombed-out back streets of London? She really did feel she did not want to give Betty up. She had become a faithful friend to Evvy and in the chaos of the night shifts, riding around London in the damage and danger, she trusted Betty to get her through.

She was fond of the staff car she used to drive Lewis Bailey around too. It was a good, sturdy Austin Ten and she was teaching herself how to read the engine. She remembered that her sister Grace had said to her once that something she'd learnt in the Wrens was that there were different types of intelligence and even different types of reading. She had now learnt that for herself. For she had always been a brilliant reader from the earliest age, a reader of books. And now she was learning to be a reader of car and motorbike engines. It was a different skill and just as testing. It changed her view of the world, knowing first-hand that people had all sorts of skills and expertise you might not know about at first glance, that you could never judge a book by its cover, just as Sam had proven with his beautiful letter. She had asked and asked him for another one, but he had wriggled out of it so far, claiming he was too tired and busy. She loved the kissing and caresses they stole in the all-too-brief moments of privacy. But as well as his handsome face and fine body, she was hungry too for his mind and wanted another glimpse into its hidden depths. He said he'd do it soon. She couldn't wait! In the meantime, his glorious kisses would have to do.

One evening, they got a bit hot and heavy behind Suki the bus and Evvy pulled away from him. Tucking her shirt back into her trousers and fixing her hair, she left him there and suddenly bumped into Lewis Bailey, coming to find her to give her instructions for the shift that was about to start. She was flushed and dishevelled and as she looked up at Bailey – and very clearly saw his embarrassment – she felt her cheeks flush even warmer and looked away. She wasn't doing anything wrong, she knew that. She had every right to court a nice young man. They weren't actually going all the way, just kissing and fooling around a bit, and enjoying each other's beauty and youth. But something in Lewis Bailey's eyes made her regret it, though she told herself not to. There was something akin to disappointment there. Did he not approve of his younger brother? The lads had told her that the Baileys loved and hated each other in equal measure, but she'd seen little evidence of this so far, mostly because they were all so rushed off their feet, with little time for anything but work and sleep. Whatever Lewis Bailey thought of her, she realised that she wanted his approval, for he was a superlative boss, and she admired him tremendously and hated the thought of letting him down.

'Sorry, sir,' she said, desperately trying to tidy her hair and fearing, without a mirror, she was probably making it worse. Why did boys always have to mess up your hair, for God's sake?

'Nothing to be sorry for, Calvert. This is your own time. Your shift hasn't started yet.'

'Yes, sir.' As they walked across the playground together, Evvy ventured to add, 'I want you to know that I take my role here very seriously, sir. Nothing is more important to me than doing well in my job.'

Bailey cleared his throat and took a little while to reply. 'I don't doubt that, Calvert. Do you think I do?'

She glanced up at him. 'I just . . . I don't want to mess this up, sir. All my life, I've messed things up. At school and beyond. I know some people think it's charming, this rebellious act I've played all these years. But for me, I'm tired of it. I want to do something meaningful. Something good. And this is the first time in my life I've done something that isn't selfish, that doesn't serve me and me alone.'

He opened the door to the corridor and she went through. He hadn't responded and she feared she'd said too much. He was her boss after all and despite the fact that they chatted a bit in the staff car during the long nights driving about the place, she didn't think she'd ever made such a long utterance to him all in one go like that, and certainly not about anything so personal. But she wanted to cast out the image he'd seen of her as she'd come round from the back of that bus.

'I can see that all too well, Calvert. And we all appreciate it.'

'Thank you, sir,' she replied, relieved.

They reached the watchroom and before they went in, he turned swiftly to her, looked at her and said softly yet urgently, 'I appreciate it. I appreciate . . . you.'

She'd never looked at Lewis Bailey so closely before. He had a full beard now, after weeks of not shaving. She'd been right; it really did suit him. In fact, he looked rather splendid with a beard, black and closely trimmed; it framed his jaw so well. Maybe he'd keep it, even after his skin had healed fully. He should keep it. She'd rather like to reach out and touch it, feel how soft it was—

Oh God, she thought. *What the hell am I thinking?!*

Chapter 7

October 1940

Rosina stood on the landing halfway up the stairs, looking out at the grounds of her family home. A new world had been created, a land of tents and huts and barbed wire. She was spying on the Army, through a small, clear pane of glass within the stained-glass window her mother had designed. It was based on the Lazenby coat of arms, in bold shapes of *gules* (red) and *argent* (white), accented with *or* (yellow). Rosina felt quite rebellious, since this was not the designated staircase of the family and instead was the one used by the Army, now that they had invaded and occupied her territory. And invaded was indeed the right word, she considered now as she watched them ranging all over Raven Hall.

The Lazenby family had been in Yorkshire for hundreds of years, mentioned in the *Domesday Book* and beyond that to Anglo-Saxon times, its origins likely from the Scandinavian invasions, the family name meaning the 'farm of the free men'. *How ironic,* she thought, as although the north-east coast of England had been invaded many times over the centuries, she had now been occupied by her own kind.

Looking through her mother's window, she wondered what her parents would have made of all this, if they had survived long enough to see it. Rosina was glad in some ways they had not lived to see their home used thus. She was glad too that George was not here, as she believed he would have hero-worshipped the interlopers and taken over, giving them whatever they wanted and joining in with it all like a boy at Scout camp. He'd been in the Army during the Great War and, despite some grisly stories, seemed to miss it when he came back. He'd wax lyrical about army life, time spent exclusively with chaps and no women about to spoil things. Yes, he would've heartily approved of Raven Hall's invasion and no doubt would've been delighted to join up again in 1939, to do whatever they'd ask of him, as long as it involved escaping from home and family responsibility.

With a shudder, Rosina felt grateful, as she did often, that George was gone, despite her loneliness. How ill-suited they'd always been and what a fool she had been to marry him. And she thought again how relieved she had felt when she had found out he was dead, as terrible as she knew that sounded. But it was true. And she mused that George had provided the model for her of what a man was like. Only when she met Harry did she know, for the first time in her life, that a man could care for her, just the way she was, without demands, without cruelty, without lies.

'Mrs Calvert-Lazenby?'

Rosina was startled from her reverie by the now familiar voice of Colonel Vaughan, whose first name was Allan, she had recently learnt.

'Yes, yes. I know I'm in the wrong part of the house. I'm moving.'

She turned to nod at him, as he stood at the bottom of the stairs. 'Not at all,' he said. 'I merely wanted to inform you that we are expecting a delivery of new light bulbs today for all the rooms used by the Army. We need a higher wattage, you see. They'll be arriving shortly and I have assigned some men to fit them throughout the house. I've informed them not to disturb certain areas, but just in case they do stumble into the family section, I wanted to pre-warn you.'

Rosina said, 'Thank you. But with a higher wattage, surely that will mean even higher electricity bills? At present, we have a percentage split, but I will have to ask you to recalculate the Army's proportion, as I don't see why I should be paying more for your brighter lights.'

'Understood. I will draw up a new arrangement and have it delivered to you for your agreement.'

'I will certainly scrutinise it before any sort of agreement, I assure you.'

'Of course,' he said and nodded at her, before turning on his heel and walking stiffly down the corridor.

Rosina sighed and came down the stairs into the corridor that now led to a number of offices filled with Army staff, officers and soldiers of various ranks doing clerical jobs, as well as a number of female secretaries who were bussed in each day. The Army had also taken over Rosina's study, the library, the billiards room, the ballroom and all other rooms upstairs that were unused. The girls – even though they were away at school, thank goodness – and Rosina had kept their bedrooms, thankfully. The officers slept in the other upstairs rooms, as well as a number of other staff, along with the officers' batmen in the servants' quarters. Bairstow had kept her room too, but had little privacy from the invading forces.

Rosina walked down the corridor away from the bustling offices to the family section, where she was permitted to occupy two sitting rooms – the comfy lounge and the more formal drawing room – and the games room. A partition was supposed to be erected to shut off the two areas, but this hadn't happened as yet. Instead, someone had put masking tape across the carpet to separate the two sections, which was already horribly scuffed and a tripping hazard.

She stepped over this imaginary barrier and tutted, annoyed at its scruffy pointlessness.

Once in the lounge, she went to her desk, now positioned by the window beside the drinks cabinet – since her study had been invaded. From this side of the house, she was very happy that much of her view was taken up with the small part of the grounds that was still in her control: the greenhouses, vegetable plots and animal areas, as well as the modest lawn enclosed by box hedges behind the greenhouses that was referred to by all as the 'family garden'. Thank heavens for it. It was the only place she could go outside in her grounds that still felt vaguely normal . . . that was, if she put her fingers in her ears so she couldn't hear the constant noise of Army men and held her breath so she couldn't smell their stink. Sometimes the wind caught the latrines and wafted their odour towards her and she wanted to gag. At least they were heading into winter soon and she wouldn't feel the loss of the outside so much. The gardens were autumnal and nature was preparing for its winter sleep.

She saw Throp appear from the greenhouse and light up a cigarette as he watched the invaders with a cold eye. She had bonded with Jessop and Throp over this, as they often stood in that spot and moaned about the Army, how much the officers ate and how late they stayed up talking ridiculously loudly. Throp had been moved from his room and yet was still surrounded by Army types, which he had to accept, of course, but clearly was not happy about. All of Raven Hall felt the same about the trespassers. Basically, they all knew that they had to do their bit for their country, but they all agreed that didn't mean they had to like it. The truth was, they hated the Army.

Bairstow was probably the most openly hostile, particularly as her kingdom of the kitchen had been invaded by an Army chef. A new range had been installed in one of the outhouses and this was used by the Army cooks, but they did use Bairstow's kitchen for some tasks, which infuriated her. She was often to be heard shouting at a cook or a soldier about muddy footprints or rubbish piles or other incursions into her previously ordered world. Rosina felt Bairstow took it even harder than she did, yet she was proud of Bairstow for taking them all to task.

As Rosina settled down to her desk to write a letter to Harry, detailing the latest litany of small tragedies, she heard a knock on the open door and turned to see Bairstow with a face like thunder.

'To see t'mess they're making of t'whole place makes my blood boil!' she ranted.

'Oh, I know. It's infuriating. But what can we do? I do tell Vaughan things when I can, but there's so much to complain about, I have to let some things go.'

'I know, I know. Tha's doing a grand job with Lord Muck. Tha dun't let him get away with owt. Anyway, there's summat else. They've gone too far this time.'

'What is it?'

'Young Ronnie Holt. Two officers wanted to go to t'wine merchants in Whitby and didn't know t'way. So they found Ronnie at t'greenhouse helping out and they commandeered t'lad to ride with them in their infernal truck to Whitby and when they got there, they let him try some of t'wine and he had too much and now he's sick as a dog. I've got him in one of t'servant's rooms throwing his guts up into t'chamber pot.'

'Oh, for heaven's sake!' cried Rosina. 'He's only sixteen!'

'I know he might look older to them, but truth is he's just a bairn.'

'All right, I'll have a word with Vaughan. If they're corrupting poor Ronnie already, it terrifies me to think of the girls coming home for Christmas. Maybe I shouldn't let them. Maybe I should take them away for Christmas?'

'It might be prudent. But then again, they're not daft, thi girls.'

'I don't have your faith in them, I'm afraid. Especially Connie. But . . . I hate the idea of being away from home at Christmas. And, in all honesty, I don't feel able to leave the place for a second to Vaughan and his gang. Anyway, I'll think on it. In the meantime, let me find him and give him a piece of my mind.'

Bairstow nodded and went off, Rosina following soon after. She walked down to Vaughan's office – latterly her own dear study and now filled with paperwork and a typist and maps on the walls – and luckily found him in.

Vaughan's secretary was a very pretty, dark-haired girl with long legs – *I wonder how she got the job*, thought Rosina sarcastically – who always gave Rosina a filthy look when she came in. 'Colonel Vaughan is not present,' she'd say, when Rosina could see with her own eyes that his desk chair was empty. And she'd never give Rosina any clues as to his whereabouts or return. But that day Vaughan was there, on the telephone when Rosina marched in. She didn't bother knocking. Why should she be polite when the Army were camped out in her own house?

'I need to talk to you immediately,' she demanded, while Vaughan was still talking on the phone.

'Colonel Vaughan is taking a telephone call at present!' cried the secretary.

'I can see and hear that,' snapped Rosina. 'I'm not blind or deaf.'

Vaughan looked sharply at Rosina but did finish his phone call abruptly. 'What is it, Mrs Calvert-Lazenby?'

'But, sir,' said the secretary in a whiny voice, 'you have your meeting with—'

'Never mind, Holness. You may leave us.'

Rosina was very pleased at this turn of events.

The secretary stood up, her cheeks pink with annoyance, and gave Rosina a withering glance before walking out.

'And close the door, please,' called Vaughan.

There was a slight pause before the door was closed, unnaturally slowly: Holness's petty little way of making her presence felt.

'Please, sit down,' said Vaughan. He was being too damned polite all round, Rosina felt. She was spoiling for a fight.

'No, thank you. I've put up with a lot these last few weeks, but now something has happened that has gone too far. There is an evacuee lad who helps out our gardeners here whom we have all taken under our wing since his parents died in a bombing raid in Hull. He's just a lad and an orphan, though he's kindly been adopted by a local family. Well, it has come to my attention that two of your men took this boy to Whitby and got him drunk on wine and now he's very sick upstairs, vomiting copiously. He is *sixteen* years old.'

'Oh dear . . .' muttered Vaughan.

'Oh dear? *Oh dear*?' She was warming to her theme now. 'Is that all you can say? This poor lad has been corrupted by

149

your men! How dare they take one of my charges and force him to drink!'

'I doubt they forced him . . .' ventured Vaughan and there was that slight hint of a smile at the corner of his moustache.

'Do you find this amusing?'

'A little bit, yes.'

He was actually smiling now.

'Do you really? You find the near poisoning of a young boy funny, do you? Well, I must say, I'm assuming you don't have children of your own, because otherwise you'd be showing yourself up as a very poor parent indeed.'

Vaughan's face clouded for a moment. He looked down at his lap and seemed visibly affected.

Rosina paused and felt distinctly uncomfortable. What had she said? 'I didn't . . . or rather . . . have I . . .?' but he didn't let her finish.

'I will look into this and ensure nothing of the sort happens again.' The smile was gone and the usual military visage replaced it.

Rosina was still feeling that she'd said something wrong but was not sure what. 'I say, are you all right?'

He looked up at her momentarily and there was a haunted look in his eyes. It was unmistakeable and disturbing. 'Of course,' he said quietly. 'What happened to this boy was wrong. I see that.'

'Thank you. I am glad you can see my position. It's . . . most upsetting.'

'As I say, I will look into it.'

He did not look at her again. She said a brief thank-you and left, walking past a livid-looking Holness waiting outside the door with her arms folded.

Rosina walked the length of the corridor and then took the servants' staircase. She wasn't sure which room Ronnie was in but saw Bairstow coming out of one with the evil-smelling chamber pot. She found Ronnie in there curled up in bed, white as a sheet. She sat with him a while as he slept.

He had grown so much since she first saw him, he looked like an older brother of himself. His brown hair had had the chop now, short back and sides, instead of the over-the-ears thatch he'd had when he arrived. He was much better looked after these days, now he'd been adopted. The rumours were that his parents had treated him badly, so as much as it seemed cruel to think it, perhaps it had been a blessing in disguise that they had been lost to Hitler's bombs. Ronnie didn't speak much to Rosina. He was very shy with her. But sometimes, in the summer holidays, she'd caught the sound of him talking animatedly with Daisy out in the garden and he was full of life, gabbling away about his ideas and his joys. Harry had really warmed to him when he had stayed there, the two of them playing chess sometimes for hours, whilst Jessop and Throp were extremely fond of the boy, she could tell. Especially with Daisy so close to him, Rosina really felt he was an honorary Lazenby these days. To think of him sick because of those Army idiots made her fume.

But something odd had happened with Vaughan and she couldn't stop thinking about it. His whole face had changed when she had mentioned children, as if somebody had turned the lights out. She wondered what it could possibly mean. And to see some emotion in that wooden face was quite shocking, like peeking at something secret, something private, that shouldn't be seen. For the first time, she began to wonder what might be going on in the mind and life of Colonel Vaughan, beyond the invasion of her house, beyond the confines of this war, to his real life beyond, the one he had left behind. What kind of man had he been, before his whole persona became subsumed by war? She had to admit, Vaughan intrigued her.

As she sat and watched over Ronnie, Rosina nearly found herself settling into a nap, but Bairstow came in and handed her something she'd been praying she might receive for months now: a letter from Harry. She snatched it and smiled at Bairstow, mouthing a 'thank you', to which Bairstow responded with a broad smile and a nod. Bairstow was very fond of Harry and thoroughly approved of him.

The letter was battered and looked brown with age, wear and tear. Stamped in bold letters on the front was

PASSED BY CENSOR. She hoped this didn't mean that too much was cut out. In his August letter from the port, not one word had been blotted out or struck through or even scissored out, so she hoped the same this time.

Rosina was desperate to rip the letter open with a flourish, but she didn't want the sound to awaken Ronnie, so she eased a finger in and edged it open with quiet care.

Date: 14 September 1940
From: Sgt H. Woodvine
To: R. Calvert-Lazenby of Raven Hall, Ravenscar, North Yorkshire

Dear Rosina,

I write from the hottest place on earth. A slight exaggeration perhaps, but it certainly feels this way. I thought I knew heat from my time in Spain, but this is something else. When we were on the ship, there were at least the sea breezes and forward motion of the vessel to cool us – when we were on deck at least. Arriving in port, the heat settled over the bustling city in a purplish haze. Small boats of local people came bobbing up beside our ship to sell us fruit, so I bought some bananas and oranges and shared them about with my team, which we enjoyed immensely, the oranges particularly as they were thirst-quenching. But, my God, the heat! It hits you with a slap the heaviness of tungsten. I exist in a constant state of dampness. You may even see the sweaty stains on this very letter, as my hands are wet with it as I write. If you were to look upon me now, you would not find me a very fine fellow since I resemble a cat who's had a bath: bedraggled, sopping wet and hopping mad to be so.

Now we are ashore and working, I can tell you little, but I can assure you that the heat is worse than ever. Whenever one meets a chap who is about to sail back towards home, one's opinion of him changes immediately from affability to hatred, caused purely by jealousy. We are homesick waifs and strays, we sorry lot, stranded in the outermost reaches of the empire. It is hard to be so very far from home and everything that is normal. And the distance between us and loved ones is felt keenly, especially with no word from home for weeks now.

Every day, we wait for the mail ship, with no success. I have not received a letter from you at all, though I know you will have written. I've seen other chaps receive letters, sometimes in a big bundle all together, which are all disordered and full of questions, the answers to which will become quickly irrelevant if they write them down, as we always seem to move about much faster than the mail can reach us. I would ask that from now on, if you haven't already done so, you date each of your letters and perhaps number them, so that if they do ever arrive, I can at least see the order they were written in, even if they arrive in the wrong order.

Anyway, I realise this letter is mostly a catalogue of moaning, so I will stop that now. Since we can write of so little, due to the dreaded censor (I wonder if the censor will censor the word 'censor'?), I will have to resort to telling you interesting facts from the world of science and nature, as surely none of that will help the enemy war effort. So, for example, since you told me you have a beehive at Raven Hall, did you know that, according to the laws of physics, they say that bumble bees shouldn't really be able to fly at all? These portly chaps are far too fat, they often carry their own body weight in snacks and their wings flap about all over the place. But these furry little fellows don't give a jot for the opinion of physics and so off they buzz. But I think whoever 'they' are who said bees shouldn't be able to fly . . . well, I think those chaps are looking at it wrong-headedly. They're comparing bees to aeroplanes, which use static wings, thrust and lift to ascend. But if bees flap backwards and forwards, they would create a little whirlwind under their wings which would lift them up. So perhaps it's this that makes them fly. As you can see, I'm continuing to use my Cambridge education in physics and mathematics to inform my RAF work – or at least, to think about bees. I've been pondering this in my sleepless nights in order to distract myself from lying awake worrying about what this next phase of the war will bring.

I think of you all of the time, and of the girls and the hall. I think of the beauty of the English countryside, swathes of green that are verdant yet contained and therein lies their charm. Everything here is too much: too hot, too bright, too everything. I feel the same way about England as I do about the study of my favourite subject: physics. I feel that both England and physics have in common a beauty derived from order. The first time I saw Bohr's models of the atom, it struck me: nature is ordered, it carries symmetry. Physics teaches us that the physical world is comprehensible and can be mapped and patterned. I feel that way about my home country too, that being a small island of modest climate, it is defined and precise. I love the calmness in that. I miss it dreadfully.

I could write a book about how much I miss you. But I don't want the censor deriving his entertainment from my paltry attempts at romance. Suffice to say, my feelings have only grown with our separation and I think each day of how many more days this war will last and how many days that means that we will not be together, and the only thing that keeps me going is that – one fine day – I will return to you and we will then have countless days before us to live in and share. That is my great hope. In the meantime, I work hard and manage my little team here with as much *enthusiasm as the heat allows. We are a merry band despite the privations of life, keeping our smiles and sarcasm to cheer each other and face an uncertain future.*

Please keep writing to me often, so that if many letters are lost, at least I may receive one. You have no idea how comforting it is for us weary travellers to receive the scent of home in a letter from our loved ones.

Give my heartfelt best wishes to your girls and my kind regards to all at the hall.

With love,

Harry

P.S. See you Sunday. (You thought I'd forgotten, didn't you?)

Rosina's eyes had feverishly read the letter through at top speed before starting it all over again and reading through slowly, in order to relish every word. It was dated a month after the last letter she had received and it had taken over a month to arrive. She realised now that their previous practice of writing often to each other was to be seriously hampered by the postal service for those stationed abroad. She'd suspected as much but was dismayed to see that this letter was so out of date already, when she had only just received it. However, she was delighted to receive any news and reread the letter over several times, before putting it back lovingly into the envelope.

There was so little in the letter to hold on to, due to Harry's care not to be censored. But at the same time, there was so much of Harry in there, of his character. She was struck again by what a fascinating young man he was, so mature for his years, so exceeding the personality of most men she had ever met, let alone one in their twenties as he was. And yet, because of his youth, she felt protective of him and dismayed that his experience abroad sounded so uncomfortable and difficult.

As she sat with the letter in her hands, watching Ronnie slumber, she felt protective of them both – the orphaned evacuee here and the brave young soldier there. She felt the same way about every person she cared for – her daughters of course, but also her staff and her tenants. Yet, she realised, this was an emotion she'd never felt for her husband. Throughout most of their marriage, he had been gallivanting around the world partaking in dangerous activities, such as mountain climbing, car racing and skiing, yet she had never once worried about his safety. But when it came to Harry, she found that every day he popped into her head, she immediately would say a little prayer for him, to keep him safe and sound, something she'd never done once for the father of her children. This revelation shocked her. And not for the first time, she frowned at the perplexity of her feelings for this extraordinary young man, Harry Woodvine.

Chapter 8

To escape the daily grind of the hall, Rosina had recently begun to pay regular visits to one of her tenants of the Raven Hall cottages, Phyllis Precious. She was a lovely young woman with her small girl, Elsie, and twin babies. And she was a tragic young woman, as her husband Wilfred had been lost at sea only a couple of months ago. Rosina had agreed with Phyllis that she would drop by every Wednesday for a quick visit and check that everything was all right. She had suspended Phyllis's rent for a time to try to help and, as well as wanting to provide support, the truth was that she loved going to see Phyllis. Rosina was missing her girls and it was nice to be around little ones for a bit, to watch Elsie's little dark-haired head bobbing as she played with a toy Rosina had brought, and it was heaven to hold the warm packages of the twins, another girl called Jill and a boy called Wilf, named for his father, sorely missed. It was welcome too to escape the Army and have some conversation beyond the confines of the occupation of Raven Hall, which is all she seemed to talk about with anyone there these days.

A foggy Wednesday morning in October, Rosina put on her mackintosh and went out of the side door and, in order to avoid as much of the Army as she could, took a back route beside the farmers' fields to get to the lane where the Raven Hall cottages were. She walked the short distance to Phyllis's cottage, carrying a little something for Elsie. She always took something with her, mostly old toys and books that she knew the girls had no particular affection for but Rosina had never got around to giving away. Today, she had a cloth doll with a stiff little body and a sweet face. She had tidied its mohair wig – auburn, just like Grace's, to whom the doll had belonged – and mended its little chequered dress, as well as sewing up a hole in one of its red felt booties the night before.

When Rosina arrived, she knocked on the door and waited. There was always a bit of a kerfuffle inside at these moments, as Elsie was determined she would be the one to let Rosina in. And so she did that morning, opening the door with grand ceremony, even though it took her a while to turn the handle successfully.

Rosina always said the same thing to her. 'Are you the lady of the house?'

'Yes!' Elsie would cry and giggle infectiously.

Rosina followed her in and heard one of the babies fussing in the next room. She knew Elsie was waiting for her gift, so she pulled it out of her inside pocket with a flourish and gasped at its beauty, which made Elsie gasp too and she reached up very slowly with the appropriate reverence.

''Ow do, ma'am,' called Phyllis from the next room.

'I've told you, no more of this ma'am business,' Rosina called back. 'It's Rosina.'

'Ro-zee,' said Elsie, and Rosina replied, 'That'll do.'

'Is it mizzling out there?' called Phyllis.

'A bit misty-moisty, as my mother used to say,' Rosina answered as she took off her coat, hat and scarf and hung them up on the hook in the hall. Elsie waited patiently for her. 'Come on, then.'

Rosina followed Elsie into the next room and the little girl held her new prize with outstretched arms so her mother could see it in all its glory. She then sat down on the rug beside the fire and play-acted with her new treasure, whispering things in her dolly's cloth ear.

'Ah, tha mustn't keep bringing her things,' said Phyllis, sitting on the settee and holding Wilf in one arm and Jill in the other. The baby girl was nodding off, while the boy was making little grumpy noises.

'How are they?' said Rosina and went over, reaching out to take the sleepy one, who Phyllis gladly handed over. Rosina sat down in the snug armchair opposite the settee. Jill surfaced a moment from sleep, then fell back into a stupor again. The warm weight of the baby on Rosina's arm was the most comforting thing in the world for her. She had always loved little babies. Their needs were so simple. They had no guile about them. It was only later that children learnt to lie and dissemble.

Phyllis stood up and jiggled Wilf about and shushed him as she paced up and down. 'Wilf's been mithering all morning. Who knows what about?'

'Important baby business. This little poppet is fast asleep now. Would you like me to put her down? Or can I hold her for a bit?'

'Hold her as long as tha likes. She likes a cuddle that'un. Likes to be swaddled. This'un hates to be wrapped up or held for too long. But he mithers when I put him down too! He can't make up his mind.'

'All babies are such different little souls,' said Rosina, remembering how she thought she had babies solved after Grace, who was a dream child, until Evvy came along with her tenacious naughtiness and blew that theory out of the water.

'They are that. Elsie and Jill are just like my Wilfred were. Patient and sweet. But baby Wilf is nothing like his father. He's worrisome. Maybe he gets that from me. I were always anxious. Wilfred used to calm me down and look after me. He were grand at that.'

There was a sad pause. 'Well, I think you're doing a grand job of looking after yourself and your little ones. It's never easy on your own.'

Rosina glanced up from the baby's perfect little sleepy face to note that Phyllis's eyes were shining with tears, which she fought to hold back.

'Is it a bad day, today?' Rosina said gently. She knew that Phyllis had some days that were better than others. Her grief for her dead husband was still so raw.

'It gets to me when t'bairns are bothersome. I miss him summat awful then.'

They sat in silence for a while, Rosina wondering if Phyllis would let her tears overcome her today. Rosina had learnt to let her do it, with no comment or fuss. Sometimes a person just needed to have uncomplicated company.

Baby Wilf was muttering less now and starting to look a little more drowsy. Phyllis slowed her pace and began rocking him gently. She turned her face to Rosina, who glanced up, and the two women looked at each other, a small unexplained smile of friendship passing between them.

'Does tha miss him, thi husband?' asked Phyllis.

Rosina had had this question before. She never knew how to answer. She knew what the answer should be, but it always felt uncouth to say it.

'Would you like the blunt truth or the acceptable lie?'

'Truth.'

'Then the answer, I'm afraid, is no. I don't miss him. I'm sorry.'

'What are tha saying sorry for?'

Rosina thought for a moment, watching Jill's mouth purse into a moue in her sleep. 'It feels wrong to admit it to anyone, that I felt that way about him. It feels doubly wrong to say it to you.'

'Nay, tha mustn't feel like that. Honesty's always t'best policy. I'm just wondering . . .' Phyllis trailed off.

'Ask me. I don't mind talking about it.'

'Just . . . I wonder why tha married a man tha didn't like.'

'Well, I did like him at the beginning. He was very charming. And I'd had a rotten time. My mother died, then my brothers died too and my father turned to drink. And George came in and swept me off my feet. He seemed like . . . the answer to everything. He knew just what to say and do to make me adore him. Once we were married, it all stopped, like someone had switched off a light, as sudden as that. He showed his true colours then. Mocking, cruel, petty and mean.

I knew I'd made a dreadful error. But it was too late, as I was expecting Grace by then. After that, he veered between a fake kind of jolliness and his true, mean self. I was so lonely, I just kept having babies to make myself feel better. And we grew further and further apart as he went off on his gallivants all over Europe, with various women, or so I'm told. I . . . well, I'm afraid I grew to hate him.'

Rosina looked up to see Phyllis staring at her wide-eyed, while baby Wilf finally slept in her arms. 'I never heard of such a person. How could he? How could he be so cruel to thee?'

'Some people are like that. Born that way, I think. As if there's something missing in their brain. Something to do with empathy, with feeling how others feel. It's just not there. I don't think people like that know how to love. I don't think they know what it means. They just copy it from others, they ape the signs of it. And so we get fooled into thinking they feel it. But they don't. They're empty, those people. Hollow things.'

'I never knew a person like that,' said Phyllis, shaking her head. 'My folks were good people, my neighbours were too. And Wilfred . . . well, tha knows what a diamond he were.'

'I wish I'd known him better,' said Rosina and smiled at his sleeping daughter. 'I only met him that once when you moved in. But, I must say, he had a lovely way about him.'

'At least I knew him a while,' replied Phyllis with a philosophical tone. 'At least I had that. I'll be always grateful for that.'

Rosina found her own eyes were pricked with tears. What did she have to cry about? It would be unsupportable to cry in this young widow's home. She willed her eyes to dry up, but found herself sniffing and Phyllis looking at her and coming towards her.

'Oh, I'm fine. I am sorry. What a silly woman.'

'There tha go again, putting thissen down. Tha's a habit of that, ma'am.'

'It's Rosina, please,' she said emphatically and some-how that set her off and she heard herself let out a little sob.

'If tha'll forgive me, I'd wager tha's taken sad not for t'loss of him, but for t'lack of love in t'first place. My old ma said to me after my father passed that it's better to have loved and lost than never to have loved at all.'

'Tennyson,' murmured Rosina, remembering reading that line with Grace when she was a serious young girl, prone to reading tragic poetry.

'Nay, 'twas my mother said it.'

'My mistake,' said Rosina gently and blinked away her tears.

'She were a wise old bird. I miss her too, now more than ever with t'bairns. She were took a few year back, before Elsie came. She'd've doted on them.'

'Oh, she would. How could anyone not?' Rosina looked down at Elsie, still playing quietly on the floor with her doll, the two babies now fast asleep in the two women's arms.

'If I may . . .' began Phyllis, now sitting opposite Rosina on the settee. Rosina looked up and smiled, thinking Phyllis wanted to take the baby, but she was looking very intently at her. 'I think tha should see who else is out there in t'world. It's been a few year now. If tha don't mind me saying, it's time enough to grieve for a man tha didn't even care for. It might be time to look for love again? If tha don't mind me saying. If it's not too forward of me.'

How Rosina wanted to blurt it out! It was so tempting to tell Phyllis that at last, after all these barren years of the lack of love, she now had a surfeit of it, full to bursting with love for Harry Woodvine. How she would delight in telling Phyllis Precious every detail of Harry's beauty, inside and out! It very nearly spilled from her lips. How fun it would be to share all the details with another woman, a friend. But she did not do it. She pursed her lips, as if to dam the flood.

'I've offended thee' said Phyllis dolefully.

'Oh, no, not at all! I don't mind you saying it at all, I assure you. You're absolutely right. And very wise advice it is too.'

'Chuffin' 'eck, tha rattled me then! I thought tha were right mardy!'

They both laughed and the moment passed. Rosina was glad she hadn't announced how lovesick she was for Harry. Her instinct was, firstly, that it should continue to be her secret – after all, she had not even told her daughters. Yet, also, she felt it would be in such poor taste to wax lyrical about a young RAF chap who was very much alive – as far as she knew – when Phyllis's young husband had been lost in the Navy. Lastly, though Rosina knew that she and Phyllis were fast becoming friends, just as with Bairstow, she had the feeling that their relationship was still based on that of unequal status, as Phyllis was her tenant and she the landlady, however well they got on. She breathed a sigh of relief that she had kept her mouth shut. Instead, she updated Phyllis on how things were going at the hall with the dreaded Army occupation.

'I just wish I'd offered the hall to be requisitioned as something else, before they foisted the Army on me. It could have been a jolly bunch of schoolgirls there now, instead of that horrible lot.'

Could tha's had a school there then? Could tha's had a choice?

'I'm not sure I'd have got my choice, but I could have offered apparently. I didn't realise that until after the decision had been made. But if I get a chance again, if the Army ever leave, I'll certainly be offering it to a school or something. Something with women and girls if possible. I'm sick of men everywhere and their boots and their muddle!'

'How about a maternity home?' Phyllis suggested.

'Now, there's an idea!'

'I heard on t'wireless about expectant mothers being sent all over to big country houses. Just imagine that, surrounded by new bairns. I'd be in heaven. I love new bairns. I love t'feel of them, t'smell of them.'

'Oh, me too. I wish I'd thought of that – a maternity home at Raven Hall. How super that would have been. You could've come and helped me, Phyllis. We'd be a fine team.' Rosina sighed, her head filling with images of Raven Hall overflowing with happy new mothers, midwives and nurses in starched white uniforms, instead of men and mud and mess. 'But it's my duty now to put up with the British Army instead. We all have our duties to perform. I mustn't grumble.'

Later, on the walk back from Phyllis's cottage, Rosina dreaded going back to the Army. She thought of her vision of a house filled with women and realised how much she missed her girls and how sick of the sight of men she was these days. Well, not all men, of course. Her male staff were marvellous. And, of course, there was Harry. She considered what would have happened if she had thrown caution to the wind and told Phyllis all about Harry. How would she have responded and what would she have secretly thought about it afterwards?

Rosina had considered many times how it would look: the so-called lady of the manor having it away with a man in his twenties. Socially, she might well end up being a laughing stock. Now that she began to interrogate it, under the potential gaze of another, she had an alarming feeling that the love that seemed a citadel against the world had started to crumble. How could she explain to Phyllis that this beautiful young man loved her, a woman in her forties? She could not explain it herself. It was obvious why she loved him: he was young and beautiful. That's what everyone would think. But she scolded herself for this simplification. She knew it to be untrue. But what if there was a nugget of truth in it? What if her love for him came largely because he was in the right place at the right time, with the right kind of beauty about him? Perhaps all it boiled down to was that she was ready to fall in love with someone and there he was, young and beautiful.

Then her doubts turned to Harry himself. Was it the same for him? Was she just in the right place at the right time? She thought of his letters, of how he had kept in touch with her so faithfully. So maybe it was not a flash in the pan. Maybe he really did love her. Could she be that lucky? What had she done to deserve it? How could it be fair that Phyllis Precious must lose her loving husband and Rosina gain Harry? It wasn't fair. Well, she mused, they were apart now and she feared that the passion of their summer romance might wane with the distance. She was still expecting him to tire of her, especially as he was abroad. He'd probably meet some nice WAAF – they must be crawling all over him, surely – and she'd hear nothing more from him. Maybe he just felt indebted to her for looking after him – like those wounded soldiers who fell in love with their nurses – and maybe he'd keep writing to ask after the girls from time to time, but one day he'd write that he'd met a nice young girl to have babies with and that would be that. She was preparing herself for the worst by thinking all this, but of course she didn't want any of it to actually happen. The truth was, she wanted Harry, but she also knew that she loved him so much that she would be just happy that he was in the world, and that even if she never saw him again, she would still love him, always. This revelation made her feel content and miserable in equal measure, as she brushed past the few rose bushes left at the edge of the family garden, their browning leaves heavy with rain which slapped wet hands of drizzle on her coat as she passed.

She trotted into the side door of the house as the rain started to really pelt down and pulled off her hat and coat as she walked down the corridor, patting her damp hair as she did so and nearly tripping over with shock when she saw Allan Vaughan standing in her lounge, looking out of the window, his head tipped back as he watched the clouds of the coming storm.

'I say, what are you doing in here?'

He turned round, caught unawares.

She did not care a jot for decorum with these Army fellows any more. If they annoyed her, she felt quite justified in saying so, as she did now. 'These are my private quarters. Please leave!'

'My apologies. I wanted to catch you and thought this would be the best place. I will leave. Please accept my apology. It won't happen again.'

'Well, since you're here now, what was it you wanted?' She couldn't make this chap out. One minute he was all official and militaristic and tiresome, the next, there was this softness there that always surprised her.

'I have something for you. A gift . . . look at it as partial recompense for the inconvenience of our proximity.'

'I really do not need anything from the Army, or from you, thank you,' she said. She was annoyed. She'd had an emotional morning and thoughts of Harry and wanted to sit at her desk and read Harry's letters in peace.

'I'm afraid you already have it, or your housekeeper does. It's been delivered to the kitchen.'

'Well, what on earth is it?'

'Will you follow me, Mrs Calvert-Lazenby?' he said and walked past her, expecting her to follow. This annoyed her intensely but she was also becoming rather too curious about this gift in the kitchen than she cared to admit, so, begrudgingly, she followed him as he walked through the Army section of the house and crossed over the threshold into the servants' areas of the kitchen and scullery. He stood to one side when he reached the kitchen door and held his hand out for her to enter – her own kitchen, for heaven's sake! How infuriating the man was! Inside, he led her through it to the servants' hall, where she saw a large wooden crate placed in the middle of it. Bairstow was nowhere to be seen, off doing jobs of some sort, no doubt, as she wouldn't have let Vaughan anywhere near her kingdom otherwise.

'What is it?' asked Rosina, stopping at the other end of the room.

'Come and look,' said Vaughan and actually smiled. His face looked quite different. His eyes looked kinder and his face softened. She had to admit it improved him, but he was still irritating.

She marched over with a sigh and peered inside, as the lid had been removed and was propped up against the wall behind him. Inside the crate was a selection of wonders. Food. Food the like of which she'd not seen in many months. Food in tins and jars and packets. She reached in and pulled out a tin of peach slices in syrup. Beneath were more tins of peaches and others of pineapples and mandarins. There were packets of chocolate biscuits, as well as several tins of salmon and ham. There were a couple of boxes of Kellogg's cornflakes – made from real corn, it read, not like the ones they had these days made from the inferior wheatflakes that simply did not taste half as good. Also, there was another box of breakfast cereal she'd never seen before called Cheerioats. A large packet of icing sugar and another of caster sugar sat beside a couple of bags of dried mixed fruit. And lastly, the oddest thing, several tins of butter. Who knew they even put butter in tins?

'What is all this? Where is it from?' said Rosina and stared at Vaughan, still holding on to the tinned peaches, reluctant to let them go.

He was smiling broadly at her now. 'They're for you. As I said, a gift.'

'But how?'

'My little sister married a wealthy Canadian chap after the last war and moved out there. She sends me things when she can. This came today. Normally, I'd share it out amongst my officers, but I decided that if anyone deserved a treat, it was you.'

'But I can't possibly take all this. It's yours. And it's . . . too much.'

'Not at all. I will refuse to take it.'

'Well, well . . .' she faltered and shook her head, still marvelling at such riches. 'I can't possibly keep it all myself. And I know precisely who should have it.'

'Indeed not,' said Vaughan, grumpily. 'I won't hear of it going to anyone else.'

'But it's mine, isn't it? You said it was mine. So I can do whatever I please with it.'

His face relaxed a little and he smiled at her, with an eyebrow raised. 'And what would please you?'

'Bairstow shall have some butter, sugar and fruit to make a cake and we'll all have a bit and she can keep the rest for her own use. The staff will all have a couple of tins of something each, with the lion's share of the meat and fish going to my tenant Phyllis, who needs to build up her strength for her three little ones.'

'That's what I would expect of you. You are inordinately kind to your staff. It's quite remarkable.'

'They are inordinately kind to me, so it's purely reciprocation.'

'But you must keep something for yourself. I insist.'

Rosina gazed down at the treasures again and could not help but lick her lips. 'All right, then. I'll take one tin of salmon and one of peaches. How's that?'

'Is that it?'

'Yes, and I'm going to sit at this table and eat them from the tin with a fork, right here, right now for my lunch. It will be the ultimate decadence.'

Vaughan laughed – the first time she'd ever heard a joyful sound from him. 'May I join you?'

'Ah, I see you want a bit of my gift. I'm not sure that was part of the deal!'

'Absolutely not. I'd just like to . . . well, I was going to say, I wanted to watch you enjoy it. But that sounds peculiar.'

She raised her eyebrows at him and said, 'It does a bit!'

They both laughed. What a turn-up this was. Allan Vaughan, the Army machine, had a little sister who'd married a Canadian soldier and sent her brother treats, and more interesting even than that, Vaughan had a soft side to him.

'I suppose I ought to say thank you,' Rosina said.

'You're welcome.'

'No, really. I mean it. It would be very easy for you to keep this and I do appreciate the gift. It will mean so much to my staff and my tenant.'

'And to you? Does it mean something to you?' He looked at her quite intently.

'Ah, don't push your luck, Colonel Vaughan. I'm still angry as hell about you lot being here!'

'I know, I know,' he said as he drew up a chair opposite her, where she was now using her tin opener to prise open the two cans, one of peaches bathed in sugary syrup and the other red salmon, lounging in oil.

She took two forks from the sideboard drawer and handed Vaughan one. She started with the peaches, in defiance of table manners, pushing the salmon across to Vaughan. The slippery peach slice tasted like heaven as it slid into her mouth. She had not tasted sugar like this for so long, it almost overwhelmed her taste buds with an explosion of pleasure as she closed her eyes to savour it. She felt a sticky drip of syrup ooze from her lips and reached up to wipe it away, opening her eyes to see Vaughan staring at her with abandonment. She laughed with her mouth half open, knowing that her total lack of etiquette had gone completely beyond the pale. But he laughed too and she laughed again and, for the first time, she felt she saw a little of who he really was.

'So,' she said, when she had eaten a couple more slices and needed a break from all the sweetness. 'You have a little sister.'

'I do,' he said, picking at the salmon, but clearly far more interested in talking to her than eating.

'I can't imagine you having a little sister. I can't imagine you ever being a child!' She knew it was personal, the way she was speaking to him. She barely knew the man and, what's more, she had quite hated him until today. Well, perhaps not hate, more intense dislike. But then she recalled the look in his eyes when she'd talked about being a parent and it sobered her for a moment.

'I assure you I was indeed a child, at some shadowy stage in the distant past. And you? You grew up here? And then your daughters too?'

'Yes. My childhood home, their childhood home.'

He nodded solemnly and looked down glumly at the uneaten salmon. Something had changed in the air of the room again, just like before.

Rosina glanced down at his hand and noticed a wedding ring there.

'Where is your family stationed? Are they local? Do you see them much?'

Vaughan did not look up and did not respond.

Rosina waited, but the silence continued to grow. She cleared her throat and put down her fork. There was something so heavy in the room, she could feel it like a weight on her shoulders.

Suddenly, he looked up. 'I had a boy once. John. Johnnie. He was nine. He got very sick. In his bones. And it . . . He died.'

Rosina made a sharp intake of breath. It was the last thing in the world she had expected to hear. And yet it made perfect sense. 'I'm so dreadfully sorry to hear that,' she said.

He was looking at the table again now, still holding his empty fork.

'My wife and I. It . . . We tried. We tried afterwards. But we couldn't make it work in the slightest. We . . . It broke us, I'm afraid. We separated and then divorced. She's in Scotland now, with her mother. I never see her.'

All that heaviness, those dark clouds, that haunted look she'd seen in his eyes, it all added up.

They sat in silence for a time. Strangely, it was a comfortable silence, though she had no idea why. Maybe it was all the time she'd spent with Phyllis, listening to her grieve. Or perhaps it went further back than that, to the shocked grieving of her daughters for their absent father. And again, years before, to the death of her father, her brothers before him and her mother before that. Rosina had been a companion to grief many times – too many times in one life, for one person, perhaps. But at least she could comfort others who felt it. At least she had that left from all the loss.

'Peaches?' she said.

'What?' He looked up, genuinely confused, as he'd clearly lost himself for a minute.

'Have some peaches,' she said and pushed them over to him.

'I don't think I can.'

'Give me the fish then,' she told him, softly.

He pushed across the salmon tin and she ate a forkful, the fork still coated in syrup. The contrast between sweet and salt was strangely delicious. She watched him stare at the peaches.

'Eat,' she said simply.

He glanced at her, then put his fork in and fished out a peach slice and ate it. Then he ate another.

'They're so good,' he said in a whisper, with a ghost of a voice.

'Good,' she said.

Chapter 9

November 1940

For the rest of September and the whole of October, the bombardment of London continued, night after dreadful night. The Luftwaffe's tactics had changed in the second month, from huge formations targeting the docks and industrial targets, to smaller groups ranging over the full city, causing more domestic damage and civilian death. The crew of Substation 73V continued to work their legs off, and still nobody had been seriously injured, or worse, for which Evvy found herself saying a little prayer for her crew every time she went to sleep. She'd never felt much about religion either way, but these days it felt like an insurance policy to hedge on the side of caution and pray, just in case.

By the beginning of November, there had been some injuries amongst the crew – from cuts and bruises, to various degrees of burnt hands and faces, to eye injuries due to sparks, as well as one man with a broken arm when he fell from a crumbling ruin. They were utterly exhausted yet dogged in their perseverance in the face of constant threat. And then, totally unexpectedly, the night of 4 November, no warning came, no siren came and no bombers came. It was the first time without bombing in fifty-seven nights.

Nobody knew what to do with themselves. They were on high alert all night, expecting the hum of planes any second. But they never showed up. The next night was the same and soon after they began to relax a little, getting used to the new equilibrium where some nights brought death and disaster and others brought peace and tranquillity. Again, they had to accustom themselves to a new reality. The mood at the station calmed, as the pressure subsided somewhat, though there was still plenty to do.

One day, someone new arrived at 73V, a middle-aged man walking in to the station and up to the watchroom, no uniform, just dressed in slacks, pullover and an overcoat. He was carrying a carpet bag, bulging with stuff, that made Evvy wonder what on earth he had in there. Sid asked him his business and the man requested to speak to the station commander. Evvy volunteered to take him to Bailey's office.

'What's in the bag then?' she said, the moment she was out of Sid's earshot. She'd learnt to curb her cheeky ways at work, but this chap wasn't anything to do with the LFB, she could tell that a mile off.

'My materials and equipment. I'm an artist,' he replied.

Evvy stopped dead and so did the man, looking at her curiously. 'An artist? Me too.'

'Really?'

'Yes, I was painting propaganda stuff and theatre sets earlier this year.'

'And now you're at the front saving London from the flames.'

'I suppose so. But I still sketch, or at least, I'd want to, if I had the time.'

'How charming,' he said, with a hint of a smirk she didn't quite like. 'Your superior officer?' he said and gestured forward.

Evvy took an instant dislike to him. He was the one who seemed superior, or thought he was.

She walked on and knocked loudly on Bailey's door, before hearing his usual call of 'What?' She opened the door to the now familiar facial expression that seemed to say with exasperation, 'What *now*?'

'Some artist bloke here to see you, S.O. Do you have the time?'

Bailey looked annoyed and shrugged his shoulders. 'Well, all right then. If it's quick.'

Evvy stepped back into the corridor and said, 'Make it quick. He's a very busy man.'

The artist did not acknowledge what she'd said and simply walked past her into the room.

Evvy pulled the door to, but didn't shut it entirely, so that she could loiter in the corridor and listen. The man introduced himself as Saxon Cavendish. *That sounds like a made-up name, if ever I heard one*, thought Evvy. He said he was an official war artist and had been tasked with painting the portraits of some of the London Fire Brigade staff. As he lived in Bloomsbury, he thought he'd start here and was going around the area's substations looking for models to sketch, before choosing his subjects, which would comprise three or four people to paint in oils. He asked if Bailey wouldn't mind if he hung about for a day and night there, sketching the staff at work. He said he'd not trouble anyone.

'Well, as long as you don't interfere with anything. And I can't have you going off on a run with my lads. Far too dangerous for a civilian to be hanging about.'

'I wouldn't dream of it!' said Cavendish. 'I intend to keep myself far away from harm, believe you me.'

Of course you do, you coward, thought Evvy. She wished Bailey would say no to him and send him packing with a flea in his ear. Then she heard Bailey's chair scrape back and she hurried away down the corridor, lest they should appear at the door and discover her snooping.

So, for the whole of that day and into the evening, the great war artist Saxon Cavendish hung about the station with his sketchbook. Evvy came and went, on driving jobs for the boss. Every time she saw Cavendish, she did not speak to him, but made sure she caught a glimpse of his work. She didn't want to like his work but had to admit that the man could certainly draw. But what she noticed was that each sketch he did of the men of the Fire Brigade had them standing in valiant poses staring resolutely into the middle distance. And every sketch Cavendish did of the women had them sitting at a desk, looking demure, with dark lips and long eyelashes – she could testify that neither Lynn nor Pauline had eyelashes anything like as long – with an elegant hand draped over a telephone or writing with an ink pen. He wasn't actually sketching what he could see, but his own idealised version of what he wanted to see. Evvy thought this was absolute poppycock and was also intensely annoyed that Cavendish didn't once choose to sketch her. After all, she was a dream of an artist's model and unusual in her driver's trousers and jacket.

A couple of times, during a lull in duties, she'd sit conspicuously on the corner of a table, one leg hooked up beneath the other, showing off her well-fitting driving outfit with the laces at the shins. She was waiting for Cavendish's attention to turn to her, but it never did. When he left that night, he showed the chaps the sketches he'd done and everyone murmured in appreciation, saying he'd made them look like heroes. He did not deign to speak to the women, who all gave each other eyerolls. Once Cavendish had gone, Evvy was fuming. She went to her bag in the library and got out her own sketchbook and pencils, which had sat untouched since she'd arrived in August. She came back to the watchroom for the last half-hour of duty and sat opposite Pauline and Lynn and started to sketch them. She wanted to right the wrong that Cavendish had displayed and focus on the women. She drew detailed, careful sketches of both of them at work: one of Pauline standing at the board, writing up information; Lynn filing papers in the cabinet; both of them focused on the phones, scribbling down vital information on jotters with sharp pencils.

Evvy got a bit of a ribbing from the fellers, accusing her of copying the great artist and what did she know about drawing anyway?

'She is an artist, actually,' said Sam, defending her. 'She gave it up to come here and help you idiots.'

Evvy smiled at him, before going outside with her sketchbook to find Vera, who she thought might be cleaning her bike. She found her in the garage, admiring her brand-new American motorcycle, which she'd received at last after angling for one for weeks. Evvy had not sought out an American bike, still happy with Betty.

'How's the new beast?' she asked.

'Oh, it's a beauty,' said Vera, glowing. 'So much more powerful than our old ones. You must get one, Evvy. Or do you think it might be too much for you, eh? Chicken, eh?' Vera winked at her.

'I'm no chicken!' replied Evvy. 'Maybe I will get one. Maybe I'll give you a run for your money.'

'Maybe you will. But I'll win. We both know that, Calvert,' said Vera and laughed.

They joshed each other like this all the time, a friendly rivalry. But Evvy knew inside that she would never want a monster of a machine like that. The power of it scared her. She was all talk. Or, as Sam said once of a fireman he disliked, 'All mouth and no trousers.' Evvy knew that she was good at putting on the bravado, but underneath she was afraid of some things and speed was one of them. She liked a bit of risk, but she also wanted to live a long life and have many adventures. And coming off a powerful American bike at top speed was not an adventure she desired in the slightest. And as much as she liked Vera, she wasn't ready to admit that. She had a reputation to keep up, as a bit of a daredevil. Evvy Calvert-Lazenby, the posh girl who wasn't afraid of a thing. She'd had to cultivate that image when dealing with a workplace full of men and she kept it up for the women too. People liked it about her, they admired her for it. Only Evvy knew it wasn't entirely true, but she kept it up for appearance's sake.

'You better get practising then, Vera. It would be embarrassing to be run off the road by the new girl.'

'Well, well, that's fighting talk! Let me know when you've got the nerve to ask for one of these, eh?'

Evvy laughed and said, 'All right, all right. All in good time. But right now, I'm after a bit of sketching practice. Mind if I draw you while you're tinkering with the beast?'

She perched on the low wall of the playground and sketched Vera working on her magnificent new machine, looking magnificent herself in her driving clothes, her hair pinned back but a lock of it escaping over her forehead as she wielded a spanner, her hands filthy with grease.

Evvy finished her sketches and looked at them. *Yes, this,* she thought. *This is what the women of war look like.* Hard-working, committed, skilful and talented. Not afraid to get their hands dirty or break a nail. She thanked Vera, who loved the sketch, and Evvy took it back inside, spreading her new work out on her bed and having a good look. They weren't her best efforts – she needed more practice on hands, she was never very good at those – but she liked the spirit of them.

She heard footsteps behind her and turned, expecting to see the ladies come in, and she wanted to see what they thought. But it wasn't them, it was Lewis Bailey.

He came across the room and stopped beside the bed. He looked at her drawings without speaking and she looked at them again with him.

'You have a gift,' he said. 'You're better than him.'

'Oh, nonsense!' she laughed. 'Thank you for the compliment, but I know how talented he was. He just annoyed me.'

'Why?'

'All the sketches of women he did were like artist's models, all graceful and feminine, carrying out their duties in full make-up and never a hair out of place. It's not real life. It's an insult to the real work these women are doing. I used to love those posters, with the glamorous girls in uniform. I thought they were terribly attractive. Now I'm in it and I see the hard work women do, day in, day out, all night, with little rest and often doing a thankless task, sometimes even under fire . . . I think of those posters now and they look ridiculous. And it makes my blood boil to see that man come in here and idealise people that way.'

She was breathing heavily after her rant and when Bailey said nothing in reply, she picked up her sketches hurriedly and put them on the library desk, placing a couple of large books on them to keep them flat. She could feel Bailey watching her. What was he thinking?

'I think you're absolutely right,' Bailey said at last. 'I've never thought of it that way. But it's true. There were a lot of folk who never wanted women in the fire brigade – senior men and ordinary blokes. They all said women wouldn't cope under the pressure, would scream and faint at the first sign of trouble. I wasn't sure, to be honest. I just knew we'd need as many warm bodies as we could get. Turns out that women have proven themselves to be as good as the fellers – better in many cases. And I never saw a woman panic or fuss these past months. You lot just get on with it.'

'Of course we do. How do men think children were raised and households managed without any gumption or perseverance? And all the other jobs women have been doing out in the community forever? I'm sick of hearing what women can and can't do. Maybe after this war is over, men will truly understand what we're capable of.'

'If that happens, then we can say that some good has come of this bloody mess.'

Bailey sighed and rubbed his eyes. He was looking absolutely exhausted these days.

'You never give yourself a break, S.O.,' Evvy said. 'Why don't you go for a sleep and I'll come and fetch you if there's anything desperate?'

He looked at her and smiled gently. 'Are you my nursemaid now, Calvert? It's a role that doesn't suit you much, I'd say.'

'God, no. I'd rather gouge my eyes out with a spoon than be a nurse. All those bedpans and bedbaths and . . .' She gave a mock shudder. 'All that awful *intimacy* with the human body . . . yeuch! No thanks. But the truth remains, you look terrible.'

'Thank you, Calvert. I can always rely on you to rally my spirits.'

'Oh, I didn't mean it that way, sir. I mean . . .' She'd put her foot in it again. The truth was, he looked incredibly tired all the time, with deep circles under his eyes. But his new beard still suited him well and she found herself watching him sometimes. He had such an interesting face, as if all his experiences were etched into every line and angle. He'd be a pleasure to sketch.

'I know you meant well. Right, back to business. You're off now, Calvert. Get something to eat.'

He left and, once alone, Evvy picked up her sketch pad and sat on her bed, leaning back against the bookshelf behind her. She closed her eyes and pictured Lewis Bailey's craggy face. Then she started drawing. When she'd finished, she was pleased with it, but it wasn't quite right. It looked like him, but there was something missing from the eyes.

When he spoke, there was an intelligence in them, a kind of fierce gaze that showed he was thinking – thinking, all the time. That's what was missing from the sketch. She'd have to keep trying, to get him right. She wanted to get him right.

* * *

As the November days went on, the enemy's tactics changed again as they turned their attention to other British cities. Liverpool and Birmingham took it bad and, worst of all, on the fifteenth, Coventry was decimated. The Germans had not invaded yet, but they were certainly making their presence felt.

In London, 73V continued their hard work, with some very close scrapes, one lad getting a rather nasty eye injury from flying sparks that rushed along on the winds created by bellowing flames. He would survive, but his eye would take a long time to heal and might never be the same. They did a collection for his mother, who'd lost her husband already in the war. Evvy shuddered when she heard stories like these, closing her eyes and crossing her fingers – her philosophy since childhood, a mishmash of half-hearted Christianity and robust superstition – and saying another prayer, that Gracie would be all right if she was sent abroad and Mummy and the girls would never be in danger and that none of their chaps at 73V would be injured, that Vera would ride safely back to the station every time, where Pauline and Lynn would never be bombed. She said a little prayer for herself too and invariably one for Lewis Bailey and always one for Sam.

Was she in love with Sam? She surmised she was definitely in lust with him. The thought of his hands on her always gave her a twinge in her belly that annoyed her. She'd usually found boys and men a bit of a lark, but never felt a real pull towards them. Sam had changed all that. When they were together, she found she could not stop looking at him, drinking him in. He did that with her too and she felt they were going through some kind of bonding phase, where they stared and stared, like babies do with their mothers, or so she'd heard. It was as if they needed to imprint the image of each other on their brain, to memorise it, in case it was somehow lost. Maybe it was passion, maybe it was something to do with the danger of the times. She remembered telling her mother earlier that year, when she was working as a painter, that London at that time was full of passion, fondness and urgency, due to the war. People knew they might never see each other again, especially those girls with sweethearts in the forces. Evvy felt lucky that her chap worked alongside her and wasn't going anywhere. But, of course, it wasn't only about the fear of them going abroad to fight; it was the very real fear of injury and death, either somewhere far afield or, in Sam's case, it could be down the road. He could die any night of the week, and so, for that matter, could she.

Evvy tried to analyse whether her strong feelings for Sam were due to his own merits, or purely the dramatic situation they found themselves in. So she decided that, in order to ascertain whether she felt something deeper for him, for Sam Bailey as a whole person, she wanted to see more of this other side of him he'd revealed in his writing. Since that miraculous first letter, after much badgering, he had now given her three more letters, all on similar themes, the ways he thought about her, the stark strangeness of the nights full of flames, sparks and smoke, how his thoughts of her were his escape from the madness of these times. Each time, she was overcome with how sublime his prose was. She again begged him for further letters, but none had been forthcoming for a while. She so wanted to see more. To Evvy, it was just as exciting as being in his arms, if not more so.

'When are you going to write me another letter?' she said when they were canoodling as usual behind Suki the school bus.

'Come on, love. You don't need a letter when you've got the real me. We're bunking in the same building, aren't we? If I was abroad like the soldier boys, I'd write to you, of course I would. But not here. It's not needed, is it, eh? Not when we have the glory of all this.' He kissed her again, running his fingers into her hair and tugging at it, which gave her a thrill.

She was lost for a moment in the kiss, but the interruption of their conversation rankled a bit. She pulled away.

'But it's not about that. I see a side to you in your writing that I don't see when we talk. Or, rather, I hear a side to you I don't hear. It's amazing how different you are in writing than in speech. It's that person I want to get to know. He's extraordinary! *You* are extraordinary, in your letters.'

His expression changed and he pulled away from her slightly. Then he turned away fully and got out a cigarette and lit it, without offering her one, as he always did, and took a few steps away, pacing while he smoked.

'What's wrong?' she asked.

'Nothing. I just can't see why you go on and on about these letters when you have me, every inch of me.'

'And I don't know why you can't do this simple thing for me. It would only take you a few minutes.'

'I'm here, I'm standing right here in front of you,' he said urgently and, stepping towards her, put his hand firmly around her waist and drew her in for a hard kiss.

'Get off!' she said and pulled away. 'Don't you pull and push me around. You can't shut down a conversation with muscle and get away with it. Why won't you write to me?

Or talk to me? Is this all we are, just bodies? If that's all it is, then it's over. I'm not interested in sex for its own sake. You can clear off if that's all you want.'

He looked at her desperately and said, 'That's not all I want. It's more than that. Much more. Surely you know that by now?'

'Then we need to get out from behind this bloody bus. I'm sick of it. All I asked is for you to write a few words. You'd think I was demanding a June wedding and a honeymoon in Monte Carlo, for God's sake.'

'All right, all right. I'll do another letter for you. Maybe then you'll stop bending my ear about it all the time.' He really did look angry and could barely look at her, puffing away furiously.

'Don't bother,' she said and walked away. She had an intense dislike of moody men. Her father had been like that and she would never put up with it again.

What a ridiculous argument, she fumed as she marched back inside. She went up to the watchroom, where she thought she'd see if she could pull Pauline aside for a chat about it. They had a few minutes before their shift started. But there was suddenly no time, because Lynn was taking a call and it was a yellow warning. The bombers were on their way.

Chapter 10

It was shaping up to be a bad night. They called in the other shift, as the bombing was so heavy. Evvy saw Sam briefly between fires and they gave each other a longing look, followed by a half-smile across the watchroom, but had no time to resolve anything and then he was gone again, off out into the night, and so was she, off on Betty delivering messages and, later, driving Bailey about as usual. She had also recently been given the extra duty of delivering petrol cans full of fuel to various pumps at work during the raids. It was the most nerve-wracking task she had, knowing she was driving into a fire situation with highly flammable materials. She dreaded it and it exhilarated her at the same time, the thrill and horror of danger pumping through her as she ferried the precious yet deadly cargo.

After delivering fuel to a few teams that night, at about three in the morning, Evvy came back to 73V for her next orders and went into the watchroom, where both Pauline and Lynn looked up at her and stared, eyes wide. Even Sid was frowning at her, then looked away.

'What?' she said. 'What's happened?'

There was an agonising pause, then Pauline said, 'It's Sam, love. He's been injured. He's in hospital.'

'Oh my God,' said Evvy and felt faint. She'd never fainted in her life, but she grabbed for the nearest chair, as she was sure she was going to collapse.

Her friends rushed to her aid and got her into the chair. Sam was injured and all she could think about was that it had been non-stop for hours and she hadn't had anything to eat or drink that night, as she'd been fooling around with Sam and then arguing with him, when they should've been having their tea. So it was probably overwork with no fuel that had made her weak, but it was shock too.

'Is it serious?' she said once she'd come back to herself.

Sid replied, 'It's not good, I won't lie to you. A wall collapsed and he was under it. Broken limbs, I'd say.'

'Was he conscious when they took him?'

'No, he wasn't,' said Sid. He put a hand on her shoulder. 'I can't let you go and see him, I'm sorry. We need you on duty. Vera's gone AWOL. She's not been heard of for a while. Have you seen her?'

'What? No. Where is she?'

'Nobody knows,' said Lynn, forlornly.

Sid added, 'Look, there's some safety gear – helmets, capes, boots, mackintoshes, et cetera – I need you to take over to Camden, as some of theirs has been damaged. I've put them in the bus. Take 'em over, then go have a scout around, see if you can find anyone who's seen Vera. Then, if things die down a bit, you can go to the hospital. Are you up to it? Can you drive?'

'Yes, yes, of course,' said Evvy and she stood up. She felt all right, no longer dizzy.

Sid told her what streets the firemen were on that needed the equipment. She went to Suki and started her up.

'Oh my God, oh my God, oh my God,' she muttered, as she manoeuvred Suki out into the streets. Sam was in hospital. Vera was missing. Was everything going wrong? Were two of her fears going to come true, in one night?

She drove to Camden without thinking, meeting roads blocked by damage or fire crews and having to turn the bus in tight spots and try other roads. Some were blocked by diversion signs, which usually meant there was a UXB down there – an unexploded bomb. But as Evvy approached her destination, she found that every road was blocked, so she pulled Suki up at the side of the road and resolved to carry the gear there on foot. There was too much to take in one trip, so she was about to load up as much as she could carry, when she noticed a tin of condensed milk at her feet, just sitting there on the pavement. Then there was another one, a bit further on, and more tins strewn here and there, some completely intact, while others were twisted into bizarre shapes. She looked ahead and saw dozens of tins all over the pavements and street, along with the blasted remains of boxes and packets. A grocers must have been hit, she realised, and its contents strewn all over the adjacent streets. Then she saw more debris in the trees that lined the little street, including a large tablecloth. She tugged at it and it came free. Evvy went back to the bus and loaded up the gear into the cloth, tying it up with a knot, and then she started to drag it along the street in the direction she needed.

The only way was down a road with a diversion sign on it. She could see the fire beyond it where the crew she was heading for must be and she had to get to them. She edged around the sign and proceeded carefully on the pavement, dragging her cargo behind her. Soon, she saw on the other side of the road the reason why the diversion sign had been put there. A parachute mine lay on the opposite pavement, its carrier splayed behind it across someone's front garden. She stopped and stared at it. If she turned round and went back, she was just as likely to set it off as going forward. So she decided to go on. She swallowed a lump of fear in her throat and steeled herself.

Taking a firm grip on the sheet carrying her cargo, she began to edge forward slowly, dragging the cloth as gently as she could. She had no idea what precisely she might do to set it off, but she didn't want to find out, so she continued to inch forward, never taking her eyes off it, as if merely staring at it would hex it into staying unexploded. She could feel her heart thumping like mad and sweat prickling her forehead.

Stupid, stupid, she said to herself inwardly. But she knew she had little choice. The men needed what she had brought and she had to get on with it for their sake, for her colleagues in the fire service, those brave men she worked alongside every day. Now it was her turn to risk her life.

Those moments inching past that bomb stretched out into hours. Sam popped into her mind. She thought of him in the hospital, alive, finding out that she'd been blown to bits. She shuffled on for Sam, desperate that she should see him again, that she should survive for him. And she did. The bomb didn't go off.

As she turned into the next street and saw the men ahead, she stopped just for a moment and let out one uncontrollable sob. Then she wiped the sweat out of her eyes and grasped her cargo again, dragging it as quickly as she could to the crew who needed it. They were grateful she'd come; someone called the men over and they came and grabbed the stuff, kitting up hurriedly. It was a bad night. Firemen were running to and fro and swearing like mad, filling the burning air with blue language. Evvy was used to it and felt it was entirely justified under the circumstances. She asked them if they'd seen a despatch rider around here, a woman. But they said no and rushed back to face the fire.

Evvy knew she had to get back to the bus somehow and wouldn't go down that street again. She tried another street nearby and found it was full of debris but no bombs, so she stumbled down it, clambering over the remains of houses. Eventually, at the end, she met an ARP warden who asked what she was up to and she said she'd parked her bus nearby.

'Well, don't drive up that street,' he said, pointing to the one with the sign. 'There's a bomb up there. It's magnetic and anything metal on your uniform or in your pocket could set it off. Don't go anywhere near it!'

Evvy nodded and hurried off to find Suki, and climbed in. She sat for a moment, completely still. She could have set that mine off easily. The keys to Suki had been in her pocket. She had metal buttons on her jacket. She felt that old sensation of someone walking over her grave and she shuddered.

Well, it didn't happen. She was all right. But how was Sam? It took all her resolve not to drive Suki immediately to all the hospitals in Bloomsbury to look for him. She thought her head might explode with fear, that he was dead. Sam, beautiful, cheeky Sam Bailey, crushed, dead. Oh God, it was hell to think of it. Did this mean she loved him? It must do. She felt as if hearing of Sam's death would be the worst moment of her life, much worse than her father's death. That must mean love, surely?

She felt as if she were going mad. She had to stop thinking of him. She had to think straight and do her job. She turned her attention to Vera. Where the hell was Vera?

Evvy drove around to a few sites of fires, jumped out and asked firemen and policemen if they'd seen a female despatch rider around, as well as asking ARP wardens at observation posts, WVS workers at canteens and eventually just anyone she saw in the streets, including civilians tramping to rest centres in a lull in the bombing. But nobody had seen Vera.

Evvy stayed out until dawn looking for her, but there was no sign. She went back to the station absolutely shattered, the all-clear ringing in her ears as she parked up Suki and dragged her feet to the watchroom. She dreaded reaching it, as she imagined the minute she got there she'd see an awful look on her friends' faces and then she'd beg them to tell her the dreadful news, whether about Sam or Vera, or both.

When she got there, Pauline told her there was no news. And then Lewis walked in and came straight to her.

'Have you heard?' he said, concern in his eyes.

'Only that Sam was injured and in hospital. Is it . . . Is he . . .?' She couldn't finish.

'That's right, he's in hospital. He's alive.'

'Oh, thank God,' she answered quietly. She said a brief prayer of thanks in her mind.

'Listen, I need to supervise the clear-up, but I'll take you after that, all right?'

'No,' she said. 'I'll take you.'

He smiled at her and off they went, helping the crews roll up the hoses, find out which ones were damaged and what other equipment might be missing or broken.

Hours later, they finally collapsed in the watchroom. Lynn brought them tea, which went down a treat. There was still no news of Vera, though the word had been put out. Sid had discovered she'd been sent on a longer drive up to North London and not been seen since. Everyone was grim-faced and exhausted. It had been a horrendous night all round, but 73V had done brilliantly, finally managing to put out all the fires they'd been assigned to. At last they could rest for a while – until the next alert anyway.

'Ready, S.O.?' said Evvy, when she'd finished her tea.

Bailey nodded and they went out to the staff car.

Evvy drove them to the hospital on Gower Street. They were told which ward to go to, and when they got there, the nurse near the door gave them a peculiar look as they tramped in. Evvy realised they must look an absolute fright with their filthy faces and scruffy uniforms. The nurse shook her head as she approached them and ushered them out into the corridor again, the door swinging to behind her.

'No, no, no,' she said. 'You're not coming in here bringing all that mess with you.'

'We just want to see Sam Bailey, a fireman,' said Lewis.

'Not like that, you're not,' replied the nurse and folded her arms.

Evvy swiftly ran out of patience. 'We've been working all night saving lives, for God's sake, woman!'

'I don't care if you've been raising the *Titanic*. You're not bringing all that muck into my spotless ward. Now, go home, get yourselves cleaned up and come back at visiting time at two this afternoon.'

'Can you tell us how he is?' asked Bailey. 'I'm his brother and senior officer, Lewis Bailey. And this is his colleague. And . . . his sweetheart, Evelyn. We must know. Can you tell us?'

The nurse pursed her lips, then said, 'Bailey, you say? Wait here.' She went back into the ward.

Evvy looked at Bailey and they both shook their heads in disbelief. 'Bloody ridiculous!' cried Evvy.

'I suppose she's just doing her job,' said Lewis.

After what seemed an age, the nurse came out. 'He's doing well. Some concussion and sprains in both ankles and one wrist. No broken bones. Cuts and scratches and bruising all over, but nothing too bad or too deep. I hear a wall fell on him. He's very lucky to be all in one piece. He's been awake and lucid since he was brought in, but he's sleeping now. We'll be keeping him in tonight, but if there are no complications, then he should be out tomorrow.'

'Oh, thank God,' gasped Evvy.

Lewis thanked the nurse, and after she left, Evvy saw him turn and put his hand to his head, then he stumbled a step and put both hands out against the wall to steady himself.

'Gosh, are you all right?' said Evvy, wanting to reach out and touch him, but feeling she couldn't, not with her S.O.

'Fine. I'm fine now.' He righted himself and shook his head, raising his eyes to the heavens. 'All our lives, looking out for that lad. He's not a lad any more, I know that. But it doesn't get any easier.'

Evvy was so moved by Lewis's moment of vulnerability, his care for his little brother clearly evident.

'You're both so brave. Your parents would be so proud.'

'That's kind of you to say.'

'It's true, I'm sure of that. Everyone in the squad admires the two of you. Every single one.'

'Well, we're all made of stern stuff at 73V,' said Lewis, gesturing for them to start walking down the corridor, towards the stairs. 'Including you. You haven't stopped for hours. You must be dead on your feet.'

'Only the same as you. But I'm actually wide awake now. Completely wide awake. It's strange. I feel like I could run a marathon.'

'It is strange. Something about an emergency. Your body finds these hidden reserves and then it'll keep going like billy-o till suddenly it'll just stop. I've had that before. I'll be going great guns, then I'll just sit down with a bump and I'm asleep in seconds. I suppose that's how we get through those mad, long nights. Our bodies just keep going, even when there's danger all around. Or, I should say, especially when danger is there. It's all about survival probably.'

'Speaking of danger, I went down a street that was closed off with a diversion sign last night and ended up creeping past a UXB.'

'You did what?' Bailey stopped her on the stairs. 'That was bloody stupid.'

'Yes, it was. It didn't go off though. I'm still in one piece. And the crew got the equipment they needed.'

Bailey looked at her seriously and said, 'Don't ever take risks like that again, Evvy.'

It was the very first time he'd called her by her first name.

'All right,' she said quietly and looked at him. It was intense, staring at each other like that. In the silence, she heard her stomach groan. 'I'm really hungry, actually. Are you?'

'Starving.'

They left the hospital and went to a café nearby and stuffed themselves with greasy, fried food which was exactly what they needed. They chatted about this and that. Soon, the chat deepened into a more interesting conversation about things they loved. They talked about the films, books and music that had moved them most. He really was tremendously cultured and it was easy to talk to him. It wasn't like he was her boss, or her sweetheart's brother. He was like an old friend.

'So, of all the books you've read,' said Evvy, mopping up fried egg yolk with a slab of bread, 'imagine that you had to choose one, just one, and you had to read that book over and over again and you were never allowed to read another. What would it be? And you're not allowed to say Shakespeare or Dickens, because that's a boring answer.'

'But, what if I love a bit of Dickens? And I do. *Our Mutual Friend* is my favourite of his. Very underrated.'

'Oh, God, not Dickens. How dreary. Is that really the one book you'd read for the rest of your life?'

He chuckled and replied, 'No, actually. It's a play. By a Frenchman. I have a translated edition, very battered from where I've read it so much. It's my favourite book.'

'What is it? I don't know many French plays, despite living there for a while. I remember seeing something by Molière. It was supposed to be funny, but I didn't get the jokes.'

'It's called *Cyrano de Bergerac*.'

'Ah, I've heard of it. But never seen it. Or read it. What's it about?'

'A man with a big nose.'

'How silly!'

'But it's about much more than that. It's about poetry. And war. It's about secrets. And it's about love.'

'Ah, I'll have to read it. May I borrow your copy sometime?'

'I'll lend it to you, one day. When all this rubbish is over. When you've got time to appreciate it properly.'

'Good point. No time to read these days. I haven't read a book for ages. Too tired.' And she yawned luxuriously, her arms stretched above her head.

'Let's be on our way,' said Bailey. 'We need a rest before coming back to the hospital later.'

She drove them back to the station and they were strangely awkward with each other in the car. The spell their conversation had woven in the café had been broken and Evvy felt sad it was gone. She had really enjoyed talking with him.

Back at the watchroom, Pauline, Lynn and Sid were gone, probably sleeping. The day crew were in and managing things.

Still no news on Vera, though the police had said they'd be in touch the minute they knew anything. Bailey told Evvy to go and clean herself up and he'd do the same. They'd meet back at the watchroom at 1.45 and go to see Sam.

'And get some sleep in the meantime,' he told her.

After a good all-over body wash with a soapy flannel in the ladies, as well as washing her hair in the sink, she felt human again. Her hair still damp, she went to the library to find her friends sleeping soundly and she joined them, lying down and instantly worrying about Vera, before falling asleep within seconds.

She had no idea what time it was when she awoke, and jumped up, worried she'd missed going to see Sam. But Bailey was coming down the corridor to find her and she wasn't late. It was as if her body knew exactly what time she needed to wake up for Sam. She popped back to the ladies and brushed her messy, slept-on hair, wanting to look vaguely presentable for him.

At the hospital, the nurse nodded her approval at their cleaned-up selves and let them through. They found Sam sitting up in bed, his face covered with scratches and bruises, which looked alarming, but he was smiling broadly, so perhaps it didn't feel as bad as it looked. They asked him about what had happened, how it felt. He hardly remembered a thing.

He asked about everyone else in the crew. He was far more worried about them than himself. Evvy told him about Vera, still missing.

'That's my cue,' said Bailey. 'I'm going to walk back, Calvert.'

'But, S.O., I can drive you.'

'No, it's not far. I'm going to chase up the police on Vera, see what I can find out.'

'I'll take you.'

'No, Calvert. You stay and chat up this young feller. He could do with a bit of that.'

The brothers nodded at each other. Evvy could tell that, despite the formality of the gesture, there was true regard in that nod, a relief in Bailey's eyes that his little brother was all right and a reassurance in Sam's that he was fine. It touched her to see it and she thought for a moment of her sisters and how much she missed them, even when they drove her up the wall. She felt so lucky to have siblings, especially so many of them, and sisters in particular. She'd always wanted a brother when she was little, but now she was glad she had sisters. The thought of a brother of theirs going off to fight was horrible, the fear she'd feel for him in this war unthinkable. She knew how strongly she'd feel about it because of how keenly she felt it now, as she looked at Sam, beaten, bruised and battered in a hospital bed. She wanted to hold his hand, but both wrists being sprained meant no hand-holding and she couldn't even touch his face, it looked so sore. She smiled at him instead and blew him a kiss, which made him grin.

'Are you really all right?' she said.

'Yes, beautiful. I'm all right. You're a sight for sore eyes.'

'I nearly fainted when they said you were injured. I've never fainted in my life.'

'Well, that's a turn-up! You must like me a bit then!'

'Of course I do, you idiot.'

'Enjoy insulting blokes you like then?'

'Only you.' She paused. 'Look, Sam . . . I'm sorry about earlier. I felt rotten that the last thing we'd done was argue before you got hurt.'

'Oh blimey, Ev, you've got nothing to be sorry for. It was all me, this idiot. And I really was a bloody idiot. I'll write you a hundred letters if you want. Whatever you want, darling. Whatever you want.'

He looked desperately worried and she wanted to take his hand so much.

'Don't get all hot and bothered. You should be resting. Nurse Goebbels will be shouting at me if I upset you.'

'I'm all right. But honest, Ev, don't say sorry again.'

'It was silly of me to go on about the letters. But I would like to talk more, you know? Just go to a café and talk.

About things you like, the things you love. What moves you most.' She was thinking of the conversation with Bailey.

'What moves me? Sounds a bit deep for me, Ev!' laughed Sam. 'I'm sure you don't want me to write you letters about the finer points of engines, because that's what I know most about!'

'Books and films and things. Music.'

'I like swing bands. I like a good dance and I'm a great mover. I'll take you dancing when I'm back on my feet.'

Evvy thought again of the way her conversation with Bailey had soared so easily, to the heights of literature that had changed their lives and the depths of symphonies and string quartets they both had listened to and loved.

'I'd like that,' said Evvy and looked down at her hands.

'You like a dance, Ev?' he said, his voice concerned.

She looked up at his face. He was frowning.

'Yes. Who doesn't?'

'It's important to me. That you're happy with me. I want you to be happy. When that bloody wall was falling on my head, do you know what I was thinking? I was thinking of you. Only you. You're the thing I care about the best. I love you, Ev.'

Evvy wanted to cry. The thought of losing Sam had tortured her last night. And she was so happy that he was alive, intact, all right. But now as she looked at him, she knew there was something not quite there, not quite right between them. What was it? She couldn't put her finger on it. And, in her hesitation, his face fell.

'You don't love me,' he said sadly and looked away.

'I do!' she said. 'Of course I love you, you idiot.' And she smiled at him, a forced smile, because, inside, her mind was twisted and muddled.

He beamed back at her. Even though his face was marked with injuries, his beauty shone through, dazzling as always. How stunning he was to her. How moved she was just to look upon him. She must draw him. And inside him somewhere was the man who had written those incredible letters. She just had to find him somehow. Maybe if they had more time, to talk and walk, maybe that meeting of minds would come. As much as she desired him, as fond as she was of Sam Bailey, there was something missing. She knew as she looked at him that, if it weren't for the letters, she wouldn't be here now. She wanted him to be more than he was. And with a sickening feeling, she realised something. She wanted him to be Lewis Bailey. For the truth was that she loved them both and wished they were one man, an amalgam of Sam's beauty and Lewis's mind. A cruel thing to think, surely? Selfish and unfair to both brothers. But it was how she felt. It was what she wanted. And it was impossible.

She drove back to the station in a haze. She was still tired from the night before, confused by her feelings and consumed with worry about Vera. If there was still no news, she resolved to find out where in north London Vera had been driving to and get on Betty and drive the same route herself, looking for bombings or road closures or any sign of what might have delayed Vera and could explain her absence. If she'd had an accident, she could have been taken to a hospital in the north of the city and maybe Vera had lost her ID in the chaos. So Evvy would drive around the hospitals up there too.

She parked up and went inside, resolved as to her next course. In the watchroom, Lewis Bailey sat with Sid, talking seriously in the corner, in low voices. The day crew were there and quiet. Then Evvy saw one of the telephone girls was crying. They glanced up at Evvy and looked away again.

Bailey stood and came to her.

'Come with me, Calvert,' he said softly and left the room.

'No,' she said. 'No.'

Bailey turned and touched her arm. 'Come with me.'

She heard a girl sob and she followed him to his office, as if walking in a dream with no will of her own, numb and automatic.

Bailey shut his office door.

'How?' said Evvy. 'Was it a bomb?'

'No, it wasn't. Vera came off her bike. It was that new American machine. It was too powerful, they think. There have been other DR accidents on it, they said. She would have gone instantly. Head injury. No pain.'

Evvy nodded, and kept nodding. She couldn't stop nodding. Her lips were pressed together, her mouth turned down. She felt blank. Then, she felt anger boil up in her.

'That bloody American bike,' she snapped. 'I should've told her not to have it. I didn't want it. I knew it was bad news. I should've stopped her. But, I always think other people know more than me, that they're more capable than me. I always put on this show of being brave and reckless and not caring about anything, but I do. I put on this front and inside I don't know what I'm doing. I'm just making up everything as I go along and it's all pretence. I'm a fraud. I'm just a fake and a fraud. If I'd been thinking more about her and less of myself, I'd have told her not to get that bike. But I only thought of myself, that I didn't want it, but I didn't want to admit I was afraid of it. Why didn't I tell her? Why?'

She was sobbing now and put her hands over her face, to cover it, to hide.

He said, gently, 'It's not your fault.'

And she felt Lewis Bailey's arms go around her and she leant into his chest and she sobbed there. He didn't say anything. He just held her and let her cry. The feel of his arms around her was balm. It was all she needed. He always seemed to know exactly what she needed.

Chapter 11

December 1940

Winters could be harsh at Ravenscar. The snowfall could be so heavy that the village was essentially cut off. Food, fuel and postal deliveries might be unable to get through, power to the houses might go down, as well as the local school closing, sometimes for weeks. The clifftop folk were accustomed to it. In bad weather, the whole community helped out, clearing snow where they could and taking their own toboggans to the railway station to collect food and essentials for other villagers. And so, every winter, Rosina made her preparations for such circumstances. She ensured she had a store of paraffin lamps and candles in the basement, as well as coal and wood for the fires. She also had two accumulators for her radio – one to leave at the post office where they were charged and the other to use at home.

However, this winter, she had the Army and assumed they'd take care of any adverse weather conditions. Surely a tank would make an excellent snowplough! But she still made her own arrangements, just in case. She didn't like to rely on the Army for anything, if she could help it, as they had felt like the enemy since they had moved in, despite the fact they were all on the same side. Yet, she had to admit to herself, her friendship with Allan Vaughan had improved a lot. After their conversation over the peaches, they now met formally each weekend to go over the week's events and any matters arising, but, in truth, it wasn't very formal, starting with a pot of tea and often ending with a little drink of something a bit stronger, if Allan had managed to get hold of a nice sherry or port, for example. Their conversations had deepened over time, starting with the business of the day and progressing to their own interests and thoughts. He was fifty-one years old, six years her senior, yet still of similar enough age to be the same generation. They had that shared allotment of time as their upbringing, as well as having both lived through the Great War as adults – she at home and he in the Army, sent to France, then Italy. He told her he was wounded twice and received a number of honours. There was something comforting about sharing these major events in their own personal histories. Were they becoming friends? It felt as if they were. Rosina began to look forward to their meetings, as a little oasis from the relentless push of domestic concerns. He was interesting, handsome and good company. What was not to like?

One cold, crisp day in December, they were in the drawing room having one of their weekly meetings, when a knock on the door announced the arrival of Allan's secretary, Miss Holness, with an urgent signature required from Allan. Rosina had had little to do with her but had taken a dislike to her after her rather rude and dismissive treatment of Rosina in the past. Once Holness had gone, Allan looked curiously at Rosina.

'You don't much like my secretary, do you?'

'In truth, I don't know her. But, yes, she is a bit . . . brusque with me.'

'Well, what you don't know about her is she's actually my niece on my wife's side and thus she looks after me. She's rather protective of me since . . . our loss. She adored her cousin John and actually looked like him a bit. So I like having Eunice around.'

Rosina suddenly saw a whole different side to Miss Eunice Holness and marvelled at how one fact could shatter a first impression and open up a person's humanity to you. The same was true of Allan. Now they talked often,

Rosina saw that his hard exterior housed a cultured man who enjoyed reading, particularly biographies of world leaders, such as Napoleon and the Roman emperors. He was captivated by world history, especially military. He told her little-known stories about the greats of the past, which were amusing and fascinating. Rosina realised how little you knew about a person when all you saw was their façade and how liberating it was to watch someone open up their true self to you. Humans were endlessly surprising that way. And now she felt bad for misjudging Allan. She also felt she had unfairly done the same to Eunice too.

'I wish I'd known that earlier!' Rosina said. 'I rather took against her. I feel like a fool now.'

'There's no need. We both have a similar kind of hard exterior, Eunice and I. Perhaps that's another reason we get on. I feel quite fatherly towards her, since my wife's sister's husband died and so she grew up without a dad. We both present a tough carapace towards the world, I think. It's only once you get to know her – and me – that you find we both have soft centres.'

'It's a good lesson for me. Not to judge by appearances. That's one of my faults, I think.'

'Faults are what make us human. I have a particular distaste for the kind of romantic gesturing in films and books that suggests one's love object is perfect. Perfection is ugly, I feel. Faults and flaws are the stuff of life. And if one can admit to them, that is even more attractive.'

Rosina liked his no-nonsense approach to life. It went hand in hand with his military exterior and somehow it was strangely comforting at this time of such uncertainty.

'I like your philosophy,' she said.

'Do you? I wrote a poem about this once, about flaws making a person more beautiful.'

'You write poetry?' Another surprise. The military man with a penchant for poems.

'I dabble. I've never had anything published, so I'm a complete amateur. But it helps me. To guide my thoughts. To exorcise them, I suppose. Stops them swimming about in my head and instead orders them in meter on a page.'

'I know that feeling. I write stories. It's always a relief when one is finished. It's cathartic.'

'You write as well?' He looked intrigued.

'Yes, as often as I can, which is not much lately. Not published either. In fact, barely anyone has seen them.'

Except Harry, she thought. He adored her stories. How he waxed lyrical about them! He saw depths in them she hadn't expected. It was a joy to hear his thoughts on them. She wondered, though, if he were too positive, too adoring. Perhaps he wasn't telling her the truth about how good they were, just adoring them because he adored her. Was that a bad thing? She wasn't sure.

'I'd be interested in critiquing them, if you'd critique my poems,' said Allan, bringing her back to reality.

A critique did interest her. Perhaps this no-nonsense military man could provide something more akin to a cold eye for her work. She welcomed the idea of an honest opinion. 'I think that would be a splendid idea.'

Another knock on the door and it was Miss Holness again, saying that Allan had a meeting in five minutes he might have forgotten about.

Rosina stood up and went to the door and held out her hand. The secretary stared at her in confusion.

'I'd like to shake your hand, Miss Holness and make a proper introduction. I feel we got off on the wrong foot and I'd like to rectify that. Please, while you are working here, do feel free to call on me at any time if you need anything. I want your time to be happy here.'

Miss Holness glanced at her uncle, who must have smiled or nodded at her because her face lit up in response and she shook Rosina's hand warmly.

'I say, that's most kind of you, ma'am.'

'Not at all. Do call me Rosina.'

'Well, only if . . .'

Again she glanced at Allan, who replied, 'Of course, Eunice.'

'Well, please call me Eunice too,' she said.

'All right, I will. I have five daughters, Eunice, so I'm used to having lots of girls around and all their paraphernalia. So if you ever need anything or any advice, please don't hesitate to ask.'

'Thanks again, ma'am. I mean, Rosina.'

She left and Rosina looked at Allan, who was beaming at her.

'You've just made her day. She terribly admires you.'

'Surely not! I thought she couldn't stand me!'

'Not at all. My sister-in-law tells me that she talks all about you in her letters home.'

'How extraordinary. Well, it's nice to know. You sound very close to your family.'

'I am, I suppose. I'll be going down to Dorset to see some of them around Christmastime. My parents are down there, as well as Eunice's family. That's where I met my wife. We're both born and bred in the land of the fossil hunters.'

'I've never been to Dorset. I'd love to go to Thomas Hardy's Wessex. I adore his novels.'

'And I love his poetry. You won't renege on our deal to share our writing, will you? I'm looking forward to it already.'

'I won't renege, never fear,' she said. 'But now, if you don't hurry along, I think you'll be late for your meeting.'

'Hmm, tiresome things, meetings. But you're right. I must get on. Mrs Calvert-Lazenby, a pleasure as always.'

And off he went.

Rosina went into her lounge, sat down on the settee and got out her knitting. She smiled to herself thinking on her conversation with Allan and the reconciliation with Eunice Holness. She counted up the squares she'd already knitted for a blanket for Evvy and noted she only had two left until the blanket was ready to assemble and be completed. She had knitted something for all her girls for Christmas, using unravelled wool from her husband's old jumpers. A scarf for Grace, to keep her warm on her long nights on duty, doing whatever it is she did. A blanket for Evvy, to keep her warm in the fire station. Gloves for Connie and the twins, and socks for Ronnie were all finished. She'd also ordered books for each of her girls and for Ronnie.

As she knitted, she mentally went through the other Christmas gifts she'd been sorting recently, making sure she hadn't forgotten anyone. She'd hand-made presents for the girls in order to try to save money on gifts. She wanted to ensure that the money the estate had was protected, because of the uncertainty of the times. The Army were paying rent for using the hall, but the damage they were doing to the exterior – and now the interiors too, purely by the volume of boots tramping in and out all day – would cost a lot to rectify and she had no idea how much money she'd get from the government for repairs, if any. So, other gifts were similarly conservative, including war bonds to all staff and tenants; chutney to Jessop and Throp; a silk scarf of her own for Bairstow; toys for the Precious children and – in a moment of weakness – she'd ordered a Red Cross nurse uniform for Elsie, who she knew would look absolutely darling in it. She had jars of home-made jam and also found a pretty yet warm peach-coloured pullover of her own to give to Phyllis. There was soap for the gardener's wife, Mrs Jessop, as well as for the maids Mary and Sheila. And she'd kept jars of honey ready to give to her other tenants and farmers, none of whom had their own hives. Then she realised she had nothing for Allan. And now she wondered if she needed something for Eunice. Would that be appropriate? A few weeks ago, it would have been unthinkable that she'd even consider giving Vaughan and his bossy secretary any seasonal gifts. But they were not those people any more. They were Allan and Eunice now and she'd have to get her thinking cap on to come up with something nice for them both.

From what Allan said, it sounded as if both of them might well be able to visit family in Dorset at Christmas, yet Rosina also felt it was her duty to provide some seasonal cheer for them here too. She was so looking forward to the girls coming home from school, as she knew they would throw themselves into decorations and getting into the Christmas spirit. How they'd always loved Christmas, all of them. And how sad it would be to spend a second one with her two eldest far away. There had been German bombings in Bristol, Sheffield and Leicester this month already, as well as poor London getting the worst of it, of course. Rosina was constantly on edge about Evvy being in the capital and even Grace in Hertfordshire, because she often went into the city. Rosina knew she had little hope of seeing either Grace or Evvy for ages, but she lived in hope that, one day soon, either one would appear at the lounge door and throw their arms around her for a much-needed hug, or better yet, both of them. They would be much missed at Christmas. She thought then of Harry, in a faraway land, hot and dusty, away from the snowfall, holly and mistletoe of an English Christmas. Her heart ached for him and she whispered a small Christmas prayer that her girls would come home and that Harry would suddenly turn up too and they would all be with her for Christmas. It was a fantasy, she knew that. But, oh, wouldn't it be marvellous if it came true?

As she sat there, knitting and thinking of her beloved girls and Harry, and of the hall bedecked at Christmas, and her kind and good staff working hard and meeting troubles with a smile despite the war and the Army occupation, and Allan and Eunice on such good terms with her now, Rosina felt a sense of well-being warm her that she'd not felt for some time. Perhaps things were getting better. Perhaps the

Army weren't as bad as she'd thought. Perhaps everything would be all right.

She gazed out of the window at the greenhouses, the chicken coop, the hedge around the family garden and sighed happily. She was lucky. She still had her home, her little outside patch of ground, her family. She had a lot to be thankful for. But then, she heard the shocking sound of glass shattering. She looked up, staring at the greenhouse. But it wasn't that. It had come from within the house.

She put her knitting aside and went out into the passage-way. She walked forward, noting as she did every day with distaste that there were new stains and wear on the floors, carpets, walls and staircases, with some balusters and stair rods missing that would need replacing. Hurrying along the passage, she peered into each room, looking for broken glass, and was met with nonplussed looks from busy Army workers. Had nobody else heard it but her? And if they had, did they not care?

She huffed and walked on further, then spotted something on the carpet in front of her. She slowed and picked it up. It was a football, filthy with mud. She took a few steps further, reaching the staircase now used by the Army. She looked up at the landing. And there it was. The stained-glass window depicting the Lazenby family crest, designed by her dearly departed mother, had been shattered. Its ruins lay on every step, exploded by the force of the football she now held. She stepped hesitantly between the shards of glass and looked out of the jagged hole to see a group of soldiers staring up at her, some with their hands on their heads or hips breathing heavily, others with their hands over their mouths to hide their embarrassed laughter.

'Sorry, missus!' called one.

'Can we 'ave our ball back then?' called another.

Without a word, she tipped the ball out of the window and watched it bounce off the wall and skitter away. One of them chased and retrieved it and they moved away from the area, giving her looks over their shoulders that were at once dismissive and somewhat shamefaced.

She had nothing to say. What good would it do, to scream at these soldiers? They were infuriating and careless, but they were just boys. They were far from home, about to face transportation to an unknown destination, to fight for their lives and for the country's freedom. She knew it would be wrong to make such a fuss about one window, when other people in English cities were having their homes and everything in them destroyed by bombing, when her very own daughter was helping to fight the fires that engulfed them. Rosina felt she would be inordinately selfish to cry over a single pane of glass. But she felt her eyes fill up and she stifled a sob. She'd had to put up with her home being taken from her and perhaps she could allow herself a little grieving for that. She felt very alone.

She looked down at the shards of glass and recognised the red and white plumes of feathers that topped the armoured helmet that featured on the Lazenby crest. Unthinkingly, she picked up that piece; a sharp edge pierced her skin and she watched as her blood seeped out and ran down the piece of glass, dripping on to the floor.

'Oh dear,' someone said. 'How did that happen?'

It was a young officer who said it as he carried on down the staircase, not stopping to hear her response but disappearing around the corner to one of her rooms, now his office, no doubt.

'Mummy!' came another voice. And it was so incongruous that Rosina guessed she'd imagined it, that she'd breathed into life one of her daughters to comfort her. So she didn't look up for a moment, until a soft hand was on her arm and she raised her head. It was Connie. Behind her, coming carefully up the stairs, stepping between the bits of glass, were Daisy and Dora. Her girls. Her girls were home!

'My darlings!' she whispered. What was wrong with her? She felt frozen to the spot.

'Gosh, you're bleeding, Mummy!' cried Daisy.

Then, Bairstow was suddenly there and there was lots of fuss. Allan turned up and apologised on behalf of the Army, saying it was most unfortunate and they would of course board it up and pay for a new window to be constructed and fitted, while Bairstow rushed Rosina off to bandage up her finger where she'd cut it quite deeply on the glass. The girls came eagerly behind, full of excitement at everything, the Army being there, the men everywhere, the drama of the broken window.

When Rosina was bandaged up and the girls had been allowed back in to the kitchen by a very grumpy Bairstow, they all gave their mother hugs and kisses.

'I'm so sorry about our window, Mummy,' said Connie, 'but I must say, I do think the Army are smashing.'

'Smashing?' cried Dora. 'Yes, they are smashing – quite literally smashing the place up!'

'The whole place is an awful mess,' said Daisy. 'Are you quite all right, Mummy? You look dreadfully pale.'

Bairstow must have thought the same, as she brought Rosina some tea with precious sugar in it, for shock.

'It's so silly,' said Rosina quietly, the first thing she'd said for ages.

'Not silly,' said Bairstow. 'That window were thi mother's pride and joy. I could kill t'idiot that kicked that damned ball.'

'Yes, Mummy, poor you,' consoled Connie and put her arms around her mother's shoulders. 'But we're here now, to entertain you and take your mind off all the chaos and destruction.'

Sipping the hot, sweet tea made Rosina feel she was coming back to life. 'So, why are you here early, my darlings? School keep doing this. Not that I'm complaining. I'm so happy to see you all.'

They all started to speak at once, but Connie's strident voice won out, as usual. 'School said snow was probably coming so they wanted everyone to get home in good time for Christmas in case the railways were disrupted.'

'I'm so glad they did,' said Rosina and all her girls kissed her and started talking at her, telling her about the journey and an amusing dog at the station that chased its tail and how heavy their cases were because school had told them to take as much as they could just in case they couldn't get back because of bad weather and how they'd been making Christmas crackers for the Christmas lunch table and also they'd made decorations out of newspaper and they were going to do the same at home and how their mother mustn't worry because they were here now to help and weren't the officers in the house a bit marvellous and how rough the soldiers outside were, although they were rather exciting too, and wasn't it all so odd having all these people at home, but all rather thrilling. And so on.

Rosina sat, sipping her tea and now eating fruit cake that Bairstow had brought for the five of them sitting around the kitchen table, the girls gabbling away and pushing lumps of cake into their mouths without forks, while Bairstow smiled and Rosina still felt a little overcome by the strangeness of war and how different it was for everyone. She knew she had to get over the destruction of the window, how minor it was in the scheme of things. She knew it was because of the link to her mother. It was her Achilles heel, anything to do with dear Mama, long dead and gone, but the grief was still keen when it came to her. But there were families all over the country who had lost their own, their men, their children even. And Rosina knew she had to pull herself together and continue to do her bit, without self-pity. It was, after all, just a window. And it could be repaired. And now her daughters were home again, she felt as if she could stand taller and firmer with their love and support. Thank heavens for her girls. What a joy they were in her life. What a gift.

* * *

The days leading up to Christmas that year were some of the happiest Rosina could remember in years. Three of her girls were home and throwing themselves into seasonal activities with gusto. They filled the family part of the house with joyfulness – and a few customary squabbles. They were true to their word on the newspaper paper-chains and got straight to it, daubing newspaper sheets in different colours using Evvy's paints, then ripping them into strips and pasting the strips into links that grew and grew across the games-room floor. They collected holly and mistletoe from the gardens and – upon Ronnie's advice, who apparently used to do this with his mother in Hull – dipped sprigs in a solution of Epsom salts to make them look frosted, then hung these all over the house.

Throp brought in a medium-sized pine tree that he had chopped down from somewhere on the estate and set it up in a pot weighted with sand in the corner of the lounge. The girls enthusiastically dragged out the box of heirloom decorations and hung them all over until it was groaning with seasonal cheer.

Rosina helped here and there, yet was busy with the work of the house and estate. She had also tidied up her most recent short stories and had given them to Allan to read, awaiting his response with interest, and he said that he'd give her his poems soon. She looked forward to that. This new friendship that was forming, as well as the girls being home, lifted her mood so much, she actually felt happy for the first time in months, the first time since Harry had left, really. Although, whenever she thought of Harry, it was always shot through with a dash of anxiety, about where he was and how safe he was, as well as her doubts about the wisdom of their relationship. But, mostly, she felt very happy and each day approaching Christmas she was delighted simply to watch her girls having fun and bringing cheer to the house.

The girls paired off somewhat, with Connie and Dora joining together, largely because Daisy and Ronnie were often off doing their own thing. Rosina watched their friendship with interest, wondering if there was more to it. She mentioned it to Dora, who said casually, 'I should think they'll marry one day,' then changed the subject.

Rosina approached the subject with Daisy one night at bedtime, when she came in to say good night.

'I see you and Ronnie are fast friends.'

'Yes, he's really such a super person,' said Daisy, sleepily, after a long day of tramping about the frosty winter moors with Ronnie and helping the girls with more Christmas preparations. 'We've been writing long letters to each other since September.'

'Is it . . . Are you . . . romantically involved, you two?'

Daisy snuggled down into the pillow, pretending to be too sleepy to answer.

'Are you, darling? Because if you are, I think we should have a talk. *The Talk*.'

Daisy opened her eyes and frowned. 'We had *The Talk* last year, Mummy, don't you remember? I really don't want to have *The Talk* again. It was dreadfully embarrassing for us both, don't you agree?'

She was right, it really was awkward. Rosina never felt particularly comfortable talking to her girls about sex and all that stuff, but, of course, it was a necessary evil of having children and preparing them for the adult world. She mostly stuck to biology, kept it short and sweet and said they could ask her questions whenever they needed to. But they never did. She assumed they discussed it with one another or the other girls at school, most likely swapping wildly misinformed stories, as she did as a girl. She assumed girls knew more about such things in these modern days of the 1940s than she did thirty years ago, when the very idea of discussing such things with your parents was horrifying and about as likely as pigs taking to the air in great flocks. She would always remember how utterly clueless she was on her wedding night. She wished she'd had *The Talk* before then, so she knew at least a little of what to expect. And how desperately disappointing it all was . . .

'All right, darling. Get some sleep. But do be careful and come to me to talk about it if you ever need to.'

But Daisy was already asleep, or feigning it. So, Rosina was none the wiser about Daisy and Ronnie.

She tried a different tack, asking Connie about it as they were cutting out star shapes from newspapers to paint and then string into bunting for the girls' rooms. Connie was a bit of a blabbermouth about everything, so was often Rosina's first port of call when trying to dig for information about the girls.

'Any idea what's going on with Daisy and Ronnie? Are they courting or just friends?'

'Daisy never gossips, you know that,' said Connie, carefully painting a five-pointed star in scarlet. 'Oh look, the newspaper is too thin and when we paint it, the star just curls up with the damp and it's ruined.'

'All right then, try painting the whole sheet of newspaper first, then leaving it to dry, then cutting out the stars, like you did with the strips of paper for the chains.'

'Oh yes, silly me. I forgot we did it that way.'

'So, you don't know what's going on with those two?' Rosina tried again.

'No idea. Daisy's mouth is like a mantrap when it comes to affairs of the heart. Not like me. I'll tell anyone who'll listen. I have absolutely no sense of decorum.'

'Well, that is true, darling.'

'Oh, I know. I don't see it as a fault, though. I think telling people your business is more likeable than being all shy and secretive. I've told everyone who'll listen how much I like Harry.'

Rosina looked sharply at Connie. 'Harry who?'

'*Harry* Harry. Our Harry. Harry Woodvine. He's an absolute dish. And he's less than ten years older than me. Lots of girls marry older men. It's quite normal. I know he might think I'm a bit young now, but by the time he comes back from the war, I'll be old enough, I'm sure. I say, next time you get an address from him, can I send him a letter? I've been meaning to ask you for ages.'

Rosina was dumbstruck by this little speech. She felt her cheeks redden and was appalled that Connie might notice and call her out on it. But what on earth could she say to Connie about it? If she said nothing, Connie would notice and needle her about it. She was entirely determined when it came to getting what she wanted.

'We'll see,' she replied and changed the subject to what vegetables they would be having with the Christmas dinner, but Connie was having none of that.

'Have you got an address for him now? I could send him seasonal greetings.'

'Not right now,' Rosina lied. Gosh, she really hoped her cheeks weren't too inflamed, but luckily Connie was too intent on painting the newspapers.

'All right, well, whenever you do, let me know, Mummy, won't you?'

'Of course,' said Rosina and sat quietly for a while as Connie thankfully moved on to the new subject of sports fixtures next term at school and who was the most useless out of the all the other schools they had played last term. But Rosina wasn't really listening. The sound of her daughter's voice bubbled away like boiling broth and Rosina drifted away into her own thoughts . . . of Harry.

She felt once more the same shame that had assaulted her at the railway station all those months ago – when she and Harry were engulfed in their desire and longing for each other, unable to show it in public, unable to kiss and hold on to each other before having to say goodbye, followed by the awful moment where the guard had thought Harry was her son – oh God, the humiliation of it. All of this surfaced at the thought of Connie being with Harry. The fact was that it made more sense for someone of Connie's age to hanker after someone like Harry. Connie was right: it was normal for younger women to pair off with older men, very normal indeed. It was much rarer the other way round, and even then, if it did happen, it was usually a matter of a few years, not decades, like her and Harry. She mused on how, over the last year, her monthly bleeds had begun to tail off, the curse – as everyone accurately called it – becoming few and far between. It could well be the stress of the war, but she wondered instead if it were the change of life. Thoughts of this change coming had disturbed her somewhat – though it would be a relief to get rid of the agony of pain and bleeding that accompanied her cycle. It was a marker, of course, of advancing age and becoming too old for pregnancy. And that made her feel even more odd about the age difference between herself and Harry.

Again, perennial doubts surrounded her thoughts of him. She knew she loved him. She knew he loved her, in his way. But what kind of way was it? And was it possible for a man so young to truly know what love was? When they were last together, and they had kissed and confessed their love, she had felt all the doubts drop away. And whenever she read a letter from him – always brimming with love and affection, always devoted and caring – the doubts fell to the wayside as well. But between times, the doubts would return and she would question everything. Now, she felt less sure of him than ever and had no idea what to do about Connie's request, hoping that she would move on and forget about it, so that Rosina never had to run the risk of talking about it to her again. But it also worried her greatly, that if, one fine day, Harry should come back from war, safe and sound, and who knows, might ask her to marry him and spend the rest of their days together, as she often fantasised, what the hell would she do about Connie? But also, she had had no word from Harry for over two months now. Was it simply the postal service? Or was he forgetting about her already?

All these thoughts and more mushroomed in her mind as she listened to her daughter's voice rattle on about lacrosse and hockey rules and Rosina painted red, green and white stripes on newspapers over and over again, the painting soothing her troubled mind somewhat, but not enough to banish her fears. Then, there was a knock at the open door.

Rosina looked up to see Allan Vaughan standing in the doorway.

'Is this a bad time?' he said and smiled at Connie, who stared at him.

'How's Army life?' said Connie, brazenly. Never backward in coming forward, that girl.

'Well, uh, it's going swimmingly, thank you,' said Allan, and Rosina smiled. The girls had been introduced to Allan soon after they had first arrived home. The twins had been shy with him, but Connie didn't know the meaning of the word.

'Jolly good. Be a good chap and win the war for us, will you? We're busy making Christmas decorations.'

'Connie!' scolded Rosina. 'Apologise to Colonel Vaughan immediately.'

'It's all right,' said Allan and chuckled. 'I think she's got her priorities straight. But if I could drag you away from such important work for a moment?'

'Of course,' said Rosina and gave Connie a severe look, who merely shrugged her shoulders and started humming a popular tune. How had she raised such arch girls as Connie and Evvy? Then, she realised, that characteristic came from their father.

Rosina got up and left the room, Allan saying quietly in the corridor, 'I have those poems for you, if you're still interested.'

'Oh yes, please,' replied Rosina.

He handed her a sheaf of typed pages, secured with brass paper fasteners.

'And I've read your stories. Perhaps you'd like to have a chat about them. I'm free in about twenty minutes if you are? Just need to make a quick phone call first.'

'All right. Let's meet in the drawing room.'

Rosina went down there, clutching the poems. She was excited about seeing Allan's work and about his thoughts on her stories.

She shut the door and settled on the sofa to read, looking at the first poem, typed neatly out in spare lines.

WATERFALL
And so it falls here.
The water.
Ab aqua libertas.
From water comes freedom.
The trip-trip drip-drip of water.
Bubbling bounteously.
Giving life.
Water.
Wasser.
Vερό.
Agua.
Вода.
Acqua.
Eau.
Oh, how precious it is.
For life. For lives. Our lives.
Water.

Oh dear, was Rosina's first thought. *That is absolutely not my sort of thing at all.*

She read it again, three times. Had she missed something? It seemed to say so little. So, water is a good thing. We need it to live. And . . .? Then she thought that perhaps she was not intellectual enough to appreciate it. Yes, that must be it. She assumed that the foreign words were all water in different languages. That was clever. (*Was it, though?*)

She read some more of his poems. They were all very similar, about random subjects, with few words, short lines and lots of repetition and random insertions of words in other languages and alphabets. Then, he appeared at the door.

'I got away quicker than expected. Have you had a chance to read yet?'

'Yes, I have.'

'Gosh. I'm rather nervous now. What did you think?'

What on earth was she going to say? 'I've never read anything quite like them.'

Allan seated himself opposite her in an armchair, sitting forward with his hands clasped, looking eagerly at her.

'In a good way?' he asked.

'Oh, yes, indeed. They're so . . . clever. Awfully clever.'

'Well, thank you very much. I do think about them for a long time. I choose my words very carefully.'

'I can see that. Each word is . . . important to the poem as a whole. Isn't it?'

'Absolutely. That first one, 'Waterfall', I spent six weeks rewriting that, putting new words in and taking words out, until I got it just right. I'm really pleased with it now.'

'Yes, it's . . . very profound.'

'I do hope so. I'm glad you've seen that. It is my best poem, I think. That's why I put it on top! I was rather nervous of what you'd make of it.'

'I can't imagine you being nervous about anything, Allan.'

'Oh, but I am, when it comes to impressing you, Mrs Calvert-Lazenby.'

She smiled at him and looked away. It took him six weeks of rewrites on that poem? She wrote her stories by hand, quite quickly in a few hours, then read them through a couple of times, before making the odd correction. They were usually done in half a day or so. Maybe she was fooling herself, in thinking she was a writer. After all, if a few words about water took Allan six weeks, then she must be underwriting and perhaps producing work of little polish. Maybe her work was juvenile, even. She now began to dread hearing his thoughts and looked apprehensively at the bundle of papers he held in his hands.

'So, have you read my stories?' she asked.

'I have indeed.'

'Put me out of my misery then.' Her mouth felt dry as she gulped.

'I think they are well-crafted stories. The language is prosaic and homely, which appeals to the reader at whom I assume you are aiming your work: women of a certain age.

For this audience, they work perfectly. The subject matter of each is quite similar – about families, marriage and children, domestic themes. And yet from such humble topics, you achieve something that . . . shines. Yes, it shines with humour and yet, too, they are tinged with sadness. I'd say you write very well. These are fine pieces of work. I'm impressed.'

He said it all quite quickly, so she had to take it all in swiftly as she listened. It sounded positive. Was it positive? She thought so. You write very well, he'd said. Fine pieces of work . . . something that shines. Yes, he was praising her, so why did she feel as if her stories were smaller than they'd seemed before?

'Well, thank you! I'm very relieved you liked them. If you did? I think you did?'

'Oh yes, absolutely I did. They are charming stories. You wield a fine pen.'

'Ah, thank you. Maybe I should type them up afterwards, as you do.'

'Oh, I do all my writing straight on to the typewriter. I think best when I can hear the mechanical clickety-clack. It tunes my mind somehow.'

'That's interesting.'

'All writers are different, as all humans are different. Each take on a subject is unique. There will be many writers who have written about themes such as the essential elements of life, as I have, or kitchens and babies, as you have. But it is our take on it that counts. A unique vision.'

'Yes indeed.'

She knew she ought to be saying something scintillating. She wanted to very much. He'd said a whole paragraph about her story and she'd said so little about his poem, though he didn't seem to mind.

'Thank you for showing me your work,' she said.

'And likewise,' he replied, smiling, then standing up and handing her stories back to her. She took them and went to hand his back to him, but he said, 'Ah, no, you may keep them. I make carbon copies.'

'Ah, right. Well, thank you so much. I'm honoured.'

'The honour is all mine. A privilege to read such pretty stories. Thank you again. Will I see you at our weekly meeting tomorrow, as usual? I have a quite fine tawny port just arrived.'

'Of course,' she said and smiled.

He nodded and took his leave. She looked down at her scruffy bundle of stories in one hand and his neat pile of poems in the other and threw both on to her desk. It went well, she thought, considering that she wasn't intelligent enough to offer any comment on his poetry. She believed she'd said enough to persuade him she wasn't a complete fool. And Allan had said nice things about her work, that made her feel that she must be getting somewhere. After all, Harry adored them. She'd felt proud of them when Harry wrote about how much he loved to read them and she must send more. Yet perhaps the reason she felt confused was because Allan had been more honest with her about them, not letting feelings get in the way of a critique. Maybe that was what she needed as a writer, to have an authentic, clear appraisal of her worth. The truth might be that Harry adored her stories because he adored her, whereas Allan gave her his insights as another writer, despite the fact that he seemed to be rather keen on her too.

She found she admired his reserve, that it was becoming obvious to them both that they got on well, they enjoyed each other's company and she found him comforting to be around. He was so very capable and secure, making her feel that whatever came along, he would deal with it efficiently, without fuss. Perhaps it was because he was a senior officer, or older than her, or simply a coolness in his demeanour that was impressive. He was so very different to Harry, there really was no comparison. But Rosina found she compared them constantly, in her mind, and could come to no conclusion, other than that she was glad Allan was around, especially in the chaos of the Army occupation of the hall. She imagined for a moment how awful it would be to have a fool in charge, who could not communicate so easily with her and was indifferent to her concerns. She shuddered at the thought of it. And then she thought of Harry with a pang. She began to wonder if their love had been real, truly real, then again she tortured herself with the idea that it was merely a symptom of the heady days of summer and being cooped up together for a time. She knew that she still ached for Harry, but his distance and absence were beginning to have the effect of diminishing her clear vision of him. He seemed more and more to her like a cloud shadow upon the sea, distant, fleeting and out of reach.

Chapter 12

During the week leading up to Christmas Day, Rosina was often to be found in the kitchen with Bairstow. It was warm, comforting and quiet in there, a little haven from the madness beyond in a house full of Army personnel and three daughters. The government had given extra rations of tea and sugar for the week before Christmas, so they baked some tea loaves, which made a lovely treat with a smear of Canadian tinned butter on. They also made Bairstow's rationed version of mince pies, as well as preparing the Christmas pudding, using the dried fruit from Allan's hamper and some grated carrot for extra sweetness, as well as plenty of breadcrumbs, the choice addition for padding out any recipe with bulk to make up for rationed ingredients.

On Christmas Eve in the morning, Rosina went down to Allan's office to present two mini hampers – actually, a pair of tiny wicker baskets that Rosina had received soap in once – with some of the mince pies and two small tea loaves for Allan and Eunice's Christmas gifts. But the office was empty, which Rosina was quite pleased about, as it would be nice for them to have a surprise to come back to on their desks. She then joined Bairstow in the kitchen, where they assembled all the accoutrements and ingredients for their meal on the morrow. The gardener's wife had killed a large chicken for them for the feast and Rosina had collected potatoes, parsnips, Brussels sprouts and winter cabbage from the family garden. Bairstow would make the gravy to her own special recipe, as well as a kind of stuffing she fashioned from breadcrumbs and oats and various herbs and spices as there was no chance of the extravagance of sausage meat.

Rosina was plucking the chicken when she felt a sharp tap on her shoulder. She looked round to see Bairstow grinning and couldn't imagine why Bairstow would touch her shoulder like that, so hard and over-familiar. Then she heard a giggle and turned the other way . . . and there was Evvy!

'Darling!' she cried and threw her arms around her daughter. Evvy laughed and gave her such a strangling hug, Rosina felt slightly winded.

'It was me tapping your shoulder, Mummy. Don't blame Bairstow! I dodged out of the way.'

'I did wonder!' laughed Rosina. 'I'm over the moon to see you! How on earth did you get away?'

'There's been a slight lull in the bombings, so my boss gave me a couple of days off, because my family are so far away and most of the others are Londoners so they get to see their families all the time. I came up on the night train. Here today and Christmas Day, then I'm back down on Boxing Day, as long as we're not snowed in.'

'Oh darling, let us be inundated with snow so you have to stay longer!'

'Oh no, Mummy. That wouldn't do. I'm needed down there. I feel bad enough as it is. But I knew it would please you, so I wanted to do it for you.'

'Thank you for that, my love. It's made my Christmas.' And she kissed Evvy on the cheek and held her tight again. What a treat to have her confidante daughter home again! How they could talk and talk! Of course, she adored all her daughters equally, but Evvy was the one she found easiest to talk to.

'Thought it might!' said Evvy and winked at her.

Bairstow made them a pot of tea and some slices of tea loaf and they took it into the lounge. Evvy popped out to find Connie, Daisy and Dora to say a quick hello, then came back for a cup of tea with her mother and sat down to chat properly.

'So,' said Evvy, looking annoyed. 'This place has been overrun by the marauding heathens then. What an absolute bloody mess they've made of it all. Are you devastated, Mummy? You must be!'

Rosina sighed and said, 'It's our part in the war. We must do our best.'

'Well, yes, of course. Everyone must make sacrifices. But I'm livid about the grounds. They've dug everything up and demolished the lawns and all the shrubs. The parquet floor in the hallway is ruined with scuff marks and dents and even the staircase is falling apart. What are they doing, for God's sake? Kicking in the bannisters for fun on their way up and down?'

'It's wear and tear. There are so many people working in the house now and endless visitors day after day. The house wasn't made for all that traffic.'

Evvy huffed and crossed her arms. 'I'm all for giving things up in wartime. We all have to do it, some more than others. But I don't understand why they have to be so bloody careless. This is our home and they're ruining it.'

Rosina had considered all of these thoughts over the past weeks and in one way it was good to hear her thoughts echoed by another, but in another way it was depressing to have it reinforced. 'Listen, darling, I've got used to it now. I have to think brightly about it all or I'll go mad. I have to feel I'm doing a good thing and it'll all be worth it in the end.'

'All right, but I don't have to like it. Who's in charge, anyway? This colonel fellow you mentioned in your letter?'

'Yes, Allan Vaughan. He's actually been very good.'

'Well, I might give him a piece of my mind when I meet him.'

Rosina gasped and said, 'No, you will not! Don't you dare, Evvy!'

'Why not? You're not scared of him, are you?'

Was she scared of Allan? Rosina had felt a prickle of recognition when Evvy said that. But she shook her head to get rid of that unsettling idea. No, surely not afraid of him. 'Of course not.'

'I just know how nice you can be, Mummy, and people take advantage, especially these military types. They're so often bullies. Don't be afraid to stand up to him.'

'I do argue my case when it's needed. But also I've spent weeks building an understanding with him and I'm really getting somewhere. He's given us a hamper of food from Canada and he's always available to help with problems in the house.'

Evvy narrowed her eyes at her mother. That piercing look of hers. It really did feel like she could see right through her! 'Is he sweet on you, then?'

'Gosh, I don't know.'

'Yes, he is. I can see it in your face. You're not sweet on him, are you? What about Harry?'

Evvy had spoken to her about Harry before, suggesting there was something exciting between them, but Rosina had denied it and she did not want to go into all that again, especially at that moment where they had little privacy. 'Oh Evvy, you are brutally scientific in your analysis. It's too much. Leave me be.'

'All right, Mummy. Let's not fall out in the first five minutes. Tell me you haven't got me anything for Christmas. I don't need a thing. And tell me also what I can do to help. I want to be useful.'

Rosina was relieved the topic had changed. Connie came bouncing in just then and soon after Dora arrived and they all chatted awhile and it was lovely. Daisy must have been off with Ronnie again, which Evvy remarked upon and shockingly said, 'He better not get her in the family way,' for which Rosina scolded her, but she had wondered the same thing herself, with a cold fear, usually in the middle of the night. She did not want any of her girls to give up their freedom too young, as she had done. She wanted them to see some of the world, to decide if they wanted to try for a career and make their mark, before they were swallowed up by marriage, babies and domesticity. Then, Daisy turned up, alone, and gave Evvy a hug and they all sat around and talked, which made Rosina warm with happiness. Four of her girls were home for Christmas and that was more than she could have realistically hoped for, so she was thrilled. Evvy told them sensational stories of her war work with the London Fire Brigade, all of which excited her sisters beyond measure, and yet, for Rosina, gripped her icily, that her daughter was in daily danger and could be injured or killed at any moment. As usual with Evvy, Rosina had to damp down the screaming anxiety in her mind that Evvy was forever a risk-taker but somehow always came out unscathed. Rosina prayed that Evvy would do so again this time. It was awful to know your child was in danger, when all your instincts cried out to remove them from it and yet you were unable to do a thing about it.

That afternoon, Rosina and her girls trooped down to the Ravenscar village hall for the annual Nativity play put on by the younger pupils from the local school. It was something the Calvert-Lazenbys always did as a family and every year it felt like the sign that Christmas was nearly here and seasonal magic was weaving its spell upon them. The girls whispered about the funny costumes and flat delivery of the children and Rosina always had to nudge them to get them to behave, all except Daisy (and Grace, if she'd been there). Ronnie turned up in the interval and Daisy went to sit with him in the second half. Rosina surreptitiously glanced at them from time to time, to see if she could divine merely by looking if they were physically involved. They didn't hold hands, just sat shoved up against each other on a bench and whispered conspiratorially at times. Maybe it was innocent, maybe just a very pure friendship. Rosina was quite envious in a way. It made her think of her conversations with Harry, and though Allan was very interesting to talk to, it wasn't quite the same.

Afterwards, the girls came with Rosina as she took Christmas gifts to Phyllis and children, the houses of Mary and Sheila the maids, as well as farmers and tenants nearby. It was a crisp day and the sky looked white and expectant, as if snow would come and it was holding its breath. That night, she sat in her room and wrapped the girls' handmade woollen gifts and books in crepe paper she'd had in the craft box and put the finishing touch to cards she'd sketched for each daughter, with a tiny little Christmas scene on, a snowy field with a sprig of holly in the corner, drawn out in pencil and gone over in black ink. She wasn't much of an artist, she felt, but she could pass muster for a Christmas card. Rosina went to bed that night feeling decidedly Christmassy. She read the final chapter of Dickens's *A Christmas Carol* in bed, before she put the light out. She did it every year and loved the enchanted aura it left her with as she drifted into sleep on Christmas Eve. But that night, she lay awake and listened to the sounds of soldiers outside shouting to each other across the dark grounds, or a random engine somewhere starting up, or footsteps on the pathways. The Army never slept, it seemed, even at Christmas.

On Christmas Day, she was up at dawn to help Bairstow with the last-minute preparations, until the girls came down in pyjamas and dressing gowns and they all had breakfast together in the kitchen, as it was cosiest there. They went to the lounge afterwards and opened their gifts. They loved their books and gloves and so forth and gave their mother lots of kisses and hugs. Rosina did not expect anything from her girls this Christmas, due to rationing and all the disruption, but she was touched when they produced a gift wrapped in brown paper from behind a cushion, that someone must have hidden earlier. Rosina opened it to find a handmade cushion cover, the front adorned with four squares of embroidery in different designs and on the back a larger square.

'We all made a square each,' said Connie excitedly. 'It was my idea.'

'And mine!' cried Dora.

'No, it was not!' snapped Connie.

'All right, it was your idea to do it. But I said we should do four squares on the front and then one on the back and I said the big one on the back should be done by Evvy because she's the only one who can do decent sewing.'

'It's true,' said Evvy. 'I am the only one who can use a needle and thread with any skill out of this motley lot. But the girls did their best and, I must say, it doesn't look half bad.'

'It looks perfect!' said Rosina and could not stop looking at it. Each square carried the personality of its owner precisely: Grace's was neat and straightforward; Evvy's was a gorgeous complex design of interlocking circles in a range of colours; Daisy's had tiny stitches in a swirly pattern, just like her musical mind; Dora's was in boxes, regular and accurate; Connie's was just a mess. 'How on earth did you girls organise all this, with you being all over the country?'

Evvy said, 'We talked about it on the telephone and I met with Grace before Christmas and collected hers and posted them to Connie at school. She sewed it all together on a school sewing machine, which is why the outside edge is a bit chaotic.'

'Oh, shut up, Evvy! It is not!' protested Connie.

'Yes, it is,' said Evvy, nonchalantly.

'It is perfect,' said Rosina and surprised herself by starting to cry.

'Are they happy tears, Mummy?' asked Daisy and gave her a hug.

'Decidedly happy tears. I'm so glad you're all here, almost all of my girls home for Christmas. Thank you, darlings. Thank you.'

Afterwards, she left the girls to go and get dressed and went back to the kitchen to assist Bairstow. The girls came down and helped lay the kitchen table with the crackers they had made at school and instead of one big centrepiece, they'd all made little ones with holly and pine cones and greenery, each with a candle at its centre they had found in the cold-weather store in the cellar. The table looked lovely and the meal was delicious. They ate with Bairstow and all had a jolly good time. Despite Grace's absence – and she was sorely missed – Rosina felt it was one of the best Christmas Days she could recall.

After dinner, they all cleared away and helped Bairstow with the washing-up and drying. Well, they helped for a bit, but Bairstow sent them packing as they didn't do it the way she liked it and they were all complaining that they felt fat, so Rosina sent them to the lounge to relax and read their new books. Rosina decided to open a bottle of port and let all the girls have a little sip, as a Christmas treat. She was bringing it up from the cellar when she saw Allan coming out of his office.

'Merry Christmas!' she said to him.

'And to you!'

'Working on Christmas Day? What a shame.'

'Well, somebody's got to. I let many of the others go home, but someone needs to stay here. It's easier for me.' He meant without family, but there was no need to say it. 'Listen, I wanted to say thank you for your kind Christmas gifts for Eunice and me. She was very touched. We both were.'

'Oh, it was nothing. Just a token.'

'Well, I have a token for you, if you'll just wait a moment?'

'Of course. But you shouldn't have.'

'One moment.'

He disappeared into his office and soon returned, handing her the small gift, wrapped in tissue paper. She opened it and found inside a book. *The Waste Land* by T. S. Eliot. She'd vaguely heard of it, but knew nothing about it.

'Oh!' she said. 'How kind.'

'It's a Hogarth Press first edition, typeset and printed by Leonard and Virginia Woolf.'

She'd heard of them too, but never read anything by them, or was it just Virginia who was a writer? She didn't know. 'That is so very generous and thoughtful of you. I will look forward to reading it. I need a good new story. I've not found a good novel for ages.'

'Erm . . . it's a poem, a long poem.'

'Of course,' said Rosina and felt like an idiot. 'I haven't read any decent poetry for a while. Excepting yours, of course!'

'Ah, you are too kind. Well, see what you make of it. I happen to think it's the apotheosis of British culture. It is unparalleled in its beauty and form. It's my favourite thing ever written, I think.'

'Well, I must say, that is quite the ringing endorsement. Thank you again.'

'My pleasure,' he said and looked at her. Then, he reached over and took her hand, the one without the book in it. He squeezed it, then lifted it to his lips and gently kissed it. She watched his head bow as he did it, saw his brown eyes close and open again and stood quite still the whole time. Afterwards, she watched him, as he let go of her hand and put his hands behind his back. He looked at her steadily, neither of them speaking. His eyes were wide and questioning, waiting for her response. It made him look handsome and yet boyish at the same time.

'Thank you,' she whispered and turned away, walking down the corridor. She did not look back. What was she thinking, at that instant? She hardly knew. It was such an odd moment, a mixture of old-fashioned charm – the grazing of his lips on her knuckles – and an intense invasion of her person, which she felt concurrently irritated about and stimulated by. It was a long time since she had had any physical contact with a man, since Harry left months before. Allan's act confused her, invigorated her and annoyed her all at once. She looked up to see Evvy standing in the corridor, arms folded, staring pointedly at her.

'I saw that,' said Evvy.

'Saw what?' Rosina tried to gloss over it, in case Evvy hadn't seen everything.

'You know very well. Him, kissing your hand. That Allan fellow.'

'We are just good friends, that is all.'

'We need to have a talk about this, but I'm not going to ruin Christmas Day with it now,' said Evvy. Her tone was absolutely infuriating! As if she were the adult and Rosina the naughty child! When did that happen, that your children became your judges?

'Oh, do give it a rest, Evvy,' said Rosina and laughed at her, though inside she was still quite shaken by what had just occurred.

She went back in to sit with the girls and listen to the King's speech on the wireless. It was so heartening to hear his voice on Christmas Day and, though its tone was undoubtedly sombre, she was encouraged by the feeling of unity, of the whole nation facing an uncertain future together. Rosina felt settled by this and also was happy that the tasks of the day were over. As he spoke, there were even a few flakes of snow beginning to fall outside, drifting down on to the churned-up ground of the gardens and giving a touch of sparkle to the Army-ridden landscape. It wasn't heavy enough snow to cover, but it added to the general seasonal magic.

After the King's speech, they all went to the games room and stood around the piano and sang a few Christmas carols, while Daisy played the accompaniment. The girls took turns in singing the descants and they linked arms and had a splendid singalong. It really had been a smashing Christmas Day.

That night, Rosina went to her bed weary but satisfied, that she had put on a good Christmas for her girls, and they had risen to the occasion magnificently. Yet, the moment she was alone, memories of Allan's kiss on her hand came back and she sat on her bed and considered it for some minutes, before there was a light knock on her door. It was Evvy.

'Everything all right?' said Rosina, hoping she was just going to say good night and hadn't come to discuss what she had seen earlier.

'Yes, I was just wondering if you'd given all of Dad's old clothes to Throp or if you'd kept back some of his slacks. I want some trousers to adjust to wear myself and thought I'd "make do and mend" some of Dad's.'

'Most of them have gone to Throp. There are a few left in a drawer. You're welcome to them.'

'Which drawer? Whereabouts?'

Rosina sighed. Evvy could be so demanding! 'You don't need them now, at this minute, do you?'

'Well, just tell me and I can fetch them.'

'Oh, for heaven's sake. It's Christmas Day. Can't you wait?'

Evvy came in and shut the door. 'What are you angry at me for?'

'I'm not angry, Evelyn. I'm just tired. It's been a long day. Christmas is always tiring for parents.'

'Yes, but it's not just that. You're annoyed at me. Why?'

'Oh, please, Evvy. Not now. Please, just let me rest.'

'Look, I feel I need to put you straight about this chap.'

Rosina looked up and frowned. 'What chap?'

'Allan Vaughan, of course. I met him yesterday. You didn't know that, did you?'

'No, I didn't. What difference does it make?'

'Well, I ran into him on the stairs. He told me off for coming up the staircase, in my own house. He actually scolded me. Shouted at me! On my own staircase! In my own house!'

'Well, he clearly didn't know who you were. And it's partly my fault, because I forgot to tell you about the different parts of the house and where we're allowed to go.'

'Allowed to go? It's your house!'

'Evvy, can we please discuss this tomorrow? I'm so weary.'

But Evvy was determined to plough on regardless. 'I soon put him straight. I said, "Do you know who I am?" And do you know what he said? He called me a bluestocking flibbertigibbet! What century is he living in?!'

Rosina sighed again and let her head fall into her hand.

Evvy went on, 'So I told him, I'm Evelyn Calvert-Lazenby and you can't tell me what to do in my own house.'

'Oh, *Evvy*,' Rosina snapped.

'You're not annoyed at me, surely? He was the one being a pompous ass!'

'He was just doing his job. He must have thought you were one of the secretaries. He'd met the girls already and didn't know another daughter was turning up, as none of us did.'

'I don't care. That's not a way to talk to anyone. And he didn't even apologise afterwards. When he heard who I was, he just said, Oh. That was it. Oh, he said. Then turned around and walked away, as if nothing had happened. As if he hadn't just berated me like a child in my own house!'

'Yes, yes, in your own house. You've said that.'

'I don't understand you, Mummy. This man is not a good man. I have a very bad feeling about him.'

'You've barely met! Don't be so dramatic.'

'Look, I don't know Harry Woodvine much, but I've met him, and according to the girls – all the girls, including Grace – Harry is absolutely smashing. And Connie is absolutely mad about him.'

'I know,' said Rosina and rolled her eyes.

'And you know how rare it is for all us girls to agree about anything. But I felt the same thing, when I met him. It's obvious to anyone who'd look at him. He's a kind, gentle soul. He's loyal and nice, interesting and well read and good with children. And he's mad for you, can't you see that?'

'You only met him briefly! How can you tell all that in one glance?'

'Because I'm an excellent judge of character and you know that. You've always said that about me. It's like I sniff it out, like a dog. I sense bad character. You know that, Mummy! It's like my secret weapon, you always said that.'

'That is true. But maybe you're losing your touch as you get older. Because there is nothing bad in Allan Vaughan. There are things you don't know about him. He's had a tragedy in his life, a terrible thing. He keeps his cards close to his chest, but I've talked with him, spent time with him and seen behind that hard exterior.'

'Oh, don't tell me. He has a sob story about his past. Oh, poor him. All those self-obsessed types have a sad tale about their previous girlfriend or wife or whatever. They prey on nice people and garner their sympathy about these terrible things that have happened to them. Boohoo! It's all rubbish to get your sympathy and make you care about them, but it's just lies.'

'His son died, Evvy. Died! You think he made that up?'

'How do you know? Where's the proof?'

'Oh, Evvy, who would do such a thing?'

'Liars do such things. I've met his type before. And I see he wears a wedding ring. Where's his wife then?'

'They divorced after his son died. She lives in Scotland.'

'Why does he still wear his ring then?'

'I don't know, but that is his choice. Maybe it reminds him of his son, who knows? I do know it's none of your business.'

Evvy came over to the bed and sat down, took Rosina's hands urgently and held them tight. 'Mummy, you're too nice. You always have been. Don't forget I'm more like my father than I am like you. I know what I'm talking about, because I've seen it in Daddy. And seen it in men I've met over the past few years, in France, in London. The charmers, the liars, the tricksters, the bastards. I've met them all. And I have trusted my gut every time and it has worked for me. I have a nose for trouble. And for goodness. Allan is bad news. And Harry is goodness, through and through. How can you even think of looking at another man when you have a smasher like Harry who utterly adores you?'

Rosina withdrew her hands and sat back, frowning at her daughter. 'How do you know that?'

'Bairstow told me you've been writing long letters to each other and he's sent you telegrams to let you know where he is. That's devotion, that is. He loves you.'

Rosina raised her eyebrows and breathed out sharply, annoyed at Bairstow for gossiping with Evvy.

'And don't be annoyed at Bairstow,' said Evvy, reading her mind as usual. 'I winkled it out of her. I wanted to know what was going on with Harry and now this Allan character. She doesn't like Allan either. Doesn't trust him an inch, she said.'

'Well, that was wrong of you. You shouldn't be dragging the servants in to personal things like this.'

'Oh, don't be daft, Mummy. You and I well know those old partitions are falling down between masters and servants these days. And you and Bairstow are old friends who discuss everything. I know how close you are. It doesn't matter that you pay her. She loves you and loves this family. She'd do anything for you, don't you know that? We're all the family she has. Don't pretend you don't feel the same way. She's family, Bairstow. Now more than ever.'

Evvy had an annoying habit of talking sense, even when Rosina didn't want to agree with her.

'Listen, darling. I can see that your heart is in the right place. You think you're saving me from some great villain. But I know Allan a lot better than you do, and than Bairstow does.'

'But why would you even look at him twice, when you have Harry waiting for you?'

'Because I'm old enough to be Harry's mother!' cried Rosina, then covered her mouth with her hand, shocked at her own outburst.

'So what? Nobody cares,' said Evvy.

'Everybody cares! Society cares. It would disapprove strongly of our relationship, especially since I'm the "lady of the manor", as they say. I have a position to uphold. It's easier for you. You've always been a rebel. I'm not like you, Evvy.'

'But you could be, Mummy! Maybe this is your time, in wartime, when the usual rules of life have gone out of the window. I'm in London driving vans and cars and motorcycles around between fires and wearing slacks and helmets and nobody gives a fig. It's our time, to throw off the yoke of society! And embrace real, true love when you find it. Not this absolute rotter Allan Vaughan who's definitely a liar and may well even become a bigamist, if you let him.'

'Oh Evvy, for heaven's sake! You're wildly exaggerating, as you've always done.'

'That was when I was a child! I've grown up, in case you haven't noticed. Connie and I were terrible for lying, I know. But not any more. I'm an adult now, with plenty of experience of the world and of men. And I'm telling you, do not trust this Allan. Do not forsake Harry for a cad like

Vaughan. And he is a cad, as sure as eggs is eggs. Can't you see it, Mummy?'

Rosina suddenly felt absolutely exhausted. Her head ached and her eyelids felt like lead weights. She rubbed her eyes. She was out of words. She was too weak for this barrage from her daughter. She felt Evvy's arm go around her.

Evvy said quietly, 'You think I'm being cruel, Mummy, but I just love you. I won't go on any more. I've said my piece.'

'You certainly have,' muttered Rosina and leant into Evvy's shoulder.

'And look. I have something for you.'

Rosina opened her eyes to see Evvy reach into her dressing-gown pocket and draw out a piece of paper, folded up. 'It's a little thing I drew for you. I didn't want the other girls to see it. Because if they saw it, they'd know I'm an old softie really, like you. And I can't let them think that. I have to keep up appearances, you know.'

Evvy was smiling ruefully at her mother and Rosina felt flooded with love for her. She was infuriating, this child, this young woman, but oh, how she loved her. She took the paper and opened it. It was a sketch, in dark pencil, signed in the bottom corner, 'To Mummy, with love from Ev.' It was a drawing of a woman in a headscarf, holding her baby on her lap, sitting on the floor in a dark place, with other huddled figures around her, less defined, shaded in grey.

Yet the mother was drawn in striking, clear, black lines, the curve of her arms around the child, the curve of the baby's head, the curve of her back as she comforted it. It was a perfect moment of peace and stillness.

'It's on the underground station platform. London folk use them as shelters. They fill up with people every night. I go down there sometimes and sketch things I see. I saw this lady and her sleeping babe and I thought of you, Mummy.'

Rosina felt a fat tear drop from her eye and land on the back of her hand. She lifted it to wipe her eyes. 'Thank you, darling. It's the most wonderful gift I think I've ever received in my life.'

'I'd rather you take my advice as a gift, than this little scribble.'

'It's not a little scribble. It's utterly beautiful.'

'Happy Christmas, Mummy. You deserve to be happy. You're the finest person I know.'

Chapter 13

December 1940

On her return to Substation 73V, Evvy was glad to be back amongst her comrades, yet simultaneously exhausted at the thought of facing it all again. She knew she wasn't the only one. The psychological effects on the firemen of constantly facing mortal danger were beginning to tell. And, too, there was the horror of the things they'd seen, awful things burnt into their memories forever. Evvy had not seen all of these things herself, but had heard stories about them back in the recreation room. Yet one night, the week before, she'd seen something she couldn't imagine telling a soul about. She'd certainly not shared that ripping yarn with her family. She'd been delivering petrol to a squad, when she'd seen a fireman from another unit using his axe to chop off a boy's foot who was trapped in rubble beside a building that was about to collapse. She saw him raise the axe and knew she wanted to look away, wanted to more than anything at that moment, but somehow it seemed cowardly not to face it, as the fireman who did it had to face the terrible task and the boy had to face the unimaginable horror of having to lose a foot or die. So she didn't look away. The vignette of that moment would stay with her forever. She knew the men she worked with saw scenes like this every night. Corpses everywhere, as well as folks dying and begging for help that sometimes reached them, sometimes didn't. Evvy herself had seen the dead, as well as seriously injured people, and the walking wounded wandering about the ruins of their houses in their night-things, broken and bloody, clutching random household objects, in utter shock. They were quickly marshalled by helpers, but Evvy could not forget the blank, haunted look in their eyes. You see enough of these things night after night after night, with no hint of respite, and it can break you.

Returning from the short respite of two days at home, Evvy came into the station and immediately felt dejected at the discontent and depression that were beginning to infiltrate the usual jolly atmosphere of the watchroom. Her colleagues were tired, dog-tired, of everything. But there were things that served to rally everyone, here and there, such as the gramophone someone had brought in, sometimes inspiring an impromptu dance, with the substation women being sought after for a spin around the rec room, which could get crowded and hot at times, the air moist from the damp uniforms, steaming in the warmth of indoors and close quarters. Evvy's current favourite song was *Oh Johnny, Oh Johnny, Oh!* by the Andrews Sisters, which she'd dance to with anyone when it came on, so it turned out it was put on a lot whenever she was around, sometimes several times in a row.

The other thing that cheered everyone up were the pets. Animals found in bombed-out houses, their owners killed or missing, were sometimes brought back to the station by firemen and kept there until collected or taken on to a rehoming centre. Some never were collected though and became permanent residents at the station. At 73V, they had two cats named Bubble and Squeak – Pauline's idea, because everyone ate it so often in the café across the road. The two cats went everywhere together and slept on a blanket on top of a filing cabinet in Lewis's office, as it was next to some warm pipes. Lewis had taken to leaving his office door open all the time so Bubble and Squeak could come and go as they pleased. In the rec room, they had a budgie in one cage and a canary in another, which were called Bird One and Bird Two by Sid. Their chirping and tunes brought a merry atmosphere to the station that was desperately needed. And the star of the show was a dog that had come in that month and was so friendly and sweet-natured that he immediately became the station mascot. He was a scrappy little Jack Russell. Everyone loved him and he adored everyone in return, yet he held a special place in his heart for Lewis, as it had been Lewis who'd found him in the ruins of a house and carried him in to the station. After that, whenever Lewis was on duty, the dog would follow him by his heels to and from every room and barked and barked when Lewis had to leave him, sometimes chasing the car or van Lewis was in for a few streets, before giving up and always finding his way back home to the station. Lewis named him Cyrano, which the men thought a weird, foreign-sounding name and wanted to call him Winnie, after Churchill, of course. But Lewis insisted. Evvy was the only one who knew the reference. It was the main character of the French play Lewis had told her about, his favourite book. She really must get around to reading it soon.

A couple of days back after her Christmas trip away, having eaten her tea and started her duty at around 5.30 p.m., she went in to Lewis's office and saw he was at his desk. By his feet was his shadow, Cyrano, chin on the floor, resting but with eyes open as she walked in, scanning for threats to his master. The dog sat up and Lewis reached down to him, his hand finding the dog's muzzle and fondling it, then patting his head, to reassure him. It was a gentle, kind gesture that touched Evvy.

'Evening, sir.'

Lewis looked up and smiled. 'Evening, Calvert. Everything all right?'

'Yes, sir. Just wondered if we could do a swap.'

'A swap of what?'

'I've drawn a sketch of you, nothing special. Just a scribble. And I'd like to swap it for a borrow of that book of yours, the one named after your dog?'

He laughed and shook his head. 'I'm glad someone round here knows what I'm talking about.'

'I'd like to know more, though. I'd really like to read it.'

'Let's see the drawing then.'

Evvy retrieved it from her pocket and handed it to him. As he unfolded it and laid it flat on the table, she thought how she did want to borrow the book, but that was not why she had done the sketch and not why she wanted him to have it. She had started and stopped sketches of him over and over. Then, the day before, she'd finally finished one and got it right. It was him, absolutely him, purely Lewis Bailey. She'd caught the handsome lines of his bone structure and the intelligence in his eyes. Yet it seemed inappropriate somehow, since he was her boss, to give him such an intimate gift as a drawing of him. So she thought she'd throw in the book swap idea, to make an excuse for it.

He was looking at the sketch for a long time, not saying a word. Did he hate it? she worried. Then he looked up.

'It's marvellous.'

'Really? You really think so?'

'I do. I'm . . . lost for words.'

He looked down at it again.

'I'm pleased. It took me a while to get it right. To get your face right. It's an unusual . . .' Then she stopped. She'd got caught up in the moment and forgotten she was talking to her S.O.

'Unusual what?' he probed.

'Well, if it's all right to say, you do have an unusual face, an interesting face. There's . . . so much character in it. And that's hard to draw.'

'Well, I think you managed it. Perfectly.' He looked down at it again and touched the folds, smoothing them out.

There was a charged moment of silence as she watched him look at himself, the version of him she'd rendered and gifted to him.

He looked back up and said, 'You . . . see me.'

'Thank you,' she said. Then, to lighten the moment, she added, 'Can I borrow your book then?'

Lewis paused, then replied, 'I suppose you could. It's just a silly superstition but . . .' He paused again.

'What is?' asked Evvy, her curiosity piqued. 'What's a silly superstition?'

He undid a couple of buttons on his tunic and reached into the inside pocket. He brought out a small book. It fell open in his hand to reveal that stowed inside its pages was an envelope he hastily returned to his inside pocket and then he handed her the book. It was battered and dog-eared, bound in dark blue leather with faded golden lettering embossed on the cover which read *Cyrano de Bergerac – Edmond Rostand.*

'It's a lovely little edition,' she said. The leather had been worn smooth by use and the lettering was almost rubbed off.

'Isn't it?' he agreed.

'How come you just happen to have it on you?'

'That's the thing, you see. Since the London raids started, I've kept a copy of it in my pocket. And I'm not dead yet. So it must be my lucky charm.'

'Oh my God! Well, put it back immediately!'

'It's daft really.'

'No, it isn't. These things keep us going. Get it back in your pocket this instant!'

Lewis took it. Then he folded up the drawing and stowed it inside the book, replacing it in his pocket.

'What's the story about?' asked Evvy. 'Maybe I should see if I can get it out of the library.'

'Cyrano is a soldier and he has this huge nose and considers himself very ugly. Whenever someone bullies him about it, he has these fantastic comebacks that put people in their place, because he's so damned witty. It's like a sword fight, but with words.'

'I like it so far,' she said, 'because I despise bullies. What else happens?'

'Well, I don't want to spoil it for you. You must read it one day.'

'What happens? Tell me a bit.'

Lewis paused and looked down. Cyrano the dog yawned noisily and looked up at him, his tail starting to wag hesitantly.

'He's in love with a girl, but they're just friends. Good friends. They talk a lot and she's very fond of him. But she doesn't know he's in love with her.'

Evvy felt a prickling sensation on her skin, like the tingles she'd feel when she heard a truly lovely piece of music.

'What happens next?'

'She's in love with a soldier in Cyrano's squad, a young, handsome man. He writes . . . well, Cyrano does. Well . . . I mean . . .' Lewis stopped again and looked away.

'What? Tell me!'

'Find a copy one day and read it,' he said, shortly. 'I don't want to give it all away.'

'But now I need to know what happens with the girl and the other soldier? And does Cyrano ever tell her—'

Cyrano the dog jumped to his feet and let out a sudden, short bark.

'What is it, eh, boy?' said Lewis.

Cyrano barked again and again. Then ran around in a circle, chasing his tail, stopping suddenly and barking once more.

Then the sirens started wailing.

'He can hear them before we can,' said Lewis. 'C'mon. We're on.'

Evvy and Lewis hurried down to the watchroom. It was 6 p.m. on Sunday the twenty-ninth of December. The phones started ringing. Pauline and Lynn were on duty and repeating the information aloud, Sid writing it on the board.

'Bombs hitting Southwark,' said Pauline.

Soon after, more calls came. 'Fires at warehouses on the South Bank,' said Lynn. 'The Minories . . . Dockhead . . . close to London Bridge Station. All on fire. Squads dispatched.'

The men were gathering outside the watchroom, listening in. Around six thirty, more calls came. 'Incendiaries in the City,' said Pauline. 'Thousands of them. Fires started in Gresham Street, Cheapside, Queen Victoria Street. Fires spreading fast, fanned by strong winds. Yes . . . yes . . . all right.' She replaced the receiver and looked up at Lewis. 'Looks like they're targeting the City. Calling all units to attend.'

Lynn rang the bell and the whole squad were ready in an instant and off out to the City.

'You're with me, Calvert,' said Lewis and they went to the staff car, Lewis adding, 'Get us to 73. Sounds like the City is gonna get a hiding tonight.'

Evvy started up the car and set off, soon arriving at the main station 73 on Euston Road. Lewis got out of the car and hastened inside. While she waited, she thought of how Sam had told her recently that the City was known by firemen as 'the danger zone'. The City of London was a square mile of densely packed buildings – offices, warehouses and churches – separated by slim passageways, many of which were lined with wooden blocks. In addition, many of the buildings were built of wood, and stored materials that would make excellent kindling. At the centre of it all, in all its splendour, was the magnificent St Paul's Cathedral, one of London's most famous landmarks, designed by Sir Christopher Wren after the Great Fire of London destroyed its forerunner in 1666. So much history and it could all be destroyed in minutes.

Lewis appeared again and got in hurriedly. 'Head for the City, Cheapside area.'

'Yes, sir,' she said and started up the car.

'It's spreading fast,' said Lewis grimly. 'Wood Street, St Martin's-le-Grand, Redcross Street, Golden Lane and Ludgate Hill all ablaze. St Bride's and St Lawrence Jewry churches on fire. They're calling everyone out. And the worst news is that loads of the water mains are damaged from bombing and the bloody Thames is at low tide and some pumps are already running low on water. We've already had a message from the PM to the commander, that the first priority is St Paul's.'

'Blimey!' said Evvy. 'Churchill himself spoke to Commander Firebrace?'

'Yeah. He said St Paul's must be protected at all costs. There're firewatchers at St Paul's but not at most of the other buildings in the City, and even if there are, they're probably not around as it's a Sunday so they're not at work and back at home eating their tea.'

Evvy turned on to Woburn Place, past Tavistock Square, and now they could clearly see the German raid in the skies, in all its horrific grandeur. What Evvy saw that night as she peered through the windscreen at the London skies was utterly extraordinary. Incendiaries were falling in their thousands, a terrifying yet strangely enchanting sight of flares like fairy lanterns dropping from the skies that, instead of magic, brought destruction and death. Strong winds were blowing drifts of them here and there, some alighting on roofs and some reaching the ground, to burn in a green glare. Along with these fire setters, the German planes were dropping high-explosive bombs and Evvy could hear them falling – she thought of how they sang as they fell and if their tune was going up they were coming for you and if the tune was going down they were heading for someone else. She could hear the anti-aircraft guns – or ack-ack, as people called them – firing tremendously fast and loud, and in between these bursts, she could distinctly hear the whine of planes trying to outmanoeuvre the shells. Each flash of ack-ack gunfire lit up the houses and winter trees in moments of stark clarity.

As she drove past the university buildings, the library must have been on fire, because they saw clouds of scorched documents gliding down like birds. As she approached Cheapside, the sky was filling with smoke and flame over the rooftops. Pulling up where Lewis instructed, they both got out and she could hear the swash of hoses nearby fighting the flames, while the ack-acks still raged, the incendiaries and HE bombs still fell like confetti and the nearby sounds of damage punctuated the roar of the fires: the clatter of bricks from collapsing walls, the clink of broken glass, the jingle of shrapnel falling on to roads and roofs. And amidst it all, the odd, random cries of people – whether victims or those on duty, it wasn't possible to discern in the cacophony.

'Wait here,' ordered Lewis and ran off around the corner to the squad. Before long, he was back. 'They've still got water here. Go back to the station and get the bus and deliver petrol to pumps that call for it. Then, once you've done those, come back here as they'll probably need it by then.'

'Sir,' she nodded and headed back to 73V.

Evvy found Pauline and Lynn run ragged on the phones with calls for help and information on the rapid spread of the fires. Pauline called out, '73W, X, Y and Z have all called for petrol for pumps.'

Sid helped Evvy load up the petrol cans into Suki the school bus and off she went. Going back to the City, she could see already that many of the roads she'd just driven were now in ruins and driving through them was becoming more and more tricky. The closer she got, the more she found roads criss-crossed by hoses snaking desperately in search of a water supply. Some of the hoses were covered with hose ramps at points, so she could drive slowly over those, but otherwise, she had to bump over the pulsing hoses. Any stretch without hoses, she could hear the brittle sound of Suki's tyres going over broken glass and in the corner of her eye she spotted a few rats scurrying along away from the chaos. Sprays of hose water caught by the wind soaked the windscreen and windows of the bus.

Evvy finally reached Cheapside and pulled up not far from St Paul's churchyard. As she got out of the bus, the intense heat hit her like a wall. The air was thick with smoke, ashes, sparks and the warm mist of water from the hoses, as if the fire and the water were at war, a battle of the elements. She made sure her tin hat was on securely, as cinders were falling from the sky, some in large glowing lumps. Breathing was trying, as the air was full of irritants and the heat started to smart in her throat. It was difficult enough to breathe at this distance, so what would it be like for her boys so close to the fires up the road? Sam was back at work now and she felt her chest tighten as she feared for his safety. She saw the outlines of her comrades stark against the raging fires, the flames leaping from one side of the street to the other with joyous abandon like children hurling themselves into a summer river. It looked like her boys had just arrived at this spot on Cheapside, as the crew were connecting the pump to a hydrant, while two men with the hose were scrambling over rubble in the street to get closer to the fire, arms linked together to hold firm against the power of the rearing hose as they directed it at the base of several bursts of fire, before reaching the main conflagration and turning the hose on it, heads down to protect their faces from the cinders and heat that could burn them or take an eye out. Behind them, other firemen helped the progress of the hose by lifting it over debris and shards of shop windows, manoeuvring it to avoid kinks and snags. She could hear the men calling to each other, 'Look out, lads!' and 'Get crackin'!' and someone yelled, 'Fuck this!'

Then she saw Lewis by the pump, sending some men off to the next street with another pump to find an alternative water source, no doubt. Evvy fetched out a two-gallon petrol can. It was heavy to carry. Sid had told her once it was about fifteen pounds or so when full. She heaved it up the street, her breathing ragged with the effort and the heat. Lewis saw her and nodded his head, fixing her with his gaze. Seeing him there, amongst his men, determined and capable, yet still finding a moment to encourage her, gave her the boost she needed to swallow down the panic she felt clawing at her throat. He pointed to another pump on the next street. She lugged the can down a side alley and saw the lads had fixed up the other pump. They nodded at her as she approached with the petrol can to top up the tank. She had to lift it carefully to fill it, as the cap for the tank was very close to the red-hot exhaust manifold, so if she spilt any, the results would be instant and catastrophic. She prayed for a sturdy grip and no wobbles and her prayer was granted by her own plucky expertise at pouring the stuff in without a drip escaping. The lads thanked her and told her another on the next street needed a fill-up too. She went back to the bus to return the empty can, retrieved another full one, took it up to the next street and repeated her task.

Back at the bus, she fetched another can and went to fill the pump Lewis had been standing at. The fire was raging closer now and one of the men turned to her and shouted, 'The fucking water's running out. Retreat!' She trotted as fast as she was able with a full can and put it carefully back in the bus.

Looking back, she saw the men backing up as the fire thundered its way up the street, but a hose was still pumping away, like a live thing, coiling and slithering up the street into the thick wall of smoke. Who was at the head of it and why weren't they retreating like the rest? The men were pointing and shouting at it and, suddenly, she saw Lewis appear from a side door in a building and run towards the head of the hose. Why on earth was he running back into the fray?

'Get back!' shouted one of her lads and she called, 'Where's S.O. going?'

'Sam's in there, at the top of that ladder. We called him and called him, but he can't hear. Bailey went in to look for him. He must be on the next building.'

Evvy stared into the smoke and did not think. She ran towards the drift of smoke that writhed with life and spat out a fine mist of vapour that drenched her face as she approached, then she felt a sharp tug on her arm that almost brought her to her knees. A fireman she didn't recognise was manhandling her away from the scene, as she yelled at him, 'The Baileys are in there!' But he wasn't listening and deposited her next to her bus and walked back up the street. She ignored his act of removing her and ran back towards the worst of the fire, as her crew members were waiting for a sight of their beloved boss and his brother. Then, the bucking hose began to flatten out and go limp, as the water ran out and it collapsed, the head falling down to the ground and smashing into a pile of wreckage. Out of the smoke, a figure stumbled backwards, pointing and staring back into it, then tripped and collapsed on the ground. It was Sam! Evvy ran to him, as well as a couple of their lads, who hoisted him up to his feet and got him up the street. She looked back to the wall of smoke and called to anybody who'd listen, 'Where's Bailey? Where's S.O.?'

Suddenly, a flare of flame leapt towards them from the building and a terrible creaking and rumbling began. Evvy looked up to see the top of the wall beginning to bow out and she turned and ran hell for leather up the street, ran for her life, choking on the acrid air as she pelted along. The rushing and crashing behind her was ear-splitting and she ducked, covering her head with her arms, as if they could save her from piles of bricks and masonry falling on to her tin hat. She threw herself on the ground and debris clattered on and around her, winding her. She lay for a few seconds, checking she was still alive and her limbs still worked. She was and they did. Turning over, she lay on her back and looked up to see a cloud of dust, which made her cough. She covered her face and coughed again, then looked back at the carnage. The whole building was now in pieces in a great strewn heap and the flames danced over it in triumph, bounding across the street to create further havoc.

She felt arms pulling her up then and walking her down the street. It was her lads and she saw ahead of her Sam leaning against her bus, drinking something from a hip flask and wiping his blackened face. She ran to him and began to speak, but her lungs were full of rubbish and she choked, hacking up filth as she doubled over. She felt Sam's hands on her and his voice, croaky and insistent, 'All right, love. All right.'

The coughing fit passed and she stood up straight and said, 'Where's Lewis? Did Lewis get out?'

Sam's white eyes, glistening in the midst of his filthy face, stared at her with fear and confusion. 'I don't know. I don't know. He found me at the top of the stairs on my own keeping the fire at bay. But the water was failing and the hose was slackening off and the fire was winning. I'd been there too long. I couldn't stop coughing. I think I passed out. He got me down the stairs. I woke up and he said, "Stand up, lad" and I did. He had his arm around me. We were stumbling over the rubble and he slipped on a sheet of glass and yelled out, clutching at his leg. I turned and went to help him up and he shouted at me to get away and he got up on two feet and hobbled onwards and shouted again, "Run!" The next thing I knew, I tripped up and everything went black. And the lads had me and you were there. Then the whole bloody lot came down. I don't know if he got out. Maybe he did. Maybe he got into the next street. There was an alleyway just next to where we were. Maybe he got down there. I don't know though. I don't know!'

His voice had started as a croak, growing louder and more hysterical as he went along, ending at a cracked shout that broke him, as he bent over and coughed just as she had.

Evvy rubbed his back and held on to him, then the lads were helping him back on to the appliance and telling Evvy to get her bus out of here, if she was all right to drive, to which she nodded. Walking back to Suki, she saw that the side nearest the fire was blistering in the heat. She climbed in and backed the bus out of that hell and patted the steering wheel to soothe Suki, hoping her tyres weren't damaged from the broken glass and the heat, and drove away from the scene. Turning left, she went along the road a bit, then pulled over and stopped. She got out and looked up at the incredible sight of the dome of St Paul's stark against the orange and pink radiance of the sky, as the buildings around it had collapsed. Somewhere in all that ruin was Lewis Bailey. She peered up the alleyway that ran alongside the street they'd just been on, to see if she could see him limping down there or sitting by the wall. But there was nothing and nobody. Just the clouds of smoke and flickering flames, that now caught the wooden blocks that formed the base of the alleyway she was peering up. The road itself was melting from the fire and the flames were beginning to race down the narrow alley. That was her signal to get going. She drove Suki out of there, feeling shattered, blank-eyed and numb, her mind racing, crafting pictures of Lewis's potential fates, of Lewis slipping on the glass, Lewis's leg dripping with blood as he clambered over the ruins and escaped to another crew, who took him back to their station or a hospital to treat his leg. Yes, that could well have happened. But other images crept in as she steered Suki back to 73V, including Lewis looking up at the collapsing building and seeing his life flash before his eyes as it crushed him, killing him instantly. Or perhaps he was still conscious under there, choking on the smoke, his injured leg sticking out of the rubble blistering in the heat as he died slowly . . .

'Stop it!' she shouted aloud to herself. 'Your bloody imagination! Stop it, stop it, stop it!'

She drove the rest of the way to the station fighting back tears. Because she thought, *If I start crying, I won't stop. I won't be able to stop.*

Chapter 14

Back at the station, a few men were standing around gulping down a quick cuppa, their faces filthy and blistered, clearly worried about Lewis and beaten down by the fires, but preparing to go straight out again. Cyrano was sniffing around everyone's feet and whining urgently, looking for his master. The sound cut through Evvy's brain as she tortured herself with worry, because she knew she was as desperate as Cyrano for the return of Lewis Bailey.

Pauline gave Evvy a cuppa and told her miserably, 'Several Wren churches have been lost. And the Guildhall is now alight and the Law Courts have been hit.'

It was awful, those precious historic buildings going up in smoke, but all Evvy could think was, *I don't care a fig for history while Lewis is still out there.*

Then Sid told everyone that bulk water carriers were being ordered in from outside the City and the Thames was starting to rise, so they needed to get straight back out there. As everyone headed out to the trucks and Evvy to her bus, Sam came to her quickly and kissed her, then said, 'He'll come back, you'll see. He'll have got to a hospital. He's the smartest bloke I know.'

'I know,' she said and smiled for Sam's benefit, but she was heartsick with fear for Lewis and did not share Sam's optimism. Then, just as she was starting up Suki, the all-clear rang out over London and she heard cheering from the men as they drove off. What were the Jerries playing at? Why end the raid so early? Maybe they would come back. But, either way, the fire brigade's night was far from over, as the fires were still raging in the City.

Evvy went out delivering petrol to different pumps all over the City for hours. Each time she got back to 73V she'd ask about news of Lewis, but there was none. By 3 a.m., the river was in full flood and the firemen of London were getting a hold on the fires. St Paul's still stood, though many of the surrounding streets were devastated. The firemen moved to damping down the smouldering ruins. The planes had not returned. *Thank heavens for that, if nothing else*, Evvy thought. By 5 a.m., she got back to the station and was told by Sid that she could go and have a rest, if she was feeling rough. But, of course, she couldn't sleep. She went instead to Lewis's office and sat in his chair for a minute, with Cyrano fussing at her and whining, as if he knew. She watched the cats sleeping peacefully on the filing cabinet and looked down at the dog. 'Come on, boy,' she said and beckoned him to follow, which he did eagerly. She grabbed a scarf of Lewis's from the hook on the door before she left the room, wrapping it around her neck.

She took the staff car and drove back to the City. It was morning now as she surveyed the ruins, peopled by firemen, police officers, rescue workers and air-raid wardens looking for survivors. The roaring drama of the orange, red and black night had been replaced by a dreary, winter London day. The wastage of destroyed buildings in so many grey heaps was infinitely depressing, accompanied by the brittle sounds of broken edifices subsiding and splintering, ash on the breeze settling on the shells of buildings, shards of glass glistening everywhere, metal struts deformed by the heat into fantastical shapes and concrete blocks tossed hither and thither, as if by a giant's careless hand. Evvy saw the City workers arriving over London Bridge, many in their suits and bowler hats, gaping up at the ruins of their offices. Her artist's eye drank it all in and committed it to her photographic memory, as she'd have to paint this one day, the colours of the night before and the monochrome of today. More than ever, at that moment, she knew she was living through history in the making. She had been there at the second Great Fire of London, in the thick of it, and she had survived. But had Lewis? That was the question that filled her mind as she drove slowly through the chaotic streets.

She reached the part of Cheapside where Lewis had last been seen. She parked up and got out to find the site was now ankle-deep in black water made filthy by the fires and issuing from the firemen's hoses engaged in damping down the ruins. She waded through it, followed by Cyrano leaping in excitement through the deluge and barking wildly at the madness all around him. She took off Lewis's scarf and held it to Cyrano's nose to give it a good sniff. He inhaled it wildly, his tail wagging like mad. Then she sent him on to the rubble and said, 'Find him, boy!' She looked out keenly for broken glass and chucked away a few bits to save Cyrano's paws from damage. He eagerly sniffed and sniffed everywhere, then started barking frenziedly and shoving his nose in between the bricks. Evvy fell to her knees beside him and started hurling bricks aside.

An air-raid warden came up to her and said, 'It's too dangerous here, girly. There's that workshop there creaking and probably going to come down any minute.'

She ignored him and kept throwing the bricks aside. Then, a fireman she recognised from another 73 squad came up and she said to him, 'I reckon Lewis Bailey is under there.' He nodded and bent over, starting to clear the rubble too, soon helped by the warden. Cyrano was scrabbling with his front paws and barking and whining, so Evvy thought they were close. Then her hand touched something other than stone or brick and she knew.

His body was whole and intact. He looked crumpled yet serene. Maybe he had died quickly. She hoped that was true. His face was thick with dust, which Cyrano began to lick away. Evvy picked Cyrano up and held him as he wriggled to free himself, staring down at Lewis's dead body, peaceful in the ruins. She waited there as the warden went to fetch the stretcher-bearers.

The fireman said, 'I'll go to an OP on the next street and ring 73V and tell them, so you don't have to do it.'

She nodded. Once alone with Lewis, she stared at his face, etched in dust with dog licks in stripes across his nose and dried blood in a dark stain all down his leg. She glanced about her and nobody else was looking. They were all concerned with their own tragedies, small or large. She put Cyrano down and he sat beside Lewis's head and whimpered quietly. Evvy knelt beside Lewis and reached into his jacket pocket and pulled out the book, the precious book that was meant to keep him safe. But it hadn't. She held it in her hands and thought of his fingers holding it, when they were warm and alive. He was going to give it to her, even though it was his lucky charm. But maybe the mere act of taking it out of his pocket and offering it to her was enough to break the magic spell. Maybe that's why he'd died. Maybe it was her fault. *Superstitious nonsense*, her inner voice told her.

She realised she was crying when her blistered cheeks and chin smarted from the salty tears that overran them and she saw them dropping on to the dusty book cover. She opened the book, knowing inside was safely stowed the sketch she'd given him. She couldn't bear to open the drawing, to see his face at that moment, and was going to close it when something else tucked into the book fell out on to the rubble. She leant down and picked it up. It was a small, sealed envelope and written on the front in strokes of blue-black ink was *Evelyn Calvert-Lazenby AFS c/o Substation 73V, Argyle Street, WC1*. It was Sam's handwriting. She stared at it. Why would Lewis have a letter for her from Sam in his pocket? What could it possibly mean?

Then Cyrano yelped and she looked up to see the warden coming back with a couple of stretcher-bearers. Evvy pushed the envelope back into the book, stood up and shoved the book into her pocket. She watched the bearers get Lewis's body on to the stretcher and start to carry him away to the next street. She followed grimly, with Cyrano trotting beside her, until they reached a van and stowed the body inside.

The warden said, 'I'll call your station later with details of where the next of kin needs to go. Any idea who that is?'

'His brother. He's a fireman too.'

'All right. What's his name again? And station?'

'Lewis Bailey, S.O. of Substation 73V.'

Her voice cracked as she said it and the warden looked at her with compassion.

'Do you want a lift back there, love? I can drive you.'

'No, I'll be all right.'

She went back to her car and opened the door for Cyrano, who leapt in and scrambled across to the passenger seat. She got in and shut the door, taking the book out of her pocket and finding the envelope. Cyrano nudged her elbow and settled down. With Cyrano's warm chin resting on her leg, she opened up the envelope and pulled out the letter written in Sam's small, neat handwriting on several pages of notepaper. It was dated Boxing Day, when she'd been travelling back from Ravenscar. She began to read.

26 December 1940

Dear Evvy,

As I sit here in my office, Cyrano at my feet, you are hundreds of miles away in Yorkshire and I must admit, I am missing you keenly. I have become so accustomed to the sound of your voice and your laughter and the sight of you, your smile lighting up the watchroom. I'll have to curb my words or I'll start gushing. I won't compare thee to a summer's day, don't worry. I write to you as if you will read this soon, yet I know that I write into a void, as I have no intention of you seeing this letter, unless I am not around anymore. And as much as I'd love you to read it, I also want to be around for a while to come, if I'm able. If I am gone when you read this, you will start it believing that the hand that holds the pen is Sam Bailey's. But it is not. It is Lewis Bailey. Please, bear with me while I explain. Everything will become clear and then I hope you can find it in your heart to forgive me.

The bombing of London has been continuing apace for four months now, with no sign of abating. Our brave men and women of the LFB have fought it valiantly, but I don't know how much more we can take, to put it frankly. I see daily the usually buoyant lads weighed down by fatigue. There are even rumours of a massive bomb that Germany have developed that will lay waste to the whole of London and this does haunt my dreams. Each night that passes without the death or serious injury of someone in my crew feels like an immense victory. And yet, each day that passes, I grow more and more sure that it is inevitable that it will happen soon and it may well happen to me. The odds increase with every raid, as we get more tired and less on the ball, as we were in September, fresh as daisies.

Thus, I decided, in your absence, to write this letter to you. I am going to keep it in my pocket inside a copy of my favourite book. If the worst happens, I hope someone will find it and give it to you. You see, I have a lot to explain to you. I wish I could do it in person, but I am too much of a coward for that. I'd much rather you found all this out after my passing. And perhaps it is a mistake to tell you any of this at all. Perhaps I am being unutterably selfish in doing so. But I freely admit that I am tired of being unselfish when it comes to the subject of you. In my life I have held back and let another advance and helped him in doing so, but in death . . . well, in death, I feel that maybe I've earnt the right to tell you the whole truth, at last.

So, here it is. When you arrived at the station, I'm sure you're aware that many a fellow wanted to ask you out. But my brother was the first one to do it and you seemed to take a shine to him. As your S.O. I couldn't woo you, as much as I desperately wanted to, being your boss. But the point was moot since you and Sam seemed to develop a rapport immediately. I decided to put it out of my mind, that my feelings for you were impossible and therefore pointless. I resolved to be a good boss to you, to help you aspire to be the best firewoman you could be. And, as time went on, perhaps I could one day be a good friend to you too. But my feelings betrayed my plans and continued to grow for you. One day, I could not rid my mind of thoughts of you and I decided to write them down, because I need a clear head for this job and experience has taught me that if I write my thoughts down, then my head is emptied of them and I can focus so much better. I wrote several times and put these short missives in my desk drawer, underneath a pile of other stuff, knowing nobody here would ever rifle around in there. Sometimes, if I had a moment and wanted to indulge myself in thoughts of you, I would take them out and read them. One day, I went to do this and I noticed that one of them was missing. I had read them so many times, I could've almost recited them by heart. And one was definitely missing. I scrabbled around looking for it amongst other official paperwork, but it was nowhere to be found. I felt mortified that it might end up in the wrong hands, but for the life of me could not think who would ever look in my desk. So I blamed it on my own carelessness and hoped it must have gone into the bin with some other discarded papers. Then, one day, Sam came to me in my office and shut the door, looking guilty as sin.

I think you might have guessed what's coming next. Sam admitted he had been going through my drawer looking for cigarettes one day and found the letters, read them and stole one to give to you. He pleaded his case, saying that he was mad about you and he was sure you felt the same, but you still hadn't agreed to go out with him. He said you were a clever one and he was worried you'd get bored of him before he'd had a chance to prove himself. He said he was sorry he'd stolen it, but it had had the right effect, as you'd loved it and asked him for more. I was livid with him and told him so in no uncertain terms. He apologised and said it wouldn't happen again. The letter had done its trick and that was that. But then, a while later, he came back and begged me for more letters. I refused, of course, and told him it was despicable, lying to you like that, pretending he was someone he was not. But he said he loved you and wanted to please you, that you'd asked and asked him and wouldn't take no for an answer. He was desperate. It was wrong, I knew it was wrong. But I agreed. I've always looked out for my little brother and he was hard to say no to. But I'll admit, it wasn't just that. I loved you too, you see. I loved you so much, the thought of being able to tell you those feelings – albeit in the guise of my brother – was a heady one and I could not resist it. And it occurred to me that my life was unfolding in a bizarrely similar way to my favourite book.

I assume you haven't read Cyrano de Bergerac *yet, or you would've told me. So I'll explain: Cyrano writes letters for his handsome soldier Christian to woo Roxane, the woman Cyrano loves. He does it willingly, knowing she would never love an ugly mug like his and this is his one chance to pour out his love for her. I couldn't believe my life was playing out the story of my hero, Cyrano, although the key difference was that his letter was not stolen. I did not craft this narrative, but found myself in it and decided to play on. It felt like fate, somehow, and I will admit that, deep down, I think I hoped that I would fare differently from Cyrano – who dies in the end – and that one day, the truth of the letters would come out and you would love me, that you would choose me.*

I didn't give Sam the letters I'd already written. I decided to write new ones. He took three from me. I poured my heart and soul into those letters. I don't even know if Sam read them. He told me you loved them. I wanted to write another, but he said not to. We quarrelled about it and he told me, No more letters. He wanted you to love him on his own terms. He was sick of the lying. Of course, he was right. But by then, I was addicted. I agreed to his request, of course, and stopped writing to you. But oh, how I missed it. I was inspired by you and I felt as if my muse was there and I was forced not to answer. But I knew he was right. It was a lie and it was wrong. It needed to stop. I stopped writing them in private too, trying to forget my feelings for you. But it was folly and I could not forget. How could I? I did not write another word though. Until now.

Again, I question my motives for doing so. If I were a good brother, I wouldn't do this. I would take my secret to the grave and let you marry Sam, if that's how things work out, and your love for him won't ever be sullied by the truth about those letters. Yet, as I've said, I have had to stand aside and watch my brother be with the woman I love. I love my brother more than I love myself, that is true. Our parents passed away when we were quite young and I've been like a father to him ever since. I've always looked out for him. And by writing those letters for him, I was continuing to do that. But just this once, I wanted something for myself. Mea culpa, I freely admit. But, also, I felt it was wrong that you had been hoodwinked in this way. And it felt right that you should know him properly, as the very good and fine person I know him to be, without those letters. I knew he was mad about you and that his feelings for you were entirely genuine. He'd never met anyone like you and, oh boy, was he far gone. He was terribly protective of you, but he understood your true nature too, I believe, as he knew that he could never hope to tame you, that your independence was one of the things that made you shine. He knew you'd probably never want to settle down with him for a life of domesticity in Camden, *but he had faith that – if you both lived through this war – you two could go out into the world and make a life for yourselves, wherever and however that may be. He'd always been a home boy, Sam, but he was prepared to give that up for you. That's how much he loved you, and then some. He was planning to ask you to marry him once there was a lull in the bombing, if that ever comes. But I think too that he was putting it off. He was afraid you'd refuse him, because of the differences in your social standing. And maybe he was right about that.*

I wanted to explain this to you, so that you are not too angry with Sam for lying to you. We are both to blame. He never should have stolen the letter in the first place, but then I should never have continued the lie by writing to you after that. We were both in the wrong. So, please don't be too harsh with him, after I'm gone, once you know these truths. He is the best man I know, a true and loyal bloke who would back an appliance over a humpbacked bridge for you in the blink of an eye. More than that, I know he'd die for you. As would I. So, all I can do is apologise and plead that you'll accept my explanation that although what we did was wrong, it came from a place of love, from us both. I hope you can forgive Sam and forgive me too. Whatever happens, please know that I did love you and will always treasure our friendship, until the day I die. I have come to hate the fact that I lied to you by writing those letters for Sam. I've never been one for lies. So this whole business never sat right with me. I only hope you can forgive me this one, final act of selfishness, in telling you the truth.

Thus, I sign off my ghostly letter from beyond the grave. I hope London survives. I hope we win the war. I hope my men remember me as a good leader, who did my best to keep them safe and protect our city. And of you, dearest, I hope you find happiness beyond this war, whether with Sam or some other lucky fellow, or simply on your own, drawing your beautiful sketches, thinking your extraordinary thoughts, as you walk off into your own wonderful life. And, Evvy, it will be the most wonderful life, because you are in it.

All my love,
Lewis Bailey

Chapter 15

January 1941

New Year's Eve at Raven Hall came and went with little pomp or ceremony. The girls stayed up late with their mother, who let them try a little red wine. They rang in midnight with a rousing chorus of 'Auld Lang Syne', which nearly broke out into an argument as Connie insisted they all cross hands, but Dora protested that the Scottish way was to only cross hands on the last verse. Allan was away, visiting family, due to return soon. Eunice was also away, but she turned up a couple of days after New Year's.

Rosina was sitting in the lounge, going over the accounts at her desk, wondering when she might get another letter from Harry, as she hadn't heard from him since October. The thought filled her with a sense of unease, that something might have happened to him, or her usual worry that he had lost interest, or simply, the most logical explanation, that the military postal service from Sierra Leone was highly irregular, if indeed he was still there. She looked up from her desk periodically to watch little flurries of snow come now and again, settling briefly on the frosty ground. But nothing too bad. They'd been lucky this winter, so far. It had been cold, but not excessively so. They'd had snow, but only a bit of it, not enough to cause any disruption. She got up to go and organise some tea and spotted Eunice tidying up the office in Allan's absence. Rosina popped her head round the door and said, 'Happy New Year, Eunice!'

Eunice turned and smiled. 'Oh and to you too, Mrs Calvert-Lazenby.'

Rosina stepped into the office. 'I thought you were going to call me Rosina,' she said, smiling.

'Oh yes, sorry. I will. Did you have a nice Christmas?'

'Lovely, thank you. My second eldest came up from London for a surprise visit, so there were five of us. And you?'

'Oh yes, it was lovely down in Dorset. Uncle Allan is on his way and he'll be back later today. Which reminds me . . . can I . . . have a word with you about something?'

Eunice looked uncertain, which made Rosina curious. 'Of course.'

'It's a delicate matter,' said Eunice, awkwardly.

'I tell you what, I'm about to have some tea in my lounge. Why don't you join me there in a few minutes? We can close the door and have a bit of privacy. Would that help?'

'Yes, thank you.'

Rosina nodded and left, organising the tea tray and going back to the lounge. She'd usually invite guests to the drawing room, but she wanted to make an effort with Eunice and show her that they could be friends, so decided the less formal room would help.

Soon, Eunice arrived. Rosina set up the tea on the little table and sat in a chair, motioning to another chair opposite her for Eunice, deciding not to sit on the settee, as it seemed a little too intimate as yet. They settled and Rosina poured out the tea. She was very curious now. What 'delicate matter' might this young woman want to broach with her?

'Thank you for seeing me.'

'Not at all. As I said to you, I'm very used to having girls around and discussing things. Whatever I can do to help, I'd be happy to, in whatever dilemma you see yourself faced with.'

'Ah, it's not about me. It's actually about Uncle Allan,' said Eunice, shifting in her seat, looking decidedly uncomfortable.

'I see,' said Rosina, even more curious now.

'I thought long and hard on the railway journey up here. About whether or not this was a good idea, coming to speak to you. And in the end, I thought, well, I've nothing to lose. I feel it needs to be said.'

Rosina shifted in her seat and said, 'Well, I'm agog, my dear. Please don't delay any further!'

'All right. Well, I may as well get straight to it. Uncle Allan is in love with you. And when he returns, later today, I believe he is planning soon to ask you to marry him.'

Rosina's eyes grew wide and then she looked away. She'd wondered if this might be the truth of Allan's feelings for her. She had not looked ahead that far, though, to a marriage proposal. It shocked her but also filled her with a giddiness she'd not experienced for a very long time. She remembered the same feeling when George had proposed, all those years ago: excitement tinged with fear. And now it was Allan Vaughan, as different from George as a man could be. Reliable, dependable, organised, kind and good. A good man was going to ask her to marry him. But she had not bargained on the news coming from his niece!

Eunice added, 'And I'm sure that hearing this from me is not what you expected.'

'We can agree on that!' said Rosina.

'Yes, well, I have my reasons. You see, Uncle Allan is a complicated man. I think he had his life all planned out, from Eton onwards, into the Army, into marriage and parenthood. He's a highly organised person and his life had all gone to plan. Until John's death. And then his marriage . . . well . . . dissolving. And the war came and it gave him some purpose again. But his personal life, as you can imagine, has really knocked him for six. And then he met you.'

Rosina nodded and took a sip of her tea. Some soldiers not far from the window were shouting at each other, which distracted her for a moment.

'And I wasn't sure about you at first. In fact, I'll be brutally honest and say I didn't like you at all!'

Rosina's attention was drawn back instantly. 'Well, the feeling was mutual,' she said, somewhat snippily. She had warmed to Eunice after their reconciliation, but this conversation was so bizarrely intimate, she was feeling decidedly uncomfortable. Yet she wanted to remain polite. 'At first,' Rosina added. 'Until we got to know each other a bit better.'

'Yes, exactly. And now I know you better, I believe you would be very good for Uncle Allan. I think you are a truly nice person. And you would care for him, as he needs to be. You see, I felt I had to tell you, because everyone in the family has been worried about him so much, for the years since it happened. He has never spoken of it to anyone in the family, not really. He just carried on. And the war has given him a new purpose and direction. We've all seen it.

And then, at Christmas, he told me he was planning to ask you to marry him. And he was asking my opinion, of what I thought, of whether I thought you'd say yes or no. And I assured him of course you'd say yes, that any woman would be a fool not to. And then I decided, that if I could, I'd come and see you first, alone, confidentially. I understand it's peculiar. And I'm sure if Uncle Allan knew, he'd be livid. So I must ask you not to reveal this meeting to him.'

'If that's what you wish, dear,' said Rosina, still slightly uneasy. 'But may I ask, why you felt it necessary to pre-empt his proposal by telling me yourself? Doesn't it rather spoil the effect?'

Eunice took a deep breath in and pushed it out, fiddling with a lock of hair about her ear. 'Yes, as I say, it was a difficult decision to make. But I decided that too much was at stake. We've all seen in the family how devastated Uncle Allan has been. It very nearly broke him completely. And he's just been starting to come back to himself, this last year. And I was frightfully worried that you might turn him down and it would break him again. So I resolved to come and tell you, so that I might gauge your reaction and also so that you knew how very important it was to him and . . . well, more than anything, I wanted you to know what a very good man he is.'

318

'I'm sure he is. But I'm afraid I can't tell you my reaction, as I haven't heard from the man himself. I can see why you wanted to speak to me. And your concern for your uncle is admirable. But I can't possibly give you a reply until I have spoken with Allan. And really, with a subject this personal, it should be left to Allan and me to discuss . . . privately.'

Eunice stood up, which surprised Rosina. 'Yes, of course,' she said hurriedly. 'Perhaps this was all a dreadful mistake. I think . . . yes . . . I think it might be. And it's done now. No turning back. I'm so sorry. Do forgive me.' Eunice sniffed and Rosina wondered if she might burst out crying.

Rosina put her teacup down and said, 'Oh please, don't upset yourself, Eunice. Please do sit down again.'

'You're very kind,' said Eunice, barely able to look Rosina in the eye now, as she seated herself. 'I do think I've blundered in here and made an awful hash of things.'

'You really haven't,' replied Rosina, smiling. 'As I say, it's truly admirable, that you care so much for your uncle, that you'd try to help him in this way. It must have been such a difficult decision for you.'

'Well, please know it truly is only to help Uncle Allan. He loves you very much, you see. He's said that and I can see it in him. And there is something else. Something he's been trying to do, for you . . . well, he's seen how unhappy you've been, with your home taken over and all the unpleasantness. He's been beavering away behind the scenes, to try to get a different base for the men here. He's always said it was too small for his devices anyway, the house and the grounds. There are more men supposed to be coming, you see, so he's been working very hard to get the whole lot moved away, to another part of Yorkshire. It's not finalised yet, but he's been pushing for it hard. He knows how much it would mean to you.'

Rosina's heart leapt at news of this, even more so than hearing about the marriage proposal. The Army, leaving? Could it really be true?

'That would be great news indeed,' said Rosina, carefully choosing her words. It seemed rude to cheer at Eunice's departure, along with the Army and everything. 'Is it going to happen, do you think?'

'It's in Uncle Allan's hands, I'd say. He's doing his best to make it happen. For you.'

'Well, that is very kind and—'

They had both heard the stark rumbling of a tank in the distance, a sound Rosina had become accustomed to of late, as the Army were now doing regular exercises across her land and making a mess everywhere they went. The rumbling grew louder. And louder. And then, as her sentence ended in mid-flow, she saw something in the corner of her eye, and turned her head. A tank appeared rounding the far end of the house, going so quickly as to look quite out of control. She saw several soldiers suddenly hurl themselves out of its path, shouting and crying out. The tank rolled right over a fence and Rosina knew at that moment that it had gone completely rogue. Men were yelling from all around, producing a chaos of sound and panic as the tank rushed onwards at a terrifying rate.

'What . . . ?' she heard Eunice say. Then, within seconds, it was bearing down on the family garden. What if the girls were there? It crashed through the hedge, rolled right over the chicken coop and smashed into the front greenhouse, ploughed on right over that, crushing it utterly and careering speedily towards the windows, near which she and Eunice were sitting.

Eunice cried out. Rosina found herself leaping up and throwing down her cup, which smashed on the table, as she went to grab Eunice to somehow get her safely out of the way, when the collision happened. The tank hit the corner of the house, the windows smashed in a riotous dissonance of sound, glass breaking, brick crumbling, engine roaring. Rosina landed on the carpet, her upper body shielding Eunice, as Rosina had thrown them both to the floor.

When the noise had stopped and Rosina lifted her head, Eunice was curled up like a kitten beneath her, unmoving.

'Eunice? Are you all right?'

'Yes,' came a little voice. 'I think so.'

Eunice lifted her head and gazed about her.

Rosina stood up and surveyed the devastation. She stepped over the upturned table and saw that, very luckily, the big old settee had taken the worst of the glass, shards of it lodged in the back, sticking out at dangerous angles, whilst the settee cushions were showered with powdered glass, bricks and dust. If they had been sitting there, they might very well have been killed. She stood for a moment, hands on hips, gazing at the hole in the wall where the window frames used to be. When it was happening, she had sat open-mouthed, watching the whole disastrous sequence play out in front of her. She could not believe her eyes. Seeing it through the window like that had made it seem unreal, as if the window frame were a picture frame, or the window a cinema screen. But it was indeed real. It had happened.

She saw men coming and staring at the scene, saw the tank back up and manoeuvre itself to drive away, which it did, as if the crash had never happened. An officer appeared outside and was shouting at the men, then asking Rosina and Eunice – who now was standing behind her – if they were quite well. Rosina nodded at him, looking at how he was framed through the gaping hole in the wall fringed with jagged edges, as flakes of snow drifted in through the gap and settled lightly on the furnishings.

'Were my girls out there?' Rosina called to the officer. 'Are they all right? Was anyone hurt? What about my gardeners?' He assured her that nobody was injured, that the tank had damaged property only. Rosina put her hand to her forehead and felt somewhat dizzy.

There was lots of fuss going on around her and Eunice pulled herself together very quickly, dealing with the details and ushering Rosina into the games room, where she could sit on the girls' settee they used in there for lounging around. Bairstow appeared and came hurriedly to sit beside Rosina, while Eunice went off to find out more information on what had happened.

'Where are the girls?' Rosina asked Bairstow.

'They were all safe upstairs,' Bairstow reassured her.

'Oh, thank God,' gasped Rosina.

'T'has not injured?'

'No, I'm fine. Just a little dizzy, that's all.'

Eunice came back in and told them she'd sort everything and there was no need to worry, and how sorry the men were, and it was all just a dreadful accident involving a young soldier in training and that the Army would pay for all the damages and everything would be put back just as it was. Rosina had nodded and replied, 'Yes, thank you,' to much of this, still in shock at the whole bizarre occurrence.

Bairstow was absolutely hopping mad, at the damage, the wanton destruction of it, but also how easily it could have injured someone, including Rosina, or even killed her, if she'd been sitting on the settee. Bairstow didn't mention Eunice, as it was no secret that Bairstow didn't like Eunice, never had, and had not changed her opinion, even once Rosina had warmed to her. But Rosina could see that Eunice was doing her best and had been very shaken by it too. They had both been very lucky.

Eunice went off again to deal with things and Bairstow poured Rosina a little brandy to sip, for the shock. Bairstow said that Rosina needed to be cleaned up, that there was dust in her hair and there might be bits of broken glass and she must get Rosina upstairs. Then the girls came rushing in to the games room, aghast at the sight of their mother, dishevelled and crowned with brick dust.

'Are you hurt, Mummy?' cried Connie, while Dora rubbed her arm and Daisy let out a little sob.

'Oh, thank the lord you are all safe,' said Rosina.

'We heard it happen!' said Dora, excitedly. 'It sounded like nothing on earth!'

'Don't fuss over thi mother now,' said Bairstow. 'She's all right but needs a bit of quiet. Back upstairs, t'lotta thee.'

Bairstow ushered them all out, as they argued that they wanted to stay, wanted to help, wanted to go outside.

'Do NOT go outside!' cried Rosina, standing up too quickly and having to steady herself by putting a hand down on the sofa arm.

Then Allan appeared at the games-room door. He strode across the room and stopped short of her abruptly. Rosina thought he was about to take her in his arms.

'Are you hurt?' he said, then, looking round at Bairstow, who had come back into the room, 'Is she hurt?'

'She's well, but no thanks to thee,' snapped Bairstow, scowling. 'I need to get her upstairs, wash t'glass out of her hair.'

'Of course. Thank you, Bairstow. Please do take her upstairs. I will see to everything.'

Rosina still felt dizzy from it all. She was annoyed at herself, for being so ineffectual, for not standing up to it and taking charge. Now she realised she had an inkling of what Evvy was seeing every night in London, only an inkling though, as she knew bombings were a hundred times worse than this. But the shock of it was overwhelming and though she wanted to say things and do things, she found herself just letting it wash over her, like a dream. She kept thinking, *Who would tell Harry if I'd died?* And who would tell her, if Harry died? These questions rattled around in her mind, with no answers.

Bairstow took her upstairs and washed her hair out over the washbasin, wrapping her head in a towel and then brushing her hair through, both of them saying very little. Rosina was thinking about telling Bairstow what Eunice had said, about the marriage proposal. But something stopped her. She didn't want to discuss it with Bairstow, though she wasn't sure why at first. Yet the other part, about the Army possibly leaving the hall, that was news that needed to be shared.

'Eunice told me that Allan has been working very hard behind the scenes to get the Army moved away from here, away from the hall altogether to a different house elsewhere in Yorkshire.'

'What? T'whole lot of them?'

'Apparently.'

'Well, hallelujah for that, if it's true. If it's not, then today's shambles is t'last straw and no mistake.'

Bairstow insisted on putting Rosina to bed after that, that she must sleep off the shock. But she was only in bed for a few minutes, when she decided she absolutely could not rest. After the shock passed of knowing that the girls were safe, she was thinking about the greenhouses and how lucky it was that Jessop, Throp or Ronnie had not been inside one of them at the time. She was thinking about the chicken coop and how it had been completely crushed and all her lovely birds must have been squashed to death. And then she thought of Harry and how they'd given them all movie-star names together and now all those same chickens would be dead. And then she thought of what Eunice had told her and what she felt about all of that, and what would she say if Allan did ask her, and what on earth she was going to do.

Rosina brushed her hair through, nearly dry now, and pinned it up in a chignon. Then she got dressed and went downstairs, going out of the back door to stand and survey the wreckage. She'd forgotten to fetch her coat and shivered as she stood there, amidst more flurries of hesitant snow, looking at the flattened remains of the greenhouses and chicken coop, not even a stray feather to say there had ever been birds there, just everything crushed into the hard ground in a mess of brick, glass, wire and mud. Luckily the bees survived, as the hive was placed away from the chicken coop, thankfully. There were only a few bees left over-wintering but Rosina was grateful they were not squashed. Her teeth started chattering with the cold, so she went back in to the lounge, to find men already boarding up the hole in the wall and the worst of the glass and rubble having been removed from the room, along with the settee, though she wasn't sure where that had gone. She wanted to tell Allan that they should repair it if possible, as it was her mother's favourite settee and she didn't want it simply thrown away. She went to Allan's office and found it empty. She was about to go outside to look for him, when he turned up, striding along the corridor. The moment he saw her, he hurried to her and fussed over her, saying she should be resting.

'No, really, I'm fine. I've had a rest and I'm feeling almost normal now. Is Eunice all right?'

'Yes, she's fine. She said you threw yourself over her when it happened. How brave and kind you are. At least come and sit down. Let us go to the drawing room.'

He offered his arm and she slid hers through, the easy intimacy of it a comfort to her.

Once seated together on the little sofa in the drawing room, he updated her about the repairs and how it would all happen, again apologising and explaining the men responsible had been taken in hand.

'These things happen, unfortunately, when new men are training on vehicles and equipment that is new to them. I'm just sorry that it happened to your family area. I can't apologise enough. It will all be rebuilt.'

'Thank you,' she said.

'Listen, I know how horrible this has all been for you. And I'm loath to concern you further by adding more news to your shocks today, but it might help you. I hope it will make you happy.'

Oh God, she thought. *Is he going to do it now?* Surely not, surely he wouldn't get down on one knee and take a ring from his pocket and do it right now, while the wind was still whistling through the house from the gap in the lounge wall.

'What is it?' she said, her mouth dry.

'I wasn't going to say anything until I knew for sure, but it's pretty much settled. The Army will be leaving Raven Hall.'

'Oh!' she said, tremendously relieved it wasn't talk of marriage. 'How has this come about?' She decided to keep up pretences for Eunice's sake, though she didn't like lying.

'I've been trying to organise it for some time. The truth is, the hall and grounds aren't large enough to accommodate everything we need here and I've found another country house with more extensive grounds and larger indoor accommodation that will suit much better. We should begin moving out within days.'

Rosina's hands went up to her mouth. Despite hearing it from Eunice, the fact of it coming from Allan's mouth made it come true and it dawned on Rosina that it sounded like it was really happening now, that the nightmare of the Army occupation might really be over. 'Are you sure?'

'Yes, I'm pretty sure. Just a last couple of loose ends to tie up, but I'm . . . let's say, I'm ninety-eight per cent sure that it will happen. Are you pleased?'

'Of course! I'm just a bit . . . you know, I think I'm still a bit in shock.'

'Of course. But listen, this is important. Before we go, you must telephone the Office of Works as soon as you can, with a new plan for the requisitioning use of Raven Hall. If you don't, it's very likely they'll just send another lot of our fellows here, a smaller unit perhaps. But if you pre-empt that with another use for the hall, and if they agree, then you can head them off before they start reallocating the hall to something you don't want. I was thinking, perhaps a school? You're so good with your girls, I'm sure you'd be brilliant at hosting a school.'

Rosina thought back to the conversation she'd had with Phyllis Precious when the Army first came. 'No, actually. I have a better idea. Well, it wasn't my idea, but rather one of my . . .' She was going to say tenants, but then she changed her mind. 'One of my friends, she suggested a maternity home. And I rather love that idea.'

'That sounds ideal. I suggest you call the Office of Works very soon and put in the suggestion. But first, perhaps draw out some plans of how it would work, where you'd put everyone, how you'd adapt the hall to become a maternity home exactly. I just know you'll be smashing at that. If you call them with all these details in place, it'll give you more chance of success. I have no sway over the decision, I'm afraid. I only got this lot moved by sheer, dogged persistence and, to be fair, I always said Raven Hall was too small for our base from the beginning. Luckily, they started listening to me. And once I got to know you and could see how unhappy you were, it spurred me on further.'

'I can't thank you enough. Today really has been, as Bairstow said, the last straw.'

Allan chuckled, 'Yes, well, I can imagine that Bairstow will be delighted. She's always seen us as foreign interlopers of the lowest order.'

Rosina laughed too. It was certainly true about Bairstow. She looked forward to telling her the good news.

There was a lull in the conversation and she looked up at Allan, their eyes meeting.

'Will you miss me, when I go?' he said, softly. He looked worried. Rosina thought of Eunice's news then also considered for a moment that the Army leaving would also mean Allan leaving.

'Of course. I've loved our weekly meetings.'

'Just that?' he said.

'No . . . more than that. I've loved . . . getting to know you.'

'And so have I,' he said, looking intently at her now. 'All the time I was trying and planning to get the Army moved from here, to please you, to make you happy, knowing at the same time that it would take me away from you. That was a hard bargain to strike with myself.'

'I can see that. And I'm grateful for it. I want the Army to go, I'm in no doubt about that. But I don't want you to go.'

He looked relieved and a smile swept across his features. 'I'm very happy to hear that.'

He reached across tentatively and she let him take her hand, draw it to his lips and kiss it again. He held it there and pressed it to his cheek, whispering her name. She allowed herself to be drawn closer to him, as he leant over and kissed her softly on the mouth. It was a tender kiss. He was trembling, which surprised her. She put her hands on his cheeks and kissed him, his hands steady now and firm around her shoulders. They embraced and the feel of him was solid and real, warm and firm. After the shock of today's events, to feel herself surrounded by human warmth – and strong, male warmth at that – was the best kind of balm. She surrendered to it utterly, letting him envelop her in comfort. He settled against the back of the sofa with her in his arms, her head leaning against his chest, his arm about her and his hand gently resting on her head. She sat with her eyes closed for what seemed a long while, letting him stroke her hair. It wove a spell on her, that simple, almost parental act of tenderness, making everything dissolve into only this warmness and cosiness, of these arms and this body, sheltering her, shielding her from the world. She hadn't felt this safe in years, decades even. It was lovely. And very hard to pull herself away from, so she decided not to and instead to yield to it completely. Every human needed a bit of comfort like this.

She had no idea what would happen next between her and Allan. She had no idea what she would say or do about it, or about Harry and her feelings for him, and the silent promises their kiss had made, and all the confused feelings of love and duty that swirled around her head and her heart. But in this moment, she was safe and she was happy and that was all that mattered.

Chapter 16

Allan was as good as his word and repairs began on the lounge wall within two days. The same day, Rosina stood with Bairstow at the kitchen window and watched as the Army started the process of packing itself up and beginning to depart. As clumps of men and their equipment were dispatched in trucks, the landscape they left looked nothing short of a battlefield, its churned-up chaos frozen in place by the very low temperatures. As they looked on at this mass retreat, Rosina and Bairstow kept shaking their heads, as they couldn't believe that they really were seeing what they'd wanted so badly for months.

Rosina had taken Allan's advice and visited Phyllis to discuss the maternity home idea, to which Phyllis had responded enthusiastically, vowing to help Rosina manage it, if they could find someone to watch the children. Rosina said she'd organise a creche at the hall, so that expectant mothers with other small children could have them looked after too. Rosina had then telephoned the Office of Works and put forward the idea of the maternity home. They had told her to send written plans, which she had typed up immediately and sent from the post office. It was all coming together nicely.

Rosina saw little of Allan as he was flat out organising the move. She was waiting for him to take her aside and ask her the question his niece had pre-empted, yet nothing had happened. Had he changed his mind? Was she relieved or annoyed? Would Harry ever write to her again? Was she right to even consider Allan? Her head was a maelstrom of doubts and confusion. It was in this frame of mind that she took a call from Grace one morning, to be told to her delight that her eldest daughter had leave for forty-eight hours and was coming up to the hall for an overnight to see her. She got a room ready for Grace, with the help of the girls, who scrabbled together some ingredients from Bairstow to make Grace some fruit buns to enjoy. More snow came the night before she was due and Rosina found herself praying that it would not be too heavy and would not block the line, not quite yet, not until Grace was here and safe. After that, the weather be damned. Let it snow them all in so Grace was forced to stay – as long as the Army were all gone first.

Grace arrived at the station on a day with bright blue skies, bitterly cold, the snow glistening on the hills in the glassy sunshine. She looked even more beautiful than the last time her mother had seen her, bright and tall and confident. Grace met Allan briefly when they got home and chatted a little with him, Rosina watching how easily they seemed to get on. The girls then came and made a fuss of Grace. They all ate the fruit buns together with Bairstow in the kitchen, the warmest place in the house and where they all found themselves gravitating much of the time. Rosina watched with pleasure her girls chattering away, sharing stories and interrogating each other about their lives. Well, at least, Connie was the one doing the interrogating and the others were listening more than joining in. Connie and Grace had never been that close, but they got on well in general. Rosina remembered that Connie used to tease Grace about being a bit awkward in company, but these days, Grace was so changed, so much more confident, that Rosina could see that Connie was looking at her quite differently.

'You're so lucky,' said Connie, with a big sigh. 'Out there in the wide world, taking a proper part in the war. You're the last person I'd have thought to be engaged in secret, important war work, Gracie! The last person on earth!'

'Thank you, I think,' said Grace, with an indulgent smile. 'It's not easy work though. Don't be too envious.'

'Oh, but I am. I can't wait to leave the dreary drudgery of school. But Mummy says I must stay to the end of the year, which is *quite ridiculous*.' On the last two emphatic words, she glanced at Rosina, who rolled her eyes and ate some more of her bun, rather than reply. She wasn't going to get into this argument again.

'And Mummy is quite right, as ever,' said Grace. 'School is important. The war work can wait. I hate to say it, but the war isn't going anywhere for a while, perhaps a long while. It'll be there waiting for you when you've finished at school, don't you worry.'

Connie leant in conspiratorially and uttered in an urgent whisper, 'Is that news from your secret work? Tell me! I won't tell a soul.'

Grace smiled and put her hand on Connie's shoulder. 'Not at all. Just read the newspapers, listen to the wireless. Take an interest. You're living through history, Connie. Drink it all in and learn from it. Then, when the time is right, you'll know. And you'll take your place and do us proud. I'm certain of that.'

Connie looked placated, certainly a lot more so than she did during these discussions with her mother. Rosina thought of how good Grace was with Connie, managing her energy so wisely and channelling it in the best direction. She was kind and patient with the twins too, always had been.

She will make a wonderful mother, when her time comes, thought Rosina. Her pride for her eldest flowed through her and she felt the prick of tears in her eyes, which she took another bite of bun to dispel.

Later on that evening, Rosina finally got some time alone with Grace, curled up on the sofa in the drawing room, a roaring fire to keep them warm, while Rosina listened to her daughter tell her stories about the other Wrens, about Jim her young man, yet, of course, nothing about her work, as Grace had signed the Official Secrets Act and could say nothing of it. That very fact alone made Rosina inordinately proud, that the government itself had entrusted her eldest daughter with such important information. Rosina watched with delight as her daughter spoke. Grace was shining, she really was.

'But enough about me, Mummy. I've been rattling on for ages.'

'Keep rattling on,' said Rosina and squeezed Grace's arm. 'Keep rattling on forever.'

'But do tell me about you, Mummy. What's been going on with you?'

'Oh, mostly the awful Army occupation has been consuming my every waking thought and sometimes my sleeping ones. I can't tell you how happy I am to see the back of them. I know one mustn't grumble and we must all make sacrifices, but it's been pretty horrible.'

'Of course it has. And what an ungodly mess they've left everything in. And I'm so glad you were all right after the tank crash. I can't believe it! It could have been murderous!'

They talked about that for a while and about the Army leaving, then Rosina fell quiet.

'Mummy, it's the oddest thing, but I think I detect in you a slight regret that they're going. Am I mad to think such a thing?'

Was she really so obvious? She'd been thinking about Allan. All that week, though deliriously happy that the Army were going, she'd been dreading the moment when Allan would finally leave, with no guarantee as to when she would see him again. Yes, she wanted rid of the Army, but once they'd gone, Allan would be gone and she knew she would miss not only his company, and now his physical touch, but also the sense that Allan was in charge of everything, taking the burden of years of sole management from her shoulders, that Allan knew what to do in every situation, that Allan did what he said he'd do and made things happen swiftly and economically. These past months she had got so used to having him around, having that protection, that person to fall back on. And once they'd all gone, she'd be facing wartime alone again.

Dare she tell Grace about him? Why not? Grace was in a relationship now, a serious one. Rosina wouldn't be surprised if Grace and Jim got engaged soon. And Grace would understand about Allan, more than Evvy had, Rosina was sure of that. Her eldest had seemed to get on well with Allan when they had met. Maybe it was something about them both serving in the forces together; they had that understanding, something that perhaps Evvy didn't possess, being the eternal rebel and joining the AFS instead of one of the military arms of the services. All of this gave Rosina the assurance to share a confidence.

'Well, there is one thing I'll miss . . . It's a person actually. Allan Vaughan.'

'Oh, I'm so glad you said that. I think he's smashing!' Grace beamed.

'Do you, darling?'

'Oh, I do. He has such a nice air about him. And he's obviously madly in love with you. Are you in love with him?'

Rosina was taken aback. Again, was it all so obvious? 'Gosh, why do you think that?'

'The way he talked about you to me and the way he looked at you when he did. Has he declared his love for you? It's all terribly exciting!'

'Well, we have spoken about it, yes. And his secretary . . . She's his niece and she came to me a few days ago and told me he was planning to ask me to marry him.'

'Why on earth did she do that? That seems very odd, for a young woman to meddle in her uncle's private, personal business like that.'

Rosina had felt it was strange, too, and yet, once they'd bonded over the tank incident, she'd not considered it again. 'Well, it's complicated. He's suffered a family tragedy, you see. He lost a young son a few years back and divorced afterwards. The niece was concerned for him.'

'That's terrible, Mummy. I'm so dreadfully sorry for him.'

'Yes, it's awful.'

They sat quietly for a moment, then Grace added, 'But has he talked of marriage then, Mummy?'

'Not as yet. I keep expecting him to turn up with a ring in his inside pocket, but he hasn't thus far.'

'Well, he'd be mad not to. I'm sure he will at some point. He's probably just waiting for the right moment. But the question of the moment is this: what will you say to him? Will you say yes? Gosh, what a thrill!'

Rosina had asked herself that question a thousand times and could not come up with a reply that convinced herself. 'Darling . . . I just don't know. I'm very confused about it all.' What a relief it was to talk about it! And she felt no judgement from Grace, no disapproval either way. How glad she was that Grace had come up for this impromptu visit, as there really was nobody else on earth she felt she could talk to about Allan, nobody else at all.

'Of course you are, dear. It's a huge decision. But the main thing is, do you love him?'

'I like him very much. And I feel safe with him. I don't know him awfully well. But I do feel so good when he's around. Cared for, protected. I haven't felt like that for . . . oh, perhaps I've never really felt like that. I'm sorry to say that, about your father. I know how you adored him.'

'No, it's all right. I understand. A person can be a very different father than husband.'

A wise observation. Rosina would forget sometimes that her elder daughters were adults now and could have such insights. 'That's very true. So, yes, I'm really rather confused about it all. But since he hasn't actually popped the question yet, I don't have to make up my mind yet either!'

'That's all good then, as it gives you a bit more time to get used to the idea. I've worried about you for years, Mummy, being all alone, running everything by yourself. It would make me feel so much better if you had an equal to share it all with, someone like you, who understands responsibility and life and all its difficulties.'

'When you put it like that, the choice of Allan does begin to sound tremendously attractive.'

Grace laughed and added, 'It does, doesn't it! Evvy and I were talking about you a few months back and she had this ridiculous idea about you and that young officer that used to stay here, the one from the RAF. Harry what's-his-name. She thought you two were secret lovers! I told her it was nonsense, but she wouldn't hear of it. Imagine you, trying to run Raven Hall with a green young fellow like that, only a few years older than me! How farcical! I told her it was rubbish. You'd never dream of such a thing. And the scandal! Evvy's imagination was always over the top, but now it's getting out of hand!'

Rosina laughed to cover up her devastation at hearing such a damning portrait of Harry and her. She got up and took the poker to stir up the fire, hoping the heat of the flames would explain why her cheeks had just flared up. Grace was right. That's how everyone would view it, whereas a match with Allan would be widely understood, approved of and celebrated. But she found she could not openly agree with Grace. She could not dismiss Harry that way and laugh about him. Not Harry. All she could manage was, 'Yes, silly Evvy.' She even felt bad about that, knowing that Evvy was right about Harry, that her famous good judgement of character was spot on when it came to Harry Woodvine. But not about Allan, no. Evvy was wrong on that count, wasn't she? Yes, she was. Just this once.

'Did you really like Allan when you met him?' Rosina asked Grace. 'Evvy didn't like him at all. It worried me a bit.'

'Yes, I liked him very much. He seemed sensible and solid, yet had a nice way about him. A kind way. And, as I said, he quite obviously adores you. And I'm glad about that. I'm glad you have someone. Because, Mummy . . .' Grace stopped and sat forward, glancing down into the fire, preparing herself for something.

'What is it, my love?'

'I'm being sent abroad, Mummy. It's definitely going to happen. I wanted to come and tell you in person. I knew you'd worry about it. I dreaded telling you. I'm sorry I haven't mentioned it until now. But I was waiting for the right moment.'

'Oh, my darling girl, thinking of me. How kind you are,' Rosina said and put her arms around her daughter and they hugged tightly. Rosina felt the tears running down her face, unable to stop them. It was one of her greatest fears, that they'd put her daughter on a ship and she'd never see her again. She hadn't wanted to cry if she was told. She was hoping that if the news ever came from Grace, it would come by letter or telegram, so that she could go and cry alone. Her daughter's kindness at telling her in person had made it all so much worse, though Grace could not have known that.

'Please don't cry, Mummy. I can't bear it.'

'Then I shall stop forthwith,' said Rosina and put a brave face on, as she pulled back from her daughter and took a hanky from her sleeve to wipe her eyes.

'I shall be quite safe, I assure you. I'll be doing the same old work, which I can't tell you anything about, except that it's housed in a building far away from battle. It'll just be in a different country, that's all. They look after us Jenny Wrens very well, believe you me. I'll be just fine, Mummy. And I'll write often.'

'Is Jim going with you?' Rosina asked, hopefully. It would be good to think of Grace there with Jim to look out for her.

'No, we're in different roles these days. We'll write all the time though. And we have talked about marriage . . .'

'Have you, darling? How thrilling!'

'Yes, we've discussed it and we really want to. But we don't want to rush it before I go. We're going to plan it out and do it properly, once we're both back on home soil.'

'Now that is news worth celebrating. Congratulations, dearest.'

More hugs followed and more chat of this and that.

Afterwards, Rosina felt much more secure about her feelings towards Allan. Evvy's baseless condemnation had shaken her, but Grace's absolute faith in Allan and the match made her feel so much better. The visit from Grace really had been a godsend, despite the sting in its tail of Grace's imminent departure for some foreign field.

Grace left the next day and her mother fought to hold back the tears, though she did allow herself a longer than usual hug, before seeing Grace off on the train. She hadn't told the other girls about Grace's posting, as they didn't need to be worrying about that yet, not till it had happened for sure. Rosina held it inside, just as she held her feelings for Allan inside, feelings that were still a swirl of confusion wrapped around her memories of Harry, complicated by his long absence and silence. Luckily, she was busy dealing with the Army's withdrawal and didn't have too much time to wallow. There was still some emptying of offices to finish and Allan told her he'd be the last one standing to make sure everything had been done and left in order. He promised he'd come and see her before he went.

The house and gardens were in a sorry state and would need a lot of work to put them right. But there was no point in doing any of that until she heard from the Office of Works as to how Raven Hall would be used next. If the Army or other services were coming, then the mess might as well stay, as it would only be messed up again. If the maternity home was going to happen, then Rosina and co would have a lot of work to do, but what joyful work it would be, preparing for mothers and newborn babies, new lives at Raven Hall again.

On his last day, Allan did as promised and asked for a meeting with Rosina before he departed. It was a Sunday, the church bells ringing down the lane, as the last of the Army staff departed. Allan and Rosina met in the drawing room, on the sofa where they had first embraced. There had been no physical contact between them since that day, Allan too caught up with the move, Rosina caught up with the girls. And somehow they'd been awkward and a bit shy since that day and could barely look each other in the eye. It was something to do with him leaving, Rosina felt. They couldn't face up to it somehow. Until now.

They talked through the repairs still being done and, if the Army weren't coming back, what she could claim expenses for in terms of putting the hall back to how it was. Then their business talk came to an end and Allan said, 'Now I'd like to turn to another matter entirely, if that's all right with you.'

Was this it? Rosina still had no idea what she'd say if it was.

'Yes, of course,' she said and waited, her hands clasped together, gripping each other with the tension.

'Rosina . . . I believe I can call you that now?'

'Of course. If I may call you Allan?'

'Indeed you must! Especially now that the hall is your own again.'

It was always mine, she thought. But realised what he meant.

'Rosina, these past months have been difficult for everyone, particularly so for you. And yet, to me, selfishly, I must admit they have been a time of great pleasure, because of meeting you. Because of getting to know you and everything that you are. When I lost my son . . .' Here, his voice cracked a little. Rosina reached out her hand and placed it over his. He grasped hers and squeezed it tightly. 'Thank you, dear. I am quite all right. I can continue. When I lost John, I felt an iciness descend upon my heart. I never felt I could love again. I certainly knew I would never have another child. I never wanted to allow myself to love again, because it brought such pain. But meeting you has changed all of that. And the truth of it is that I have learnt to love again. I have fallen in love with you, Rosina. I love you. Those three little words, so simple, so plain. One syllable each. And yet they contain all the workings of my heart. I never thought I could feel that way again. And I never want to lose it. And so, I would like to ask you, if you feel the same way, of course – and I have an inkling that you might, after our beautiful embrace on this very sofa proved to me – I would like to know, if you would do me the honour of

349

considering a marriage proposal from me, if I did ask you such a question, what your response might be in such a circumstance.'

Rosina had listened to all of this, thinking she knew how it was going to finish, and it had indeed finished in sort of that way, but she wasn't sure what the question precisely was. Was he asking her to marry him? Or was he asking her if he asked her to marry him, would she consider it? She was confused and a bit flustered and didn't know how to respond.

In her hesitation, he withdrew suddenly and stood up. 'My apologies. It was tasteless and crass of me to mention such things. A terrible error of judgement. Please forgive me.'

Rosina said, 'No, no. Please, Allan. Not at all. I was just momentarily confused as to what I was being asked.'

'I thought I'd made that abundantly clear, my dear,' he said, still looking flustered.

'You did, you did. Please sit down. Please.'

He did so and she took his hand and squeezed it again, which seemed to calm him. 'I'm sorry. It's all my fault. You're right. I do think I bungled my words somewhat. You see, I'm not at all sure what your response will be. And so, I think I might have couched it in conditional verbs and all that sort of nonsense to give you room to wriggle out if it.'

'I don't need to escape,' she said softly, caressing his hand. He looked at her hopefully and suddenly she was surprised to find that she knew exactly what she wanted to say. 'If you're asking me to marry you, then my answer is let us think on it. We have got to know each other quite well these past months, but mostly under the guise of managers of this requisitioning. I know there is true affection between us and I have high hopes that this will continue to grow as we know each other longer. I believe there is no need for us to rush into anything. Let us continue to discover each other and grow in our affection and love, until we feel absolutely ready to become man and wife. Would you be prepared to do that, for me?'

'I would indeed,' he said and leant over and kissed her cheek.

They both smiled and even laughed a little at the relief of the worst having passed. It would be easier to talk, now everything was out in the open.

'But, dear, will you tell me this? Is there hope that you will say yes? Can you give me that?'

'There is hope. There is most assuredly hope.'

'So, if I were to ask you, would you say yes, at some point, in the future?'

'As I say, there is definite hope. Let us give it time.'

'But, over time, the answer may well be yes?'

He was holding her hands tight now, his deep brown eyes imploring her.

'Yes,' she said. She was going to add, *Yes, it may well be. Yes, there is hope.* But she didn't get that chance, as he beamed at her, drew her to him and they kissed on the lips, a long, hard kiss.

'You have made me the happiest man in Christendom! I can go and carry on my duties now with a lightened heart. Thank you, dearest. Thank you!'

It was a new sensation to hear him laugh. He was like a giddy schoolboy and it was infectious. She laughed too. And they hugged and kissed again.

Soon after, he left, still beaming at her, delighted with her and with himself.

But I didn't actually say yes to marriage, she told herself, as he drove away. *Or did I? No, I was quite clear. I'm sure I was. I said yes, meaning yes, there was hope.* But as his staff car trundled down the drive in the snow and reached the end, turned on to the main road and disappeared from view, she was left wondering whether her own understanding of what had passed between them was hers and hers alone, and he had gone away with quite another meaning in mind.

She told nobody about it – who could she tell? She knew Bairstow would not approve. And Grace was long gone. She went through the motions with the girls that evening and sent them off to bed, then looked forward desperately to her own, where she could truly be alone and think, or hopefully, sleep. She felt exhausted. The relief of the Army having left was immense, yet she also had that spent feeling one has when a large task has been accomplished and is over, leaving one empty.

She finished off in the kitchen, bidding Bairstow good night, who went off to her own room. Rosina dragged herself up the stairs – her stairs again now – to her bedroom and got into her nightgown, her hair tied in a plait across one shoulder. It was not as chilly as it had been recently, so she didn't put on socks before climbing into bed. Then she remembered she'd not brought up her jug of water and she always had one beside her bed. She often woke up in the night with a dry mouth and couldn't get through the night without her glass of water there. It made her anxious even imagining going to sleep without it. She was a creature of habit that way.

She sighed, pushed her feet into slippers, pulled on her dressing gown again and, turning the landing light on so she wouldn't trip on the stairs in the blacked-out house, she traipsed downstairs. In the kitchen, she switched on the small lamp over the range and found her jug of water sitting on the kitchen table. In her tiredness, she'd left it there. She tutted and went to pick it up, then heard the unmistakeable rushing sound of rain outside, spattering against the kitchen windows, covered by the blackout curtains. The snow that had been outside would probably get washed away, she thought. She was a pluviophile, a lover of rain, usually, its refreshing sound, its clarity. But at this moment, she'd rather have snow. Now Grace had gone, now Allan had gone, now the Army had gone, she had a desire to bring it forth. Let it fall, let it cover everything, the churned-up mess the Army had left of her home. Let it make it all anew, clean, pure and sparkling white. Let them be snowed in and not have to move from home for days, be cut off from the world, safe and quiet, where she could think and calm this constant turmoil of thoughts in her mind and in her heart. For she was quite unsure as to what was happening in her life and what it all meant, and who to believe about Allan – Grace or Evvy? And who to keep in her heart – Allan or Harry?

She stood and listened to the cleansing rain and had a sudden desire to see it. Her thoughts were mirrored by the chaotic sound of the raindrops splashing off the roof and clattering against the doors. On a whim, she turned the kitchen-door key and opened the back door, to look out at the rain falling. It was heavy and the air was thick with it, falling down like stair rods – siling it down, as the Yorkshire phrase had it. The hall had been blanketed by snow, covering up the worst of the damage the Army had left. But now she could see patches of earth appearing as the rain washed it away, the destruction becoming more evident in these churned-up lumps of earth, where once there had been lawns and shrubs and order. It was a depressing sight and she wished again the snow had come instead to continue to hide the damage temporarily.

As she stared into the rainfall, it seemed to thicken, and thicken, until all she could see was water. But there was something else. There was something there, in the rain, moving through the night. She strained her eyes to peer into the distance, as a shape was forming down the end of the drive, central between the trees that lined the avenue up to the house. It was a person. A person was walking up the drive. She glanced at the clock. It was nearly midnight. Who on earth would be walking up the drive to Raven Hall at midnight? And in this weather? Was it one of the soldiers from the Army camp, left something behind, or been given the wrong orders? Was it Evvy, back again from London? But as it grew closer, she could see it was male, in a greatcoat, cap pulled low, collar turned up against the rain, kitbag on his shoulder. He trudged onwards, onwards towards the house. She waited for him to get closer, then was planning to ask him who on earth he was and what he wanted at that time of night. She didn't want him knocking on the door and waking everyone. She'd have to give him a bed for the night, she supposed, though it vexed her to do so, as she'd just got rid of the rest of them. But something about this lone figure, his isolated shape shifting against the diagonal lines of rain all about him . . . something was familiar. And before he looked up, when at last he was close enough for her to see the shape of his face, the sharp line of it against his dark coat . . . she knew. It was Harry Woodvine.

He looked up and saw her. He grinned from ear to ear. Breaking into a trot, he came to her quickly, throwing his bag down as he reached her. He threw his arms around her and she felt herself lifted from the ground.

'What are you doing here on the doorstep in the rain, you madwoman?' she heard him say gladly as he hugged her close. And he didn't put her down. He carried her in through the kitchen door, as she wriggled and laughed at the sheer joy of him appearing, like that, out of nowhere, out of the night, like something from a fairy tale, conjured by the spirit of the rain itself. He deposited her on the kitchen floor and disappeared again, running back to fetch his bag. She looked through the open door and watched him. Was he real? Was this happening? Or was she asleep? Had coming downstairs to get the jug all been part of a dream and she was still dreaming now?

But he was back and coming in through the door and closing it, and shaking off the wet, dropping his coat and hat in a mess on the floor, pulling off his boots, as she stood there, unable to speak, for she thought if she said a word, he'd disappear and she'd wake up. He looked up, coatless and hatless and bootless now, in his uniform and socks, his hair plastered wet against his head, drips tumbling down his face, grinning at her.

'Now then, my darling. Are you pleased to see me?'

'Harry!' she said, still in utter shock at this apparition, standing before her. Harry Woodvine, in all his glory. And, oh, how glorious it was to look upon him again! Even with his hair dripping wet, she could see how yellow it was, how blue his eyes shone, how tanned his skin was by a foreign sun and the stunning cut of his jaw as he smiled. She felt rooted to the spot. 'It really is you. It really is. Here. In my kitchen!'

'Of course I'm here. The moment I landed, I knew it was here I'd come to, if they just gave me one night. Just one night. That's all I'd need. I'd bloody walk here from Dover if I had to.'

He came to her, his arms going around her back and drawing her close. The pull of his body was like a magnet, utterly unstoppable, a force of nature. She folded into him and closed her eyes, felt his mouth on her mouth and her lips opened as they kissed deeply, so deeply. It all came rushing back to her in that moment, the pure, incredible physicality of him, the curve of his frame into hers as they kissed and he held her close, so close. How could she have forgotten it? How could she have forsaken it? It was utterly overwhelming, the most magnificent kiss she could ever imagine, of love and passion, of longing and separation, of reunion and rejoicing. She knew him deeply and he knew her back, just the same.

And if the pantry light had not suddenly been turned on in the room next door and the sound of someone's slipper-shod footsteps shuffling about in there come to them, at which they both froze and cocked their heads . . . if that had not happened at that moment, Rosina was quite sure she would have let Harry Woodvine take her, right then, in her dressing gown and slippers, right there on the kitchen table.

A clatter of a utensil on the floor and a 'Oh bother!' alerted Rosina and Harry to jump apart, for she knew that voice better than her own.

Connie appeared at the door, holding a plate, a bread knife and half a loaf. Her mouth dropped open in a perfect O, like a cartoon figure expressing shock.

'Harry Woodvine!' she squealed. 'It's really you!'

Rosina said, 'Yes, it is, now don't wake the whole house up, for heaven's sake!'

But it was too late, as Bairstow was already on her way, and appeared in the hall and also stood there at the door with her mouth open, soon replaced by a smile Rosina had only seen in recent days when the Army were leaving, but not quite as broad as this smile.

Connie started firing questions at Harry, while Bairstow stoked up the range to put a kettle of water on it for tea, hanging up Harry's coat, hat and scarf on a rack before the fire to dry out and then placed Harry's boots beside the range too. They all sat around the kitchen table and Rosina carved up slabs of bread for everyone, spread with Canadian butter and homemade jam, which everyone said was 'proper jam', Harry's saying that came from his Shropshire childhood, which had nothing to do with jam, yet instead meant that something was absolutely lovely. In answer to Connie's barrage of questions, Harry explained he had one night's leave and that was it, that he'd got the train up to Whitby and got a lift from there, that he was being picked up again in the morning at eight and straight back down south to a new posting abroad somewhere.

'So, you had one night spare and you came all the way up here to see us? All the way up from Kent?'

Connie's eyes were sparkling with wonder at this and Rosina had to look away. She couldn't let her daughter see her own face, as she had no idea what kind of expression it held, her mind a kaleidoscope of clashing thoughts.

'That's about the size of it,' mumbled Harry, his mouth full of food.

'But why?' pushed Connie. 'Why would you come all this way? Just for *us*?'

Harry swallowed it down and said, 'Because you are my favourite family on this side of the country.'

'What about your own family?' quizzed Connie.

'Oh, do stop interrogating the poor chap, Connie,' snapped her mother.

'It's a fair question,' said Harry, smiling at Rosina with a wink, to say to her, *I can manage this*. 'The snow is bad in the west and the trains aren't running. So I came up to see you lot. If that's all right with you, Miss Constance.'

'Well, of course it's bloody all right!' cried Connie.

'Connie, language!' chided Rosina and let her forehead drop into her hand, exhausted by all this madness and feeling quite faint with it all, for reasons only she – and probably Bairstow – and Harry truly understood.

'Now then,' said Bairstow and stood up, taking Connie's plate away from her. 'Back to bed, missy.'

'Oh no, Bairstow! Mummy? I can stay up, can't I?'

'No, we're all going to bed,' said Rosina, throwing a grateful glance at Bairstow, who nodded. 'Poor Harry must be absolutely shattered.'

'But he's only here for one bally night. One night! What's the point in going to sleep? There's only a few hours till he's got to go!' she protested. At this moment, Rosina's patience with her daughter ran dry. She wanted to curse the fact that it was only two days before the girls returned to school. If only they'd already gone, she and Harry could truly be alone together in peace. Then she immediately felt guilty for thinking such a thing, but the annoyance still rankled.

In her hesitation, Harry stepped in and said, 'Now, young lady. I'll be up early, to partake of one of Bairstow's legendary breakfasts. Do you think I'd sleep through that? If you go to bed now and get some sleep, I'll see you here at this very table at six a.m. sharp. Is that a deal?'

Connie was delighted and her mother could see she considered this quite the exclusive date with Harry, despite the fact that they'd all be there.

'All right, if I must. And I will be here, six sharp. As I always am. I'm quite the early riser these days.'

'That's about as true as saying it's weather for short trousers outside,' said Bairstow and hurried Connie along. At the kitchen door, she turned and said, 'It's grand to see thee, Sergeant Woodvine.'

'Call me Harry,' he said. 'You always did, Bairstow. And it's grand to see you too.'

Bairstow added, 'Don't worry about t'mess. Leave it. I'll sort it in t'morning.' And off she went, arguing with Connie and getting her upstairs.

'Thank heavens for Bairstow,' said Harry, shoving a last piece of bread and jam in his mouth.

They were alone at last.

Still chewing furiously, he reached over and put his arms around her and she let him, moving from her chair on to his lap. His mouth still full of mashed-up bread and jam, she nuzzled his neck instead and his hands roamed up and down her back and on to her hips, shifting her closer into him.

'I can't believe you're here,' she whispered.

'Of course I am,' he whispered back. 'I said I'd see you Sunday, didn't I?'

'Oh Harry,' she said and she was crying. It was joy and it was guilt and it was shock and even fear, all mixed together. She kissed him and tasted her own salty tears, mixed in with the sweet and malty flavour of his mouth.

He slid his arms beneath her and stood up, still kissing her, carrying her around the kitchen table, through the door and into the servants' hall, shrouded in dimness, yet with the light from the kitchen illuminating the dark enough to see. She kissed him again voraciously and he placed her gently on the big table, that once served the many staff. She pulled him down as she leant backwards. There was no need for words, no discussion to be had. The months apart had brought them here to this moment, the miracle of their closeness again now was all that was needed to explain their actions, as she wrapped her thighs around his hips and soon he was inside her, and they watched each other as their bodies moved slowly together as one. All the nights since they'd had those first kisses in the summertime garden at the king and queen's seat, where she'd gone so often since then and stood, looking at the view and longing for him, wondering if they'd declared their love sooner, whether they would have made love instead of just kissing that day. And now he was here, she knew this was where he should be and where she should be, and somehow the last few months without him seemed like the dream now, a strange dream peopled by an army led by a serious, tragic officer that came and then went, leaving chaos and destruction in its wake, all covered now by a blanket of cleansing snow, as if none of it had ever happened. Here was Harry, in her arms, inside her, at this moment, where he should be.

Home.

Epilogue

March 1941

Sometimes Evvy found beauty in the most unlikely places. On that bright, cold, early spring day, she found a clump of daffodils growing out of the ruins of a house in Camden. The rubble of the house's remains must have fallen on to the front garden, here and there leaving little gaps for life to nudge through. She sat down on a low brick wall opposite and got out her sketch pad. Cyrano the dog sat down beside her. She didn't use a lead for him; he followed her everywhere, rarely leaving her side. She had a hell of a job dissuading him from jumping up on her motorcycle some nights and had taken to asking Pauline to distract him when she went out on a job, just so she could get out of the station without him. The little dog had transferred his affections for Lewis on to her exclusively.

He had little interest in anyone else at the station and positively seemed to dislike Sam, which upset him. Evvy tried to be understanding with Sam, and comfort him, but she had found it so hard, since the revelation in Lewis's letter, since they had all lost Lewis Bailey.

The effect on the whole station had been profound. What had once been a happy band of brothers and sisters facing adversity together was now a family in mourning. They were there for each other, they supported each other, they drew together and got on with the job admirably. But over everyone hung a dark cloud of sadness. Their leader was gone; for many, they felt the best of them was gone. A new S.O. was appointed, a chap called Denholm, who was all right, good enough at his job. But he wasn't Bailey and he never could be. It was difficult enough to step into a dead man's shoes, but this man had been revered by the crew.

There was a lot of help on hand for his brother Sam, everyone knowing keenly that Sam must feel it the worst, as not only were the brothers close, but Lewis had saved his younger brother's life. Everyone made a special effort with Sam, but he didn't want an ounce of sympathy. He had angry outbursts, or periods of morose indifference. Evvy felt terrible for him, losing his brother, but she also found she could offer little solace. Since Lewis's death and the truth coming out, she and Sam had broken up. They were pleasant to each other, but neither could face the other, avoiding one another whenever they could. As she saw him suffer, she wanted to help. She wanted to comfort him in his grief. But the revelations in Lewis's letter were like a blow to the cheek: shocking and hurtful, leaving her dazed. She had been lied to by both of the men she had cared so much for, as they had colluded to fool her. That's how she had felt at first: a fool. She knew something was odd about Sam and those letters; she had had a gut feeling about it. She scolded herself for not pursuing it further at the time, for not putting two and two together. If she had, maybe she would have found her way to Lewis sooner. Maybe if she'd known, she would have been with him. Who knows how things might have turned out differently? It wouldn't have stopped the Luftwaffe bombing the City that night, or the building falling down on Lewis. But at least he would have known her love for him, if she had worked it out sooner and followed her gut. She vowed always to act on her gut from now on. It was never wrong.

As she had sat sketching the flowers amidst the ruins, the bright sun had clouded over and now little flurries of sleet were whipping up. It was one of those March days where it was 'summer in the light, and winter in the shade'. She remembered her mother would always quote Dickens on a day like this. *The ever-changing march of time*, she thought, shoving her small sketchbook and stubby pencil into her pocket and walking off to find a bit of cover somewhere, Cyrano trotting beside her.

They sheltered in the cloisters of a church for a while until a brief hailstorm passed, then walked on. Her legs felt heavy and she had to force herself onwards. She'd been putting off this walk for weeks but now was determined to do it. The daffodils sketch was a delaying tactic; she had planned to walk to St Paul's Cathedral – and the nearby site of Lewis's death – and pay homage there, sketch it and say a prayer for Lewis. She'd been at Lewis's funeral, the whole crew had. It was solemn and largely silent, except for the vicar's booming voice beside the grave, in the freezing, still air of early January. He was buried with full honours. And soon after, Evvy and others had received commendations for their bravery that night, Evvy's specifically awarded for her role of delivering petrol to the pumps under highly dangerous conditions. The award was appreciated, but it felt hollow for Evvy. The one thing she should have done that night, she didn't, she believed. She still dreamt about ignoring the cries to retreat, instead staying at the scene, digging in the rubble and pulling Lewis out alive. She knew it was pointless to think that way, that everybody said the fire was raging too close, which it was. Everyone there that night had the same look at the funeral, a kind of baffled guilt, that they had to leave him, that they couldn't rescue him. Sam felt it most deeply, Evvy supposed. But they all suffered from it and she could not stop dreaming of the moment, over and over, of finding his body and waking him up, of him spitting out brick dust and wiping his eyes, alive and safe. The dreams tortured her and she began to dread sleep.

As the weeks went on, the dreams had lessened, work fell back into its normal routine – the bizarre normal that nightly bombings created – and life proceeded. The golden daffodils pushing through the ruins seemed to encapsulate it all, as did the coming of spring, which cheered everyone a little, with its promise of newness.

Evvy walked on, head down, glancing at Cyrano's eager face looking up at her from time to time as he kept in perfect alignment with her. *Thank heavens for you, little one*, she thought. Dogs always made one feel better, such pure souls they were. She found animals much easier than people. She had no idea what to do about Sam. She still cared for him and, truth be told, missed his embraces dearly. When they were in the same room at the station together, she'd often find herself watching him or look up to see him gazing at her. But it felt as if there were an invisible barrier between them, a sheet of perfectly clear glass, where they could see but not reach each other. The day after Lewis's death, Sam had come to her and she'd tried to hold him and let him hold her, but she'd blurted out about the letter and the truths it contained, leaving Sam grasping for an explanation, yet he could not find the words, only saying 'Sorry. I'm sorry,' over and over. It had felt cruel to assault him with the truth about the letter, in this, the first, aching phase of the shock of his grief for his brother. But Evvy was in shock too and she couldn't keep it inside. After that, they had seemed to step apart, as if a dance had just finished and they went to separate sides of the dance floor. Since then, they'd spoken little and not touched at all. She missed him. She missed Lewis more. It was impossible to make sense of it all, so she gave up trying and focused instead on her work at the station and, in her spare time, threw herself into her art. Drawing was the one reliable thing in all this chaos. All you needed was a pencil and paper. The simplicity of it was comforting.

Evvy reached St Paul's as the wind was whipping up again, the dark clouds scudding across the dreary sky. She found a bench and sat down to stare at the cathedral. It was spectacular even under miserable skies, white and stark against the greyness and amidst the ruins, a jewel in London's crown. Churchill had been right to insist on it being saved, of course. The destruction of such an icon of British culture and history would have been a severe blow to morale. Evvy knew that to be true. She admired its beautiful shape as she looked upon it, but there was a visceral hate in her too for it, something that took her breath away as she started to sketch it. She had to stop for a moment as she feared she might sob. This building had been saved. All around it was the legacy of that night of pure destruction. And in that debris of history was Lewis's deathbed. She stared at the spot, now cleared, but she'd never forget precisely where it was. He was buried in a small churchyard in Camden, but this was the place she knew she'd visit in homage to him, long after this war was over, she promised herself.

She pushed herself to continue drawing, sketching out the beautiful curves of Wren's vision, then below it, scribbles of grey and black to outline the carcasses of burnt buildings. Fifteen firemen had died that night, including Lewis. Was it worth it? Was a building, however historic and important, worth more than a life?

She was finishing her sketch, just as the breeze blew away the last grey clouds and out came the sun, beaming down brightly on the scene, illuminating the pale stone that now stood shining against a mid-blue sky. Evvy looked up at it in awe; it was truly a striking sight to behold. It took her breath away, even at this place of death – or perhaps because of it – a reminder to her of the majesty of life; the things she had seen these past months, stark and clear as a painting in her memory: the flares falling like fireworks, the silhouette of Sam against the crimson fire, her final glimpse of Lewis spectral in the smoke, the sleepers heaped in curves on the underground platform, the twisted wreckage left after fires had fizzled out, the wandering ghosts of London's dead and the plucky living who went on, night after night, living their intricate lives in quiet defiance. The fearsome splendour of it moved her so – life in all its complexity. Whatever happened, whatever hell she found herself stumbling through, the spectacle of it all never ceased to amaze and fascinate her. Evvy could not look away, however painful it might be; she could never stop gazing at the awful beauty of life.

* * *

The once lovely grounds of Raven Hall looked like an abandoned battlefield. After the snow had gone, the truth of its ruin became clear, a pockmarked visage of brown lumps and troughs, deep holes where the corrugated iron Nissen huts had been removed and mounds of earth left after digging, the whole landscape appearing as if terrific battles had been fought on that ground, instead of a horde of young men sleeping, training and playing football. The hall, once cleared of all its desks and chairs, filing cabinets, telephones, lamps and piles of papers, now looked like the carcass of a house recently burgled, with telephone wires snaking around rooms with no telephones left to receive their calls, whilst the walls, floors and staircases resembled the site of a recent fist fight amongst coal miners, so grubby were the stains on every surface.

After the drama of recent events – the Army's withdrawal, Allan's almost-proposal, Grace's news of her foreign posting and, last but definitely not least, Harry's miraculous midnight appearance – Rosina could have slept for a month. The prospect that assaulted her, of clearing up the mess left by the occupation, seemed almost insurmountable. Despite praying for months for the Army to leave, once they'd gone, and Allan with them, Rosina felt utterly alone. Grace and Harry gone too, she felt abandoned by the world and what greeted her eye every day upon waking was what felt like the ruins of her old life. It was unsettling, too, to imagine that, at any moment, some new class of horror might descend upon the hall, in the shape of another battalion of ruffians. Though she wanted to start working on the hall's repair, she didn't want to do too much work in case she was to discover that the Army were going to return, or another service. She was still waiting for news from the Office of Works of what type of requisitioning Raven Hall would be subjected to next. But after a couple of anxious weeks waiting to hear, Rosina decided to pre-empt the decision and start getting everything tidied up anyway. If the Army or similar came back, then so be it. It would feel like her home again even for just a short while. And if the hall was granted her application as a maternity home, then they would need to clean it up thoroughly anyway.

Bairstow was on hand, as usual, and the maids Mary and Sheila, as well as Phyllis, who turned up with her children in tow, saying she'd heard from Mary that Rosina needed help. So the clear-up began, the women working inside, the men working outside. They took turns to mind the Precious kids – who didn't need much, as Elsie entertained herself, or napped with babies Jill and Wilf – and everyone set about cleaning the walls and carpets and wooden floors as best they could, Rosina getting some old paint pots out from the garages to touch up the stains on the walls. Throp came and went, fixing bannisters and other broken bits here and there. Outside, he worked tirelessly with Jessop – and Ronnie when he wasn't at school – to rebuild the chicken coop and fill in the holes with earth, to begin to level out the ground. The builders who came to fix up the tank damage to the walls did a good job patching it up, though the bricks didn't match, and Rosina's mother's settee had been thrown away as unfixable.

Slowly, slowly, over the early weeks of the year, the hall and garden transformed from a mess into something resembling home again. Some things she could not afford to replace as yet, such as the mostly ruined carpets in the communal areas downstairs. There were also some new cracks that had appeared in ceilings here and there that worried her. She resolved to deal with these soon, but for now, she had to focus on the rooms they would use and try to get them shipshape again. It was not the same as it once was, but it was a vast improvement.

And all the while, Rosina actually relished the opportunity to clear up everything around her, largely because her mind and her heart were a complete muddle. At least her exterior could be tidied up, even if the interior was an absolute mess of mixed emotions and unmade decisions. Harry's brief appearance had been dreamlike, but the fact was, it was all too real. They had gone upstairs afterwards and made love again, slower and less feverish that time. Her years of celibacy and, before that, major dissatisfaction with her sex life had been wiped out in one fell swoop. This . . . *this* was what she had been waiting for, all those years. Exciting yet loving, thrilling yet tender. Afterwards, they had lain entwined in each other, fully naked, under the blankets, a luxurious tumble of limbs and bones and flesh and warmth. They did not speak much for a long time, just wallowing in the union of their bodies and the sounds of their breathing. Neither had slept, not wanting to miss a moment. They knew, too, that Harry would need to decamp to a spare room before morning came, to keep up appearances for the girls. After an age of lying together in beautiful silence, the hours had crept by and they began to surface, starting to talk about Harry's recent adventures and plans to come. He had told her stories about Sierra Leone, the heat and the flies, the local people he made friends and enemies of, as well as his team. The work was still secret, but there was plenty else to tell. He was going to be training some chaps for a while in London, before going on to sail to Singapore. That's all he could say. Rosina knew a bit more about Singapore than Sierra Leone; she knew it was a Crown colony, owned by the British. Though she wished the war would keep him on British soil, she felt somewhat relieved that, of all foreign places, he was going to Singapore, as it somehow felt safer, being a British colony and a small island. She'd heard mention in the press and on the wireless that it was a British stronghold and would undoubtedly be safe against attack. He had kept asking her if she already knew this or that story, as he'd told it in his letters, but then it was revealed that he'd written many that she had never received. After telling her his tales, he was impatient to hear more about hers, as he'd received so few letters. So he had quizzed her all about the Army occupation. She began with the tank accident, which appalled him. Thinking back to her fears after the tank incident, she had asked him who would tell her if he was injured or . . . worse. He had said he had a cousin called Bridget back in Shropshire, who he'd told about Rosina. She'd agreed to pass on any information about Harry to Rosina if the worst happened. Rosina was touched that he'd thought ahead and organised this on her behalf, although equally unsettled at the prospect. She told him she'd make the same arrangement with Bairstow for him. She had explained about the general chaos and damage to the hall, carefully omitting mention of Allan Vaughan, and feeling her throat tighten with guilt as she did so. But she kept telling herself, she didn't know. She didn't know Harry still loved her, after months of no word. And she didn't know love like this was real. When he was away from her, she felt as if the whole affair had been written down in a romance novel, a figment of her own longing. But when they were together, it was real and here and now, and all her doubts fell away. It was difficult to reconcile.

They had talked on until morning, Harry sneaking out at around 5.30 a.m. to get himself washed up and presentable for breakfast at six, as no doubt Connie would be there on the dot and eagerly waiting. Rosina didn't feel it was necessary to tell Harry how Connie felt about him. It was obvious to everyone and rather embarrassing, especially since Rosina understood full well that Bairstow knew exactly what had been going on all night between herself and Harry, while Connie had sat there starry-eyed, bombarding Harry with questions and conversation, eager to go a hundred miles an hour into a meaningful relationship with the object of her desire. Rosina had felt terrible about it, watching her daughter waste her affection, which would never be reciprocated, not in the way she wanted anyway. Her heart went out to her, but then, Harry was so sweet with her, kind and careful, without leading her on, trying to be avuncular but never patronising. What a natural he was with young people. And Connie was nearly grown up now; she'd get over it. She'd be leaving soon and going off into her adult life, not looking back.

As much as Rosina loved her own children, the gradual movement of them away from her into their own lives had not been something she regretted, instead something she enjoyed, feeling that she had done her best to prepare them for adult life, and one day in the future, once they had all gone out into the world, she could begin the next phase of her life, whatever that would bring. It didn't bring her fear of loneliness or being left behind, instead it comforted her, the idea of the taste of freedom from constant mothering. Would marrying Allan Vaughan give her that freedom? It would be a new life, a new adventure, with someone reliable and kind beside her to share the stresses and strains, someone to lean on, to rest with and to go out with into the new post-parenting, post-war world and explore it a little, before returning home to the hall they would run with ease together, once he had retired from the Army. And if he went on working for them for a few years, then she would keep her freedom at the hall, seeing him as and when his work allowed. It was an attractive prospect, one that would be approved of by all and sundry, a fitting new master at the hall, with his fitting wife, grandchildren coming and going over the years, growing into greyness and dotage together. After his departure, Allan had sent her a letter saying he wanted to give her plenty of space and time to consider her position and he would not bother her while she was doing so, that she should contact him when she was ready to discuss it further. All very business-like and yet, it was also thoughtful, not pressuring her by constant communication. He was a good man, wasn't he? A good catch. A good bet, some might say.

But then . . . there was Harry . . . Since their feverish meeting, which still felt somehow unreal, Rosina had assumed he'd gone on to Singapore, but then she received a telegram to say he was still in London and would visit if not shipped soon. She'd heard no more from him and was left wondering if he was still in the country or not. Wartime meant many were left in the dark about their loved ones' whereabouts, so she was accustomed to this and did not worry too much. But each morning she'd wake and wonder if today might be the day he'd suddenly turn up again. And if he did, she knew she'd fall into his arms without a moment's hesitation. But what of the future? Was there to be a future with Harry? Was it all a pipe dream, a ridiculous fantasy? Or was it her destiny?

Rosina stood by the newly mended window of the lounge, looking out at the bright cold March day, just as Evvy was doing hundreds of miles away in London. They were both thinking about two men. They were both in two minds. If only they'd had the nerve to share it with each other, what a comfort they could have been. But Evvy always kept her secrets secret. And Rosina felt she could talk to nobody of this, not even Bairstow. She knew Bairstow disliked Allan. She knew she supported Harry. But what would the rest of the world think? And did that matter? Rosina had a sudden flashback of Harry's body, the glorious weight of it crushing her into the table . . . and she felt a deep twinge in her body that was powerful yet alarming. She shook herself to come back to normal, as Phyllis was there beside her, putting the twins' cardigans on, because they were to take them outside for a walk in their pram, to get them to nap.

Rosina felt a little hand take hers and she looked down to see Elsie smiling up at her.

'Play kings and queens?' said Elsie. 'Sit on their seats?'

'Yes, all right,' said Rosina, smiling and squeezing her hand. 'You be queen and I'll be king and your brother and sister can be the naughty knaves who stole all of our tarts.'

Elsie giggled and pulled on Rosina's hand. Phyllis picked up Jill and Rosina took up Wilf and they tucked them into the pram at the back door, then they all put on their coats and went outside. The breeze was icy, but when it blew by, the sun shone down and warmed the tops of their heads. Phyllis pushed the pram and Elsie ran excitedly onwards.

'Summer in the light, winter in the shade,' said Rosina. She thought of her daughters then; of the girls back at school, Connie causing havoc and Dora working hard and Daisy thinking of Ronnie; of Evvy, bold and enigmatic, facing daily danger in the capital; and of Grace, someday soon about to board a ship to who knew where, for who knew how long. She thought of Allan, commandeering a new hall, a heavy sadness in his heart for his lost boy, thinking of her perhaps, and waiting for her answer. And she thought of Harry, she guessed still in London preparing to go abroad, where one day soon he would stand, his hair golden under the eastern sun, in the British colony of Singapore, facing who knew what challenges in his war to come, on the other side of the world.

She stopped to look over the view of her gardens, as Phyllis and Elsie went on ahead. Here, in the brown, heaped wreckage of Raven Hall's grounds, clusters of crocuses and dwarf narcissuses pushed through the dark soil. Nature renewed and brought life back to the troubled earth. The fritillaries and forget-me-nots would appear next, popping up all over the garden, bringing their colourful reminder of new life. Rosina looked forward to the Easter holidays, when her girls would be home again and she could bask in their bright vitality. They'd save up their rations and try to make hot cross buns and eat them toasted, the warm butter running down their chins. The hall would echo again with the sound of laughter. And after that, perhaps the corridors and rooms of Rosina's home might fill with the newest life of all: the sound of babies coming into the world. Rosina crossed her fingers and hoped against hope that her plans for the hall would come to pass. She felt some optimism, as she saw the sunshine burn through the patches of wispy sea fret that haunted the battlements. The sea looked calm today, to match her mood. Yet, as she looked out over the moors, she saw that dark clouds were massing. Rosina said aloud to nobody in particular, 'It's black over Bill's wife's mother's.' It's what Bairstow and the Yorkshire folk would say, when rough weather was on the horizon. Would the storm come Rosina's way or go out to sea? Only time would tell.

Glossary of Yorkshire Dialect

In this series of books set in North Yorkshire, when rendering the speech of local people, I have attempted to give a flavour of the regional dialect and accent, rather than a fully phonetic representation. This is to prevent general readers from finding the phonetic spelling of too many words a distraction when reading.

Bairns = children
Black over Bill's wife's mother's = dark clouds in the distant
      sky, signalling the coming of a storm
Chuffin' 'eck = expressing surprise
Dun't = doesn't
Grand = very good, excellent
Mardy = upset/bad-tempered
Mithering = fussing and moaning

Nay = no

'Ow do = hello (shortened form of How do you do?)

Owt = anything

Siling it down = heavy rain

Summat = something

T' = used for *the*, shortened to a half-pronounced *t* sound
      or a glottal stop

Tha = you

Tha'll = you'll

Tha's = you are

Tha've = you have

Thee = you

Thi = your

Thissen = yourself

'Twas = it was

'Un = one

Author's Note

- The setting for Evvy's fire station, Substation 73V, did exist at Argyle Street School (thanks to the London Fire Brigade Museum for this info), but the setting and characters I placed therein are fictitious.

- I used a range of sources to research the firefighters of the Blitz on London 1940-41, including books written by staff who were there. These incredibly brave people worked ceaselessly throughout the war. Many were injured or died on duty, both men and women. This story is my small homage to their courage and resilience.

- My descriptions of the night wherein the City of London was bombed were based on accounts I read by firefighters and civilians, as well as the usual artistic licence necessary when novel writing. Churchill did indeed instruct the fire service to save St Paul's Cathedral at all costs. I imagine that every time I go to London from now on and see its beautiful dome on the London skyline, I will think on those who were hurt or died to preserve it on that terrible night.

- Reading about the requisitioning of country houses during the war was fascinating, particularly learning about how destructive some of the armed forces were of country houses that never recovered and were knocked down after the war. Houses were damaged by such varied incursions as the constant tramping in and out, as well as up and down stairs, of heavy boots causing staircases and archways to collapse; modifying of the structure of the house by, for example, introducing new telephone lines, that led to terrible damp problems later; stripping silk from wall coverings to fashion gifts for girlfriends; careless discarding of lit cigarettes or even lighting makeshift fires that led to huge house fires that caused wholesale damage; and so on. As I read, I often felt torn by supporting the courageous forces who went off to fight, many of whom made the ultimate sacrifice, yet I was also shocked at the wanton destruction that befell these beautiful buildings. I would imagine few had much sympathy for the rich owners – understandably when one considers the privations everyone had to face in Great Britain during the war – but the loss of the houses and their grounds is sad and leaves a gap in our country's heritage, another casualty of war.

- It was a pleasure to use *Cyrano de Bergerac* by Edmond Rostand as not only a book mentioned in this story but also an inspiration for Evvy's love triangle. I first became aware of this play when I watched the Depardieu film version in the early 90s and absolutely fell in love with it. The stunning wordplay of Cyrano and his tragic love for Roxane stayed with me decades later and popped into my head when I first started considering the idea of Evvy meeting two firefighter brothers. With many adaptations over the years and a new film version released recently in 2021, it seems that the world is still in love with this beautiful story, first published in 1897, based on a real person from the seventeenth century and also apparently responsible for introducing the word 'panache' into English usage. Such is the legacy of great lives and great art; they never leave us.

Acknowledgements

Sophie Walter and the London Fire Brigade Museum team, for invaluable help on the fire stations and sub-stations of the Bloomsbury area during WW2.

The whole team at my brilliant publisher Welbeck, with particular thanks to Rachel Hart, my editor, for loving these women as much as I do and shaping their journeys through WW2.

My superlative agenting team from United Agents: Laura Macdougall and Olivia Davies, for advice, support, knowledge, negotiation and championing. You guys are the bee's knees.

Thank you to readers, reviewers and book bloggers who contact me via Facebook, Instagram, Twitter and my websites, for your questions and interest in all of my books, as Walton and Mascull – bless you for your support.

Particular thanks to those loyal and ever supportive bloggers who have read so much of my work and reviewed online over the past ten years – including Robert Armin, Susanne Baker, Josie Barton, Julie Boon, Rachel Bridgeman, Anne Cater, Frankie of Chicks, Rogues and Scandals, Dee Groocock, Susan Heads, Linda Hill, Kaisha Holloway, Beverley Ann Hopper, Sarah Lizziebeth, Karen Mace, Kath Middleton, Pam Norfolk, Miriam O'Brien, Faye Oliver, Sharon Rimmelzwaan, Vicky-Leigh Sayer, Lainy Swanson, Angela Thomas, Eliza Jane Tulley and Anne Williams. N.B. I've never included a list of reviewers before as I've always been terrified of leaving out someone important, so please forgive me if I've not included everyone who has supported my books throughout the years (see my comment below on my atrocious memory). Please know that I appreciate every review, mention, comment and message from readers – they mean the world to this author.

Lu Corfield, for becoming the voice of Mollie Walton on the audio books. Just beautiful work from a beautiful person.

Habiba Sacranie of W.F. Howes, for superb work on bringing my stories to life as audio books, as well as a fabulous long, rambling conversation on the phone one day that covered multiple digressions and outright abandonment of the point – it reminded me I'm not the only person who talks in this meandering way.

Sandy Rawlings and the whole team at Lincs Inspire and my local libraries, for their support for years for my books.

The saga and romance writers community, for comradeship in the face of literary snobbery against these fabulous genres of writing and for battling for recognition to give these books the place they deserve in the UK arts coverage. Solidarity, my fellow authors! Special mention for the Romantic Novelists' Association, the leading champion of us all.

All my writer and publishing pals who struggle on in this mad business of books and keep me going. We've all realised by now that there's never any magical point when you 'make it', instead that you just keep writing, just keep writing, just keep writing (think Dory. . .)

Facebook friends, who join me daily for a bloody good laugh – you know who you are (which sounds vaguely threatening, which I suspect they'd appreciate).

Friends who have looked out for me this year and kept me smiling, including Lucy Adams, Melissa Bailey, Fiona Cooke, Debbie Cowie, Lynn Downing, Iveta Drabekova, Kerry Drewery, Kerry Hadley, Kathy Kendall, Jay Kershaw, Pauline Lancaster, Fiona McKinnell, Beth Miller, Louisa Treger, Sue White and Sumaira Wilson. Anyone I've missed out is because of my terrible memory, which contains black holes unknown to science, so I apologise profusely in advance!

My family who cheer for me on and off social media and have supported me and my books for years, including my brothers and my sisters-in-law, my nephews and niece, my aunties, uncles and cousins; Poppy's grandparents, auntie, uncle and cousins, as well as her great auntie and family; and last but never in any way least, my parents, Liz and Russell Beeson. Your support means so much to me.

Poppy, for her unfailing support of my writing, wicked sense of humour, supreme holiday buddy, fellow narrative lover, superstar journalist and all-round brave and beautiful girl.

Clem for everything, but if I were forced at gunpoint to choose one thing, I'd have to say our mutual love of chonks.

About the Author

© Emma Shardlow Hudson

Mollie Walton is the saga pen-name for historical novelist Rebecca Mascull. She has always been fascinated by history and has worked in education, has a Masters in Writing and lives by the sea in the east of England. The inspiration for the Raven Hall trilogy came when she visited the stunning Raven Hall Hotel with her daughter and fell in love with the beautiful cliff-top view. Under Mollie Walton, Rebecca is also the author of the historical fiction trilogy, the Ironbridge Saga.

WELBECK

PUBLISHING GROUP

Love books? Join the club.

Sign up and choose your preferred genres to receive tailored news, deals, extracts, author interviews and more about your next favourite read.

From heart-racing thrillers to award-winning historical fiction, through to must-read music tomes, beautiful picture books and delightful gift ideas, Welbeck is proud to publish titles that suit every taste.

bit.ly/welbeckpublishing

WELBECK

ANDRE DEUTSCH

MORTIMER

MORTIMER

WELBECK